THE COURAGE
TO TRY

By the Author

Edge of Awareness

The Courage to Try

THE COURAGE TO TRY

by

C.A. Popovich

2015

THE COURAGE TO TRY

ISBN 13: 978-1-62639-528-2

THIS TRADE PAPERBACK ORIGINAL IS PUBLISHED BY
BOLD STROKES BOOKS, INC.
P.O. BOX 249
VALLEY FALLS, NY 12185

FIRST EDITION: OCTOBER 2015

CREDITS
EDITORS: VICTORIA VILLASENOR AND CINDY CRESAP
PRODUCTION DESIGN: SUSAN RAMUNDO
COVER DESIGN BY SHERI (GRAPHICARTIST2020@HOTMAIL.COM)

Acknowledgments

I would like to extend an enormous thank you to Len Barot, Sandy Lowe, and all the hardworking folks at Bold Strokes Books for all they do to help me fulfill my dream of writing. I also want to thank Victoria Villasenor and Cindy Cresap, editors extraordinaire, for helping me make this work so much better.

To Sandi, who patiently answers all of my equine questions, I'm grateful for all the ways you're in my life.

Finally, thanks to all the readers of lesbian romance. Your support means everything.

Dedication

To Annie

CHAPTER ONE

"Pull!" Kristen Eckert shouted a second before catching sight of the yellow topped black disk flying across the pale blue sky. She leaned into the shot and tracked the clay pigeon with laser precision, as she gracefully swept her twenty-gauge across her body. She pulled the trigger and focused on another disk whizzing into her line of sight from the opposite direction. She repeated the process and allowed herself a second to feel the satisfaction of watching the clay target disappear in a puff of smoke. She was on track to another perfect one hundred. She broke open her over-and-under and tossed the empty shells into the station's bin before positioning herself on station eight, the last station of her round. She took a deep, calming breath and exhaled a shout for the target. She smoked the high eight and turned her concentration to the last shot. The clay target disintegrated as she followed through with her swing, and she grinned.

"Damn, girl. You sure you ain't training for them Olympics? You're gittin' as good as that gold medal winner."

"Thanks, Tim, but Kim Rhode trains for Olympic-style skeet shooting. Our rules state we start with the gun on our shoulder, not down by our hip, the way she trains. And besides, I'm only trying to beat my own best score." Kristen walked back into the clubhouse with her craggy friend and owner of the gun club.

"You go ahead and try it. Your momma shot that way the whole time she was here. I ain't gonna tell nobody to stop ya."

"We'll see. Sometimes I think I wouldn't mind challenging myself more. Do you have any of your Italian roast brewed this afternoon? I could use a cup."

"Sure do. I'll get ya a sandwich to go with it."

Kristen wiped down her Browning Citori and carefully placed it in her space in the gun rack. Tim Roland had assigned spots for the few top shooters in his club, of which she was one. She often thought the gesture was to honor the memory of her mother, rather than her shooting ability. The year before Kristen was born, her mother had sauntered into the club as if she owned the place and challenged Tim to a shoot-off for a right to membership. She'd been the first female member of the private gun club located just outside of Novi, Michigan. At least, that was the story Tim told. Her mother had relayed pretty much the same rendition, with the slight addition that she'd mentioned bringing her heart surgeon husband with her occasionally. Tim vehemently denied that her marital status had anything to do with his decision. "That lady could shoot!" was all he'd said, and today Kristen was one of several single female members welcomed into the previously male-only domain.

"Here ya go." Tim set her coffee cup and sandwich on the round table in front of Kristen and sat down opposite her. "Everythin' okay with your dad?" he asked.

"He's no worse. I'm heading over to see him soon. Sometimes I almost wish he would get worse, you know? I can't imagine knowing everything he knew, being a heart surgeon, and then struggling to remember to brush your teeth, or to recognize your friends and family. At least if he was totally unaware of everything, he wouldn't have to deal with the…I don't know, the agony of it, I guess." Kristen took a drink of her coffee. *Is it dad's agony, or my own?* She wished she could figure out a way to keep him home.

"You tell him I said hello." Tim patted Kristen's hand as he spoke. "Ya don't know what he might understand. I gotta go back to work. We got a new member comin' in today."

"Thanks, Tim."

Kristen watched him retreat to his office, finished her coffee, and headed out to her car.

"You must be that hotshot female. The one to beat."

The voice was unfamiliar. Kristen set her gun case in the trunk of her Boxter and turned to face the stocky, broad shouldered man. His slicked back dark hair made him look as if he were wearing a cap. A thick gold chain gleamed against his black turtleneck and matched the gold in his belt buckle. His ring covered fingers wrapped around the handle of a leather trimmed gun case with Fabbri embossed across the side. He smelled as if he'd bathed in expensive cologne.

"I'm sorry. Do I know you?" Kristen asked.

"Not yet, but you will." The stranger sauntered into the gun club without another word.

She shrugged and turned away. *Must be the new member Tim mentioned.* She'd dealt with plenty of men who didn't like women being there, and it didn't faze her anymore. She had far more important concerns in life than some guy with a chip on his shoulder.

❖

Kristen steadied herself before she headed into the building. She noted the newly painted *Sundowning Care Facility* sign next to the door, and the new mat they'd put out since her last visit. She took a deep breath before entering her father's world. She found him in his usual spot sitting in his recliner with the TV on and the sound off. She automatically did a quick assessment. He was clean-shaven, and they had combed his hair. The pajamas were fresh, and he was wearing the warm socks she'd bought him for Christmas. She rested her hand on his shoulder before speaking.

"Hi, Pop. I brought you some more Rolos. How're you feeling today?" Kristen steeled herself for the answer. Last week his dementia had taken him so far into his past he hadn't recognized her.

"Is that you, Kristen? You look thin. Are you feeling all right? I'm a doctor, you know. I could write you a prescription for something." Her father's brows furrowed, and he seemed to focus on something over her left shoulder. She knew better, but she turned to look toward the blank wall at which he was now intently staring. She fought down the bile as her stomach churned with anger at the injustice of her renowned heart surgeon father sitting in front of a muted TV, grappling for comprehension from a bare wall, and completely dependent on the care of strangers.

"I'm fine, Dad." She set the ignored Rolo candy on his nightstand and noted the empty wrappers still in his wastebasket from her last visit.

"Did your mother come with you today, honey?"

This was becoming a frequent question. "No. Not today." Kristen had given up reminding her father about her mother's death from cancer six years ago.

"That woman works too hard. She's a nurse, you know. In a prestigious hospital." He creased his brow again, no doubt, in an effort to squeeze out the lost memory. "I can't remember which one it is right now, but she works way too damn much. What about you? Why aren't you working today? You know you'll never get ahead if you don't work."

"It's Sunday. I wanted to spend the day with you." Kristen watched her dad's eyelids droop and his head begin to nod. She wished she could take him home where he belonged, but she'd tried that. He'd gotten too difficult to handle. Even the caregivers she'd hired had only lasted a few days. She sighed in frustration. "Do you want to lie down and take a little nap, Dad?"

"Yes. Thank you. My daughter will be coming later to visit me. I need to rest now."

Kristen helped him out of his chair and sat him on the side of his narrow hospital bed. She gently lifted his feet onto the bed as he lay down. She covered him with the hand knitted comforter she'd brought from home, one of her mother's many creations, and kissed his forehead before heading to the nurses' station. She paused just outside the door to his room and leaned against the beige wall. The sterile looking hallway reminded her of the brown tiled hospital corridor she'd spent hours pacing as she waited for her mother to finish her chemo treatments. As difficult as that was to endure, it had given her mother a few more years of life. At least it was action. She clenched her fists and swallowed the lump in her throat at seeing her father slowly fade from existence, with nothing she could do about it. She pushed away from the wall and focused on what she could do—let the nurses know he wasn't alone.

❖

Kristen listened intently as she repositioned her stethoscope on the distended belly of the pregnant Arabian mare. "It sounds like a washing machine in there. A lot of gurgling and whooshing."

Dr. William Berglund laughed as he washed his arms in the sink outside the stall. "I expect everything will go smoothly. She's delivered two foals without our help. She probably wants us out of her way so she can get on with it."

Kristen wrapped her stethoscope around her neck and stood by the doctor. The scent of Lava soap, fresh straw, and manure mixed with horse sweat brought back memories of her father. She was twelve years old the first time he'd allowed her to *help* him deliver one of his Appaloosa foals. She was about as much help now as she'd been then, standing in awe as the mare tossed her head and stomped her front foot. She was reminded of the *Alien* movie when a foot, nose, or butt pushed out the mare's side as the foal rolled around, ready to claim its place in the outside world. The breeder, a friend of Bill's, called him more for company than for any medical reason, and Kristen was grateful Bill had called her to come along for the experience.

The horse let out a screeching whinny, went down on her knees, and rolled over onto her side. A minute later, she turned onto her belly, whinnied again, and pushed her rear end up, still on her front knees.

"She seems agitated," Kristen whispered to Bill. "I guess I'd be, too, in her position."

The mare pawed the floor before she plopped her butt down and eased over onto her side again.

The breeder chuckled. "She puts on quite a show, doesn't she?"

"So, this isn't anything new then?" Bill moved toward the stall door, watching the horse attentively.

"Nope. This foal might be a big one though."

After several more minutes of standing, going down on her knees, rolling to her side, and repeating the process, she finally stayed on her side.

"Here it comes." Bill had quietly made his way into the large stall and stood ready to assist the mare if necessary. "Come on, little one. Let's see those feet."

Bill's gentleness and concern for his patients was one of the reasons Kristen trusted him. She'd worked for him for five years before her mother had gotten sick, and she knew he warranted his reputation for being one of the best equine veterinarians in the area.

The placental sac popped out, and the foal's front hooves emerged, followed by its velvety nose. Bill carefully grabbed the front legs of the foal and pulled in an effort to help the mare. He broke open the sac, wiped out the foal's nostrils and mouth to clear its airway, and stepped back to let nature take its course. In less than ten minutes, the newborn was floundering under the onslaught of its mother's tongue.

"It's a girl, and you were right. This filly is big," Bill said.

Bill and Kristen stayed long enough to see the filly find her mother's nipple to feed before heading to Bill's van.

"I wanted to ask you something, Kristen." Bill meticulously went through the unused emergency kit, counting his supplies. Then he carefully stowed it in its designated compartment in the back of his van and turned to face Kristen. "I'm bringing another veterinarian into my practice, and I was hoping you might consider coming back to work on a part-time basis for a while to help her get settled."

"Her? Is she a horse vet?" Kristen handed Bill the empty bucket she'd carried out behind him.

"No. She stepped in for Paul last week for a standard neutering, and I was impressed with her attentiveness. I've been getting so many calls for small animal services lately that I thought it would make sense to expand." Bill nestled the empty bucket far from the rest of the equipment and closed the back door. "She'll be covering all the small animals, and I'll still be taking care of the horses. She has a practice in St. Clair, but it sounds as if she's ready to give it up."

"Bill, you know I quit the small animal clinic because I didn't want to work with barking dogs and biting cats. In fact, I think cats are better off left in the barn than brought into homes as pets." Kristen raked her fingers through her hair and paced behind the van. "I've got my dad to worry about, and the barrel racing events will be starting soon. I don't know." She knew she'd say yes. Bill had never questioned her need to take time off when she'd worked for him during her mother's illness, and when her father had started his decline, Bill had offered whatever assistance she needed in his care. He'd even given her a month's pay when she quit and tried to take care of him herself at home. She owed him.

"I don't expect you to stay forever. I know you're busy. Think about it, please." Bill leaned against his van as if he had all the time in the world to wait for her answer.

"I'll think about it." She sighed in exasperation. She'd gotten used to her time being her own. When her father had become unable to care for his affairs, Kristen obtained power of attorney, and all of his financial investments became her responsibility. She'd inherited her parents' property and all their assets, so she didn't need to work, but she'd help Bill out.

"She's coming to the clinic next Friday. If you can, come by and meet her, and let me know what you think."

"I'll take Zigzag through his keyhole practice in the morning and come over after that."

"Thanks!" Bill grabbed her hand and squeezed gently. "She's nice. You'll like her."

"We'll see." Kristen didn't even try to hide her skepticism. Her father had bred Appaloosas for years, and she'd grown up learning what to feed them, when to groom them, and when to call the veterinarian. She knew about West Nile, Lyme disease, Potomac Fever, heaves, and colitis, and she had firsthand knowledge of the tragedy of an inexperienced veterinarian delaying treatment. She sighed. *At least if this new doctor isn't any good, it'll only be dogs and cats.* She waved to Bill as he pulled away and then she went to her car.

CHAPTER TWO

G ood morning, Rose." Dr. Jaylin Meyers arrived at her clinic with a bag of assorted bagels and cream cheese varieties for her staff. "I picked up a few of those specialty bagels from the bakery this morning. Help yourselves." Jaylin set the bag of warm bagels on her office manager's desk.

"Thanks, Doc. You must've had a good day with the horses yesterday."

"It went well, yes. It was a standard gelding procedure. Dr. Berglund is good, and he has quite a support staff. So, who do we have coming in today?"

Rose brought up the day's schedule. "Bob Miller is bringing in his new bulldog puppy for vaccinations. Jenny Miles has a kitten she found living in the culvert in front of her house. She wants you to check it out to see what it needs. She doesn't know if it's a male or female. Let's see, Billy James is bringing Lucifer in for a heartworm check, and that takes care of the morning." Rose glanced at Jaylin before continuing to scroll down her day's list. "This afternoon, we have Mrs. Preston bringing in Pepper. She says he's been scratching at his left ear for three days. Then, so far, there's only one other patient scheduled. Maria is bringing Frankie in for his heartworm check."

Jaylin smiled at the thought of seeing Maria again. The last time they spoke was when Jaylin had called to wish her a merry Christmas, and Maria had admitted to falling in love and moving in with a local dog groomer. Jaylin had asked Maria out at a time when her loneliness had overpowered her fears, and Maria had turned out to be perfect for her: completely unavailable.

"I'll go tell Nancy about the bagels, and let me know when puppy Miller gets here."

Jaylin sat back in her office chair and considered how she felt about giving up her practice. She'd worked hard to earn the trust and respect of her clients in the small town of St. Clair, Michigan, and she was proud of that. It would take time to build a rapport within a new community. Starting over would be a challenge. But it was time to push herself out of her comfort zone.

Jaylin reviewed her office space and made a note to check with Bill about room for shelves in the new office. She was in the middle of making a list when Rose let her know Bob Miller had arrived.

"Good morning, Bob. So this is your new little guy." Jaylin looked at the tall man dwarfing her exam room. He cradled a bulldog puppy with hands nearly as big as the pup himself. The bulldog snorted, bounced, and lifted his pudgy front legs as high as he could while wiggling his back end from side to side. "Well, you're a friendly one, aren't you?" Jaylin smiled at his antics as she held him close to her body to listen to his heart.

"He looks pretty healthy. You've had bulldogs before, so I probably don't have to tell you to keep an eye on his skin for any sores, and watch his weight. They can get obese quickly since they tend to be real couch potatoes. Does he have a name yet?"

"I'm gonna call him Bambi."

Jaylin studied the young dog. He was fawn with a brindled coloring across his rear end. "I can see it. He looks a little like a baby deer."

"Exactly!"

"I like it. It suits him." Jaylin picked up Bambi and set him on the scale to get a starting weight. She'd miss her long-time clients like Bob. They might choose to go elsewhere rather than make the forty-mile trip to her new clinic, but she couldn't control that. She could send them a letter letting them know where she was and hope they chose to follow her. If not, she'd make new clients. *I can do this.* "He won't get his rabies shot until he's a year old. He's a healthy puppy, and I think he'll be a great dog for you, Bob."

"Thank you. I think so, too," Bob said. He bent to kiss Bambi's head.

Jaylin suppressed a grin and took Bambi's chart to the front desk.

"Thanks for your help, Rose." She spoke quietly as she handed her the file.

"Dr. Meyers. You don't need to thank me for doing my job. If I hated it, I'd quit." Rose smiled and shook her head.

"I hate doing paperwork, so indulge me."

Jaylin went to her office to relax with a cup of coffee and a cranberry bagel while she waited for her next appointment. She opened her laptop to check the latest *Veterinary Practice News*.

❖

Jaylin started at the ping of her phone signaling Rose's text announcing Maria's arrival with Frankie. She shut down her computer before heading to the exam room.

"Hi, Dr. Jay." Maria hefted Frankie onto the exam table and beamed her incredible smile from across the table.

"How've you been, Maria? Everyone adjusted to the move?" Jaylin relaxed into the presence of Maria's gentle spirit.

"You know"—Maria tilted her head, a look of wonder on her beautiful face—"it's interesting to me how little adjustment was needed. I feel as if I'm finally living the life meant for me. I'm crazy in love with Dana, and the little church where I sing feels like home. Frankie's settling in, too." She pulled Frankie into a hug and continued. "I think he's lost some weight. He has two flights of stairs to navigate to get outside, and Dana takes him to the grooming school a couple of times a week. He's gotten a lot more social around other dogs."

"I'm happy for you. Let's get this guy weighed." Jaylin gently moved Frankie to the scale. "He's down two pounds." She cupped the dachshund's face. "Good job, little guy." His butt tried desperately to keep up with his wagging tail at the attention, which made them both laugh. He didn't even flinch when Jaylin drew his blood. "Good boy." Jaylin deposited the blood sample in the lab area, grabbed Frankie's chart, and turned to Maria. "Stop and see Rose on your way out. I'm glad you and Frankie are doing well."

"Oh, no. I'll go in a minute. First, I want to know how you're doing. I don't like the worry in your eyes. I know you rescued a dog in November. Is everything going all right?"

Jaylin looked up from Frankie's chart and caught Maria's intense gaze.

"I just have a lot on my mind. Railroad, my dog, is great. I'm planning to train her for agility trials this fall."

"Good. I'm glad she's working out for you. My invitation to come to our church Easter program still stands. I'm arranging some nice music."

"Thank you, Maria. I'll think about it."

"I hope you do," Maria said. "Pastor Wright is great. He accepts everyone who wants to be there. He won't judge you. I've been singing in the choir for months, and it's really a comfortable, welcoming place of worship. I'd love to have you visit. Dana and I usually stop for lunch after the service and you'd be welcome to join us." Maria's gentle tone and intense dark eyes encouraged Jaylin.

"Thanks, Maria." Jaylin considered telling Maria about her intention to sell her practice, but she still had planning to do. Maria was one of her few friends in the area, and she would miss her. She made a mental note to keep in touch with her and gave her a tight hug good-bye.

Jaylin dropped Frankie's chart off on Rose's desk. Alone in her office, she began a list of the positives and negatives of selling. Dr. William Berglund had offered her an opportunity for a new small animal clinic attached to his equine hospital in Novi, Michigan. *Forty miles away, but closer to my brother.* She wouldn't have to worry about a mortgage or taxes on the business because Bill would take care of the billing and insurance, and he hadn't asked for any monetary investment on her part. She wrote that under positives. She'd be making less income. She wrote that under negatives but with an asterisk. How much money did she need? She'd managed to pay off her student loans, had a roof over her head, food for herself and her dog, and a reliable vehicle. She had all she needed. She would have to hire movers, probably come up with a security deposit, and monthly rent, but she had a little money saved, and she paid rent now, so there was no change there. She'd learned the lessons of doing without from her foster care childhood, and it was time for her to take a chance on something new. She opened her laptop and composed her ad for the sale of her practice. She had a couple of weeks until her appointment with Bill to see the new building and finalize the details. It was time for a staff meeting.

"I'd like to speak to you both before you head home today, if that's all right." Jaylin stood at the front reception desk as she addressed Rose and Nancy.

"Sure," they said in unison.

Jaylin collected her thoughts for a moment before continuing. "I've had an offer from Dr. Berglund to take over a small animal clinic he's starting in Novi. It'll be a big move for me, but I also believe it will also be an excellent opportunity." She looked at both her employees as she spoke. "I plan to sell this practice, and I wanted to give you both time to consider your options. I'll be meeting with Bill in a couple of weeks, and I'll know more after that."

Rose and Nancy looked at each other before Rose spoke. "I think it's great you're moving on, but I know I'll miss you."

"Me, too," Nancy said.

"Thanks, you two. I'll let you know how it goes."

Jaylin went back to her office, a sense of excitement building. Telling her staff was the first step, but somehow that made it more concrete. *I can do this.*

CHAPTER THREE

Jaylin pulled into the parking lot and parked on the shaded west side of the building. The white lines on the aged and cracking asphalt were barely visible, indicating that it probably wasn't Bill's top priority. She'd intentionally arrived early to have a chance to check out the building. This would be a huge decision, and she didn't like surprises. She took time to gaze around the expanse of land surrounding the equine clinic. The giant oak, maple, black walnut, and various weed trees grew randomly across the land as if sprouting wherever the hand of nature had thrown seeds into the breeze. Thirty-foot spruce sentinels protected the building from the winter's harsh north wind. Serenity floated in the breeze, rustling the tiny new leaves vying for first chance to offer shade from the intensifying sunshine. She could be comfortable in this natural setting. It was what she missed most about her current building, located as it was on the busy main street of downtown St. Clair.

Bill had made good progress updating the building. The neutral colored, freshly painted cinderblock blended well with the verdant surroundings. She recognized the vinyl windows as the expensive brand she would have loved to have had in her clinic. The covered entryway, lined with neatly trimmed boxwood on either side of the aging cement walkway, looked like a perfect stopping place for nervous dogs. The new steel front door had a small window large enough to let sunlight in but small enough to keep intruders out. She tried the handle on the door but wasn't surprised to find it locked. She walked around to the rear entrance, a smaller version of the front. She recognized the young shoots growing along the path to the door as day lilies. She pictured a bird feeder set away from the building and a small table with a few chairs where she and the staff could eat lunch and take breaks.

Jaylin heard squealing tires just as she grabbed the handle of the equine clinic's door. She'd finally been able to afford the Volvo she'd wanted, so her heart raced when she turned to see a sporty little Porsche convertible skid into the parking lot and stop within a yard of her vehicle. Damn fool. *Probably one of those wealthy horse owners.* She yanked open the door, then turned back to give the idiot a piece of her mind, but the woman climbing out of the Boxter Spyder held her spellbound for a moment. She was striking.

"Hello. Is that your wagon?" the arresting woman asked.

Jaylin wondered if this was Bill's vet tech. She hoped not. She shook off the disquieting reaction. "Hello, yourself. Do you always drive that way?" Jaylin stood next to her XC70 Volvo with her hands on her hips. She knew she was glaring, but this woman unsettled her.

"Huh? Oh. Sorry. I didn't mean to scare you. My name's Kristen. Are you the doctor here to see Bill?"

"You need to be more careful. You could've slid into the side of my car."

"I said I'm sorry. I didn't come close to hitting your car." Kristen pointed to the distance between the vehicles.

"You most certainly did come close. What if you'd hit some gravel and couldn't stop?"

"I'm not going to stand here asking for forgiveness. I didn't hit your car, and I was in complete control of mine. There's no gravel on this lot. Look at it." Kristen waved her hand toward the area surrounding them. Kristen set her hands on her hips and stood mirroring Jaylin's stance.

"Never mind." Jaylin dismissed her with a wave of her hand and began to walk away while resisting the impulse to lean closer.

A light breeze carried the scent of fresh hay and early spring, and a horse whinnied in the distance.

Kristen bristled at the universal dismissal. "I was running late. I'm not going to apologize again. I'm here to see Dr. Berglund." She turned to head into the building but stopped when Jaylin gently gripped her arm.

"Hey. Apology accepted. I'm here to see Bill, too. I'm Dr. Jaylin Meyers."

Kristen startled at the feeling of loss when Jaylin released her hold on her arm. Golden flecks in her hazel eyes sparkled in the sunlight. "Fine. Let's go inside." She held the door open for Jaylin but resisted the urge to touch her, a feeling that threw her off balance.

"Kristen, I'm glad you could make it." Bill Berglund slid his arm around Kristen's shoulder. "And Dr. Meyers. Did you two already meet?"

"Yeah. I've already managed to piss her off." Kristen forced a smile.

"It's all good," Jaylin said.

"Well, that's fine then. Would either of you like an iced tea?" Bill asked and walked behind his desk to the refrigerator, totally ignoring the tension permeating the room.

"No, thanks," Kristen said. She watched Jaylin eye her suspiciously.

"I would. Thank you," Jaylin said.

Bill handed a cold can of tea to Jaylin. "So, do we need formal introductions?" he asked.

"You know, I'd like to start over, if we could," Kristen said.

"Good. Dr. Jaylin Meyers, this is my former vet tech, Kristen Eckert. Kristen, this is Dr. Jaylin Meyers. She's considering a position as a small animal vet here at my practice." Bill turned to address Jaylin. "I've asked Kristen to come back on a temporary basis to help you get settled. She worked for me for five years before…well, a few years ago. She knows the clinic and most of our clients. She's a graduate of Macomb Community College's vet tech program, and I think she could be a huge asset to you if you decide to move to this area."

"I'm glad to meet you." Jaylin held out her hand and Kristen took it in a show of truce.

"How about a tour?" Bill asked.

"Sounds good," Jaylin said.

They walked outside to the adjacent building that would be the new small animal clinic. Jaylin's neatly cut brown hair feathered along her neck, barely touching the collar of her powder blue polo shirt. Kristen imagined running her fingers through the soft curls and gently nibbling on the exposed skin. Jaylin had breasts the perfect size for snuggling, and expressive, slender hands. Kristen found herself imagining their heat as they traveled across her skin. Her body looked trim and her legs long under her tailored slacks. A polished pair of penny loafers finished off her casual elegance. Those hazel eyes that had captured Kristen with their intensity had moved to take in the building and surrounding area, and she wished they were back on her. She shoved the thought aside and focused on what Bill was saying.

❖

Jaylin willed her hands to steady as she ran her fingers over the walls of what could be her new clinic. Bill said she would have full control over it. She would be in charge as far as treatments went, and Bill would take care of the financial side of things. She wouldn't be making as much income, but as she'd figured, she wouldn't have the expense of a mortgage either. But that wasn't what made her hands shake. Kristen, the annoying woman who'd sped into the parking lot like a maniac, had the bluest eyes she'd ever seen. She'd tied her thick mahogany hair back away from her tanned face, and there was a softness born of maturity in her features. She was older than Jaylin would have expected for a vet tech. She guessed her age early thirties. She was lean and wore her jeans and Western style shirt and boots as if she was born in them. Her cocky grin touched a place in Jaylin she vehemently safeguarded. She hadn't been so intensely affected by anyone since Sally. She squashed the painful memories and concentrated on the job ahead.

"This all looks great, Bill. I like the connecting door between the buildings. The clients can wait in that expansive waiting room of yours and not have to walk outside to get here. When will the plumbing and electrical be finished?"

"I expect it'll be finished by late April. You can oversee all the improvements, but please be sure to run anything by me so I'm not overdrawn on my bank account."

Bill grinned, but Jaylin knew he was probably only half kidding. The renovation looked expensive. "It looks terrific so far. The only thing I might add would be a table and chairs and a bird feeder in back. You've done an outstanding job."

"Thanks. I'm guessing from all the calls I've been getting, you'll be super busy, but I can't count on that until I see the numbers. I know Sarah's willing to take on the extra work of scheduling your appointments, and I believe Kristen will fill in for a while as your technician. If you get overloaded, just let me know and we can figure out a permanent solution."

Jaylin chanced meeting Kristen's gaze. Kristen grinned, and Jaylin ignored the flutter in her stomach. No way would she go there. Her sanity depended on it. "I'd be happy for any help you can give me, Kristen." She slid her hands into her pants pockets, straightened her spine, and returned Kristen's grin with a confident smile before she turned back to Bill. "I think I'd like it here. You have a lovely piece of property."

"I was lucky to get it. Four years after I moved here from Kentucky, the veterinarian who owned this place died of a heart attack and left it all to me. The property had been in his family for generations, but he was a confirmed bachelor and was determined that I carry on the tradition of the equine clinic. I plan to for as long as I'm able, and part of me wants to keep it only a horse clinic. But so much has changed in this area that I would be remiss to ignore the pet owners clamoring for help."

"I'm not sure how long it will take to sell my practice, but I'll be in touch next week to let you know how it's going. Thank you for showing me around." Jaylin turned to Kristen. "I'm glad to meet you, Kristen. I look forward to working with you."

"You, too, Dr. Meyers. I'll do what I can, but my expertise and interests lie in equine medicine. It's been a long time since I've worked with dogs and cats."

"But you have experience with them, correct?" Jaylin met Kristen's eyes.

"I do. But I'm not sure…hey, do you need to leave right away? We could go get lunch and talk. Novi has some good restaurants." Kristen hadn't looked away, and Jaylin lowered her gaze and took a step back. She hadn't wrestled with power struggles since Sally, and being reminded of her twice in less than two hours gave her a stomachache.

Kristen smiled and turned to Bill. "Any suggestions as to where I should take the doc?"

"You two can decide, but it's a good idea. Go wherever you want, my treat. I've got a worming appointment to get to, or I'd join you. I look forward to hearing from you, Jaylin. Enjoy your lunch." Bill left to gather his equipment, and Jaylin followed Kristen out to their cars.

"Nice ride, by the way," Kristen said.

"Thanks. I'm sorry if I snapped at you earlier. I'm a little protective of it."

"No problem. I can get a little aggressive when I drive my Boxter."

"Shall I follow you somewhere? I don't know the area well yet." Jaylin looked perplexed.

"Unless you're afraid to ride with me, I can drive." Kristen opened the passenger door of her car and waited for Jaylin's response.

Jaylin looked at her own car and back to the open door.

"It'll be fine there. Bill will be back in a couple of hours, and there won't be any workers here until Monday." Kristen hesitated. "Maybe it would be better if you drove yourself. That'll give you a chance to get to know your way around."

Jaylin clicked the lock button on her car's remote door lock and turned to face Kristen. "I'd enjoy a ride in that hot little sports car of yours."

Kristen lost herself in the sparkle of hazel and in Jaylin's shy smile. It was time for her to distance herself and find out what Dr. Meyers expected from her. She shivered slightly at the thought.

"Are you cold? I have a jacket in my car."

"No, I'm fine. Sorry. There's a nice little bar and grill with outside seating. Do you like burgers and beer?"

Jaylin settled into the low passenger seat and snapped the seat belt closed. "I love burgers and beer."

❖

"Is this place always so crowded?" Jaylin hadn't expected so many people at three o'clock in the afternoon.

"It has terrific food, and it's been a long winter. Everyone's out enjoying one of the first nice days we've had. Come on. I see an empty table on the terrace." Kristin led her to the open seats, and pulled the chair out for her to sit.

"Thanks. Are you always so chivalrous?" Kristen was quiet for so long, Jaylin thought she wouldn't answer. "Never mind."

"No, that's okay. It seems to come naturally for me."

"You enjoy being in control?" Jaylin knew she was skirting the edge of flirting, but she couldn't seem to stop herself.

"Yeah. I like being in control most of the time, but I've been known to let go a time or two." Kristen grinned.

Jaylin's stomach fluttered. *Careful*. She shifted in her seat and rearranged her silverware before locking her gaze with Kristen's. "I tried that once. It didn't work out so well."

"He was a fool." Kristen's looked at her menu, then back to Jaylin. "Or she?"

"She. And maybe so, but I was the foolish one." Jaylin set down the menu and rested her elbows on the table. She needed to change the subject. "So, you prefer working with horses than small animals. Would you be willing to help me out though? Bill speaks highly of you."

Kristen looked up from her menu and hesitated before speaking. "I'll tell Bill I'll do it. It's been a long time since I graduated, and I've been working strictly with horses, but I'm willing to give it a shot for a while."

"Thanks. I appreciate it. I don't expect it will take me long to settle in. I guess we can talk about the time frame once I get moved."

The server taking their order interrupted their conversation.

"Why do you want to move across the state, anyway?" Kristen asked.

"I was raised in the Grand Rapids area. My practice in St. Clair has been good for me, but I think I'm ready for a change." Jaylin took a sip of her beer.

"Family?"

"Nope." Jaylin looked around and stifled the threatening tears as her brother's image flashed in her mind's eye. She twirled the beer bottle on the wet ring it made on the table. "How about you? How did you end up in Novi?"

"I've lived here all my life. My parents moved here before I was born." Kristen didn't offer any further information, and they finished their lunch in uncomfortable silence.

Jaylin wished she'd resisted the impulse to ride to the restaurant with Kristen. She needed to get home, back to her safe comfort zone.

"You ready to head out, Dr. Meyers?"

"Yes, and if we're going to work together, please call me Jaylin."

"Will do, Jaylin." Kristen stood and waited for Jaylin to stand before following her out. Then she smiled that damned disconcerting smile, and Jaylin hurried toward the car.

The small sports car didn't allow much room between them, and their shoulders brushed as Jaylin fastened her seat belt. Kristen's jean clad legs moved seductively as she depressed the clutch, and her right hand tensed and relaxed as she caressed the shifter knob and smoothly shifted gears. Jaylin had felt those warm, soft fingers against her own when they'd first met, and she imagined she still felt the tingle in her palm.

Kristen had lowered the top, and Jaylin watched the sun reflect off her thick mahogany hair. Her smooth looking sun kissed skin had a healthy glow. She turned and smiled at Jaylin, tilting her head as if she could feel Jaylin's stare. She was beautiful. Jaylin wondered if she was making a mistake by moving. She couldn't allow herself to get involved again. Sally had been enough of a lesson. At least she'd only have to work with Kristen for a few weeks. She'd make sure it wasn't longer than that.

CHAPTER FOUR

Jaylin's stomach knotted with nerves as she drove to her clinic. She had arranged for Rose and Nancy to meet her before they opened, so she'd have time to fill them in on the details of her move. She worried about their futures, although she had found an excellent veterinarian to take over her practice, and he was enthusiastic about keeping them on.

"Thanks for coming in early, you guys." Jaylin waited until they'd both picked out their warm bagels from the bag she'd brought and turned their attention to her. She took a settling breath before speaking. "I've sold the practice to a young veterinarian who's moving from Ohio. I've checked his credentials, and he's well respected in his current practice. His fiancé is from Michigan, so he's excited to be able to move here, and he told me he'd love to have you both stay on and work with him. He'll stop by next week to meet you both."

"So, when is this move taking place?" Rose asked.

"It'll be the third weekend in April. The new doctor, Dylan Nash, will be spending a few days working with us the last week before I move. That should give you a sense of who he is and if you want to work with him."

"If you like him, that's probably good enough for me," Nancy said.

"Yeah, you're special, Dr. Jay, but we're happy for your new adventure. We talked about it, and we both want you to keep in touch." Rose's voice hitched and she wiped away a tear.

Jaylin allowed her own tears to form and opened her arms as Rose and Nancy moved into them for a good-bye hug.

❖

The thought of moving didn't bother Jaylin. She never minded packing and unpacking. It motivated her to rid herself of unnecessary stuff, and as she walked through her sparsely furnished condo, she knew she'd have no trouble finishing by the time the movers arrived.

She only had one photo album encompassing her childhood. Like waves receding from a beach and rinsing the sand, she allowed the flashbacks of her multiple moves within foster care to wash over her and sweep away any residual anguish.

Her other photo album chronicled her adult life. She'd torn up and burned, in a purging ritual, all but one of the snapshots she'd had of Sally. She kept one as a reminder of a life she never wanted to repeat. She gently placed the photographic records of her life in one of the open boxes neatly lining one wall of her living room. She'd been packing boxes all morning and had managed to fill and close up the last of them. The only items left to pack were the few toiletries in the bathroom she'd throw into her overnight bag.

She dropped into her favorite swivel rocker, tipped her head back, and embraced the concept of starting a new chapter in her life. She'd been shuffled from home to home her whole childhood, never able to settle in one place. Material possessions and living conditions disappeared and changed without her control, so she was excited about the fenced yard attached to the small house she'd found to rent. She could work with Railroad as often as she'd like instead of traveling to a training facility like she did now, and she planned to pick up a new bird feeder on her first day off. *This is going to be a great adventure.*

CHAPTER FIVE

"Zigzag looked great out there, Kris. I think you two are a shoo-in to win the competition next weekend."

"He did do well, didn't he?" Kristen grinned at Debby, her friend and fellow barrel race competitor. "He's getting better with each practice, aren't you, big guy?" She leaned over the withers of her chestnut Appaloosa gelding to pat his solid neck.

"Are you going to enter the Camas Prairie Stump Race next week?" Debby asked.

Kristen had considered the barrel race, which meant two horses starting at the same time but running in the opposite direction around the barrels. "I don't think so. Zig is still new at this. I don't want to spook him by starting out next to another horse."

"Shadow and I would be happy to walk through it with you. If we start out slowly, it'll be easier for Zigzag to get used to it."

"Thanks." Kristen dismounted and hugged her horse's warm head when he rested his chin on her shoulder. "Maybe I'll take you up on that. Right now, I have to go home and review my small animal notes from school. Dr. Berglund's hired a new doctor, and I've agreed to help out for a while."

"Last time he was out to worm Shadow, he said he had fewer patients lately," Debby said.

"Well, I guess this new doctor will be working on smaller animals. She probably doesn't know diddly-squat about horses." Kristen rubbed Zigzag's soft nose and turned to lead him back to the barn.

"She, huh?" Deb's eyes sparked with interest. "What's her name?"

"Jaylin Meyers," Kristen said.

"If she's a vet, she probably knows something about all animals. Don't they have to learn all of it in vet school?" Debby tugged Shadow's reins and followed Kristen.

"I guess so. I'm not looking forward to it, but I told Bill I'd be willing to help her *transition* into the practice." Kristen led Zigzag into the barn. "I hope she doesn't expect me to hold on to some feral cat while she pokes a thermometer up its butt."

"Well, be careful, and let me know if she's hot." Debby's grin was predatory.

"Geez, Deb. You're such a player."

"Come on. You aren't exactly Miss Prissy yourself."

"Yeah, but I get the impression that Jaylin isn't the type to hop into bed with just anyone. In fact, I get the feeling she's been burned before," Kristen said. She began to brush Zigzag and pondered Jaylin's "I was the foolish one" statement.

Debby tied Shadow next to Zigzag. "I know you're not interested in anything serious, but if you aren't going to try to seduce her, maybe I can."

"Fine. Once she starts and I have my schedule, I'll let you know how it goes." For some reason, she didn't want Debby near Jaylin.

"Let me know when you want to get together to practice the stump racing," Debby said.

Kristen considered Debby's statement as she waved and climbed into her pickup truck. She wasn't interested in anything serious with Jaylin, or any other woman, for that matter. Jaylin was beautiful, but she couldn't allow herself to get too close. She had responsibilities. She'd help Bill out and work with her for a few weeks, doing her job and keeping her distance. Content with her decision, she pulled out of the lot and forced images of Jaylin's gentle smile out of her head.

❖

Kristen tossed her car keys onto the kitchen counter and retrieved a beer from the refrigerator. She leaned against the refrigerator door and blew out a breath. She hadn't expected her reaction to Jaylin, and if she couldn't keep her attraction under control, it would be a long few weeks. She carried her beer to her deck, fired up her grill, and settled into her deck chair to read.

Kristen focused her attention on everything she'd learned in school about the care of dogs and cats. She might have to ignore the lure of Dr. Jaylin Meyers, but there was no way she was going to appear incompetent in any way. She spent the next hour making notes and reviewing her textbooks. She worried about the age of the material, but decided she'd rely on Jaylin to know what she was doing. She stood and stretched her back, pushing aside further thoughts of Jaylin, which kept ending with her in her arms.

She rinsed her plate and silverware and put them in her dishwasher before heading out to her barn to prepare the stalls and bring in her horse and pony. "Come on, you two. Time to settle in for the night." The pony had been her mother's, although she'd never had much interest in her. Kristen had kept her after her mother died as company for Zigzag and they'd become inseparable. She wondered why the bond between animals seemed so essential. She wasn't convinced that was the case for humans. Her one attempt at a relationship had taught her extreme caution was necessary in dealing with any feeling for her soon-to-be new boss.

❖

Kristen arrived half an hour early for her first day at work, surprised to see Jaylin's car in the lot.

"Good morning." Jaylin was already in the exam room when Kristen entered.

"Morning. I see you get an early start. I'm not late, am I?"

"No. I'm used to getting in early to check on surgery patients. Since we have none, I suppose I'll make us some coffee and we can wait outside," Jaylin said.

"Are we busy today?" Kristen followed Jaylin to the kitchenette and pulled out two coffee cups from the small cupboard.

"Sarah says we have three dogs and a cat coming in. It sounds as if the first dog needs a flea bath."

"Do you do flea baths?" Kristen nearly choked on the question. She hadn't signed up for grooming duties.

"No. If that's what's necessary, I'll send them to the groomer in town. I've already contacted her and confirmed we could refer patients to her. The owner told Sarah that the dog wouldn't stop scratching herself." Jaylin filled their cups and headed out the back door. "We'll make sure she isn't anemic and give the owner the lecture on flea control. I'm going to fill the bird feeder before I sit." Jaylin dumped seed into the squirrel-proof feeder and returned to the table.

So far so good. Kristen's nerves settled in the presence of Jaylin's calm. She pulled out a chair for Jaylin to sit and relaxed into one across from her. She watched the early morning sun glint off Jaylin's shiny hair. She looked serene and confident, and Kristen mentally shook herself as her thoughts strayed toward exploration of Jaylin's full lips.

"I just want to thank you again for doing this, Kristen. I know you'd rather be working with horses." Jaylin smiled.

"That's true, but there's a small part of me that wants to see how much I'll remember from my classes. A very small part." Kristen grinned over her coffee cup. "I know we didn't get off to the smoothest start, but I'll do my best to help you out."

"I'm responsible for a large part of that rocky start, so thanks," Jaylin said.

"Did your move go well? Bill told me you found a little house to rent in town."

"I did. I was surprised how quickly I found something. It's perfect for me and Railroad."

"Who's Railroad?" Kristen figured it must be a pet, but she wanted to keep Jaylin talking. She liked her voice.

"She's my rescue dog. I got her in November, and I've been working on obedience training with her. She's picked it up so quickly that I'm thinking of agility instruction next. Do you have any pets?" she asked.

Kristen fidgeted in her seat, watching Jaylin's beautiful hands. "Not a dog. I have an Appaloosa gelding that I ride in various events. His name is Zigzag, and he's quite a showman."

"I'd love to see you ride someday." Jaylin smiled and leaned forward on the table.

"There's a barrel race coming up at the fairgrounds. I'll let you know what time I'm riding," Kristen said.

"Cool." Jaylin sat back in her chair and watched the sparrows jostling for position on the bird feeder. "So you ride in barrel races. What else do you do for fun?"

"I love to shoot skeet. My mother taught me as a kid and I enjoy the challenge."

"Your mother? I'm surprised. Geez, I'm being sexist. I was about to say that I would have thought it would be your dad's sport. Sorry." Jaylin winced.

"Yeah, that did sound sexist. My mom was on the U.S. Olympic skeet team for several years. One of my fondest memories is traveling to Barcelona when I was thirteen to watch her compete. It was the last year the team was combined men and women. The Olympic committee introduced the women's event in two thousand, and she traveled to Sydney. That was her last Olympics. She died of cancer in two thousand eight."

"I'm so sorry, Kristen. I didn't mean to bring up bad memories." Jaylin took Kristen's hand.

"My memories of her sickness are awful, obviously, but as my mother, she was great. From her, I learned that I could do whatever I put my mind to, but from both of my parents, I learned the value of hard work and financial prudence." Kristen smiled and squeezed Jaylin's hand. Jaylin had intertwined their fingers while she'd been talking, and the feeling of rightness took her by surprise.

"I never knew my mother," Jaylin said. "My younger brother and I grew up in the foster care system. I guess you could say I've had several mothers. None of them much good."

Kristen quickly changed the subject. "What time is the flea-bitten dog coming in?" She didn't want to go into any more personal stuff, and the pain in Jaylin's eyes told her there was a larger story there.

Jaylin checked her watch. "In about ten minutes."

Kristen sat back in her chair and watched the birds flitting about the feeder. Her thoughts strayed to lunch the first time she'd met Jaylin. It had been a bit uncomfortable. They'd both shied away from anything too personal, so this revelation about her mother surprised her. For some reason, she wanted Jaylin to trust her enough to confide in her.

She'd been allowed a glimpse of some inner turmoil that Jaylin probably didn't realize she showed, and Kristen felt compelled to soothe her. She found it hard to believe anyone would have treated

Jaylin badly. She'd said her practice had been "good" for her. Kristen wondered what that meant. *None of my business.* They had to work together. Maybe they could be friends. *Nothing more.*

❖

"Thanks for helping me with this stump racing business. I think Zigzag likes it." Kristen smoothly dismounted to join Debby and Shadow standing at the end of the course.

"No problem. I enjoyed it, and Shadow needed the practice. I know this is a complete change of subject, but I want to know why you didn't tell me about this new doctor at Dr. B's clinic."

"I did tell you about her."

"Yeah, but you were supposed to let me know if she was hot. I stopped in to talk to Dr. B about Shadow's worming schedule, and I saw her at Sarah's desk. She's a knockout. She was leaning against the wall smiling at Sarah when I was leaving. Jesus, those eyes. When she looked up at me, I felt her peering inside me, searching my soul. When she looked away, I wanted her. I'd have torn open that lab coat, pushed her against that wall and reached inside to—"

"Debby. Deb, hey. I have to work with this woman. Let it go." Kristen shook her head to dislodge the thought of Jaylin naked.

"Sorry, friend. I'm just relaying the incredible fantasy she evoked. I'm getting wet just thinking about her. I bet she had on some kind of sexy black lace bikini panties. She left before I had a chance to introduce myself." Debby and Shadow followed Kristen to the barn.

"I'm sure you can catch her in the clinic any day of the week. Maybe you could grab a stray cat and make an appointment." Kristen pulled off Zigzag's saddle and blanket and picked up a brush.

"Maybe if you introduce me as your friend, she'll be more likely to accept an invitation to the club. I bet she'd look way hot in leather." Debby slid her saddle off Shadow and stowed it on a rack.

Kristen tried unsuccessfully to rid herself of the vision of Jaylin in leather. She bristled at the thought of Debby and Jaylin together at the leather bar. She had no claim on Jaylin and wanted none. Why shouldn't she and Debby hook up? Would Jaylin even want that? Kristen continued brushing Zigzag, relaxing into the familiar task and letting her mind wander.

She was better off alone. It was safer. Her father needed her, and relationships took up too much time. She couldn't allow that to happen. The occasional hookup she had with a woman at her rodeo events was more about their mutual physical need than any genuine connection. She had her Appaloosa, her skeet shooting, and her dad. That was all she needed. Her mind knew better than her heart.

"Jaylin will probably come to the fairground next week. I can introduce you then," Kristen said.

Maybe Jaylin already had a lover, although that seemed unlikely from the bits she'd gathered from the few conversations they'd had. That thought did nothing to relieve the ache in her belly.

CHAPTER SIX

Jaylin pulled her Volvo into the end spot in the Greenwood Cemetery parking lot. She opened the back door and signaled to Railroad to heel. They walked along a short path lined with purple and pink rose of Sharon to an area in the middle of the cemetery.

"Hey, you. I brought a friend with me today." Jaylin sat on the ground facing her brother's bronze grave marker. "This is Railroad. She was tied to a railroad track, left to die. Now she's my best friend." Railroad dropped to a down position on command, and Jaylin pulled her close. She removed the overgrown grass and brushed the dirt from her brother's marker. *Roy Meyers 1981-1998.* She pulled out the inset vase and filled it with the flowers she'd brought, then leaned back on her hands and sighed. She had no idea how her younger brother had died, or why he'd gone so young. She'd worried over the years about who'd raised him and what sort of young man he'd become. She hoped she'd been a positive influence in the few childhood years they'd shared when they'd lived not far from Novi, before they'd been separated. Now that she lived closer, she could visit him more often.

"I sold my practice and moved here to Novi. My new place has a bird feeder." She thought of the stories she used to make up about the birds on the days she'd been locked out of the house after school.

That one's from Ohio, and that one flew all the way from Pennsylvania.

Tears leaked out the corner of her eyes as she allowed memories to surface. Jaylin had always thought the tears would stop, or at least turn to happy-memory tears. But that day had yet to arrive. Railroad whined and settled her head in Jaylin's lap. "I'm lonely, Roy. And I miss you," Jaylin barely whispered. "Railroad and I'll be back again soon."

Jaylin stood and signaled her dog to heel on the way back to her car. The spring morning sunshine warmed her face, and after filling the dog bowl she carried in her car and giving Railroad a drink, she walked her to the dog run area. She wondered why a cemetery would bother with a dog run, but whispered a thank you to whoever came up with the idea.

Later, before getting on the road, Jaylin sat in the driver's seat with the windows open enjoying the cool caress of the spring breeze on her cheeks. She ate a sandwich, drank her iced tea, and let her mind wander. What was Kristen doing on her day off? She'd surprised herself when she'd told Kristen about her mother. She hadn't told anyone about her past in years. She wondered what it was about Kristen that inspired that kind of trust. They'd been working together for a week, and their initial discomfort had faded. Kristen showed up on time or early to prepare the exam room or surgery room, she meticulously kept track of the drug cabinet, and she never hesitated to help restrain a patient. They'd fallen into a comfortable routine of taking lunch breaks outside, and she was beginning to entertain the idea that they could be friends. She simply had to figure out how to stifle the persistent desire to kiss her. Friendship, she could handle. Nothing more.

❖

"Good morning, Sarah." Jaylin stopped at the reception desk on her way to the clinic. "Will I be busy today?"

"Good morning, Dr. Meyers. Yeah. It looks as if you're booked for the day. The small animal side of the practice is taking off."

"Good. I'm glad to hear it. Please call me Jaylin, or Jay if you prefer. I don't see any need for formalities."

"Thanks, Jaylin." Sarah smiled. "You have one patient who insisted on being first on your schedule today."

"Who is it?" Jaylin leaned over the counter to see the computer screen.

"It's a Bob Miller. He says his puppy knows you and won't go to any other veterinarian. Are all small animal owners this loyal?" Sarah looked so flummoxed that Jaylin had to laugh.

"I guess some are. I've known Bob for several years, and this is the second puppy that I've taken care of for him. What time is he coming in?"

"Ten o'clock."

"Thanks. I'll talk to you later." Jaylin ambled to her office in the adjoining building and opened her laptop. She filled her coffee cup as she waited for her computer to boot up and silently thanked Bill for his Wi-Fi. When she sat at her desk and opened her e-mail, she nearly choked on her coffee. Curiosity forced her to open it, and she stared at the e-mail from the one person she hoped never to hear from again.

I see you're working in Novi. Closer to where you started. You still belong to me, you know. We had something special and I know you want it again. I know what you need.

Jaylin's hands trembled as she set down her coffee cup and scrolled down the message.

Remember when you'd strip for me? One button at a time. We can do that again. I promise I can take care of you. You can be mine again. We were so good together. Remember?

Jaylin felt the stirring start between her legs at the memory. Damn her. If Sally still had power over her with only her words, what did that say? Was she still so weak she couldn't resist the pull of false promises? Did her desire to have someone love her still trump her self-worth? She didn't want to be owned. She wanted the mutual love and respect that Sally had deceived her into believing she could give her. Jaylin slammed her laptop closed. It was time for a meeting.

❖

Jaylin stopped in the kitchenette for a glass of water and a minute to compose herself before going to the exam room where Bob Miller waited.

"Bob. How've you been? It's good to see you." Jaylin shook the hand that dwarfed hers. "I see Bambi has grown into a handsome young dog."

Bob shuffled his feet and grinned at the compliment. "Yeah, he's special, this one. All my other bulldogs seem boring now. Bambi's real smart." Bob lifted the seven-month-old puppy to set him on the exam table.

"He looks great. What did you bring him in for today?"

Bob shifted his substantial weight from foot to foot. "I kind of wanted to find out where you were and if we could, well, if we could maybe see if he's ready for his *surgery*." Bob's face glowed red as he shifted his gaze around the room.

"Ah. I know you want a well-behaved pet, and I know you're a responsible pet owner. Having this surgery will keep Bambi calm and content. But you know that. Let's check him out." Jaylin moved her stethoscope around Bambi's chest, poked and prodded his bulky frame, and finished her exam with a pat to his head. "He looks plenty healthy, Bob. I think we could neuter him anytime. I prefer to do blood work before any surgery. I'll take a sample today, and if everything looks good, you can make an appointment for anytime you're ready."

"How much will it cost me? I mean now that you're at this fancy horse clinic and all."

Jaylin hadn't expected that reaction and hesitated before responding. "Fancy horse clinic, huh? I don't know about that, but I know I want Bambi safe. There's no extra charge for the blood work. Years ago, I had a surgery patient that had an undiagnosed, rare blood disorder. Since then I check every animal before surgery."

"Thanks, Dr. Jay. I'll make an appointment as soon as I hear from you."

"Sounds good. I'll call you with the results of the blood tests." Jaylin reached to squeeze Bob's arm. "Thanks for driving all the way out here."

Bob shifted foot to foot again. "I was glad when I got your letter. I called your office, and Rose offered to make an appointment with the new vet, but Bambi trusts you."

"I made the decision to move," Jaylin said. "And I think it's been a good one. I didn't want the new vet to think I was trying to steal clients away, but I felt the need to let a few of my long-time clients know where I was going. I'm glad you found the place."

"It wasn't hard. It only took me half an hour to get here. I think Bambi enjoyed the ride. Bye, Doc." Bob plodded toward the exit and waved as he commanded Bambi to heel.

Jaylin didn't want anything to go wrong with Bambi's surgery, and she made a mental note to request Kristen be available for assisting. She ignored the fluttering in her belly at the thought of spending time with Kristen.

❖

"My name is Jaylin, and I'm glad this meeting is still here." Jaylin paused as uncertainty paralyzed her. Could she admit how pathetic she felt? She'd fallen back into her "I'm not good enough, so I'll settle for anyone who wants me" mode. "It's been a few years since I've been to a meeting, but I recently realized that I'm not fixed yet. I may never be, but I'm willing to work toward healthier relationships. My sanity and my life depend on it."

Jaylin sat back and accepted the appreciation of the many voices welcoming her back and proclaiming her worth. Realizing that Sally could still affect her from only an e-mail, prompted her to make the twenty-mile trip to the safety of the lesbian Codependents Anonymous group where she'd found support and understanding before, and after, Sally.

"Dr. Meyers. It's good to see you again." A tall, dark-haired, sixty-something, buxom woman pulled Jaylin out of her seat and wrapped her in a hug as she spoke.

"Maggie. I'm glad to be back. I hadn't realized how much I missed it until I came tonight. I'm afraid I'm floundering with my self-worth." Jaylin snuggled into the warmth and security of her former sponsor's hug. She never wanted to move.

Maggie held her until Jaylin pulled away. She knew that Maggie would hold her for an hour if Jaylin needed it. Gratitude swelled in her heart as she stepped back and grabbed Maggie's hands. "Still calling me doctor, huh?"

Maggie clasped both of Jaylin's hands and held them to her chest before speaking. "You, young lady, ought never to forget your huge accomplishment. You put yourself through college, became a skilled veterinarian, and have your own clinic. You deserve the respect of the title you worked hard to earn. Now, let's sit and tell me what's going on in your life."

Jaylin hesitated. It'd been a long time since she'd talked about her relationship with Sally and the pitiful way she'd ended it. "Sally contacted me. That she did is scary enough, but the worst part is that I found I still react to her. I thought I'd purged her out of my life and my system." Jaylin blew out a breath, sat, and rested her chin in her hands while shaking her head.

"It sounds as if you haven't quite grasped the lesson you fought to learn with Sally. Did she confront you?" Maggie sat across from Jaylin and leaned back in her chair; her mellow voice soothed some of Jaylin's distress.

"No. I reacted to an e-mail. Not even face-to-face. She got to me with a damned e-mail." Jaylin flopped back into her chair, trying to ground herself.

"Believing you're unworthy of value and love can be the hardest belief to overcome." Maggie took Jaylin's hands in hers. "You can do it. I know you can. You're a strong woman and have a lot to offer the right woman. You deserve to be treated well."

"I guess I'll have to keep telling myself that until I believe it." Jaylin squeezed Maggie's hands and forced a smile. "It was hard to get through all the therapy after my last foster home before I went to college, but maybe I need to go back to therapy. I'm still afraid no one will stay with me. I remember when Sally chose me. I was so happy I'd finally found someone who wanted me, picked me. For the first time in my life, I felt as if I was worth something. What a mistake." Jaylin covered her face with her hands.

"Listen to me. Yes, you made a bad choice in Sally, but that does not define who you are." Maggie rested her hand gently on Jaylin's shoulder.

"I know, Maggie. Five years of therapy and many more Codependents Anonymous meetings have taught me something." She raised her head and smiled. "I'm working tomorrow, so I'd better head home. Thank you for spending time with me tonight. I needed this meeting."

"I'm happy you came back to us," Maggie said. "I know I've missed you." She wrapped Jaylin in another hug. "Be careful driving home, and come back soon. You know how it works."

"It works if you work it," they said in unison.

CHAPTER SEVEN

Jaylin filled the bird feeder before sitting at the outside table. Her meeting had helped to ground her, but she questioned her ability to ignore the pull of Sally's words. Her loneliness had been invading her dreams, as well as her days, lately. She couldn't figure out why it seemed so intense now. She was happy with her new clinic. She had Railroad and a nice place to live that was closer to Roy, and she'd reconnected with her CoDA group. *So why do I still feel lost?*

"Good morning, Doc," Kristen said.

"Hi, Kristen." Jaylin continued to sip her coffee quietly, still contemplating her past.

"Do we have a busy day?" Kristen sat across from Jaylin and poured herself a cup of coffee from the carafe.

"It doesn't sound like it. Sarah said there was an emergency on its way, but I haven't heard anything yet."

"So, should I get the surgery room prepped? Did she say what kind of emergency?"

Jaylin closed her eyes and shook her head.

"You all right? You seem…subdued."

"Yeah, I'm fine. Just a little down today, I guess. I'll call Sarah and see if I can get any more information—"

"You sit. I'll go talk to her," Kristen said. She squeezed Jaylin's shoulders before going to talk to Sarah.

Jaylin sat pondering for a while longer, then shook off her gloominess and went in search of Kristen. She found her leaning against the wall next to Sarah's desk, looking relaxed and sexy. Her smile and solid presence settled some of Jaylin's disquiet. Before she was able to interrupt and find out about the emergency, the clinic door flew open, and a large man rushed in with a nearly lifeless dog cradled against his chest.

Jaylin switched to trauma status. The dog's head moved slightly. It was alive. Barely.

"This way," she said. Jaylin led the man to the surgery room and noted that Kristen was already setting up the surgical kit and an IV bag. The dog was a large mixed breed, its fur matted to the skin. The man laid the dog on the stainless steel table, and the smell hit Jaylin before she saw the squirming fly larvae. "Fuck." The word slipped out before she had a chance to harness the rage bubbling from her core. She'd seen many cases of animal abuse in her years of practicing veterinary medicine, but each one caused the same reaction. She mumbled an apology to the client and began the process of assessing her patient.

Maggots covered the multitude of sores on the skinny, abused animal. Jaylin turned to Kristen, who already had her stethoscope resting on the dog's side.

"Weak heartbeat, shallow breath sounds. God, he's in bad shape." Kristen shook her head and looked as angry as Jaylin felt.

Jaylin checked his pale gums and felt his femoral artery for a pulse. "Weak pulse. I don't think he's going to make it. He's severely anemic, dehydrated, and malnourished. Is this your dog?" Jaylin glared at the man who had brought the dog in.

"No. He's my neighbor's dog. The jerk ties the poor thing up in the backyard all year. I fill a bucket of water for him when I can get back there. I don't know how long he's been like this, but I couldn't stand to let him just lie there and die. Was I too late to save him?"

Jaylin watched as Kristen shaved a spot on his front leg to thread an IV needle. She then began the task of shaving away the matted hair around the area with the worst of the wounded skin. She carefully poured hydrogen peroxide on his hindquarter and wiped away a mass of maggots and hair. The neglected dog never flinched.

"I don't know yet if it's too late. It's early in the year to see this many fly larvae," Jaylin said.

"The idiot doesn't clean up the dog's droppings and he tosses bags of garbage out next to the dog's area. It was buzzing with flies when I was there this morning."

"Thank you for bringing him in. If you don't mind, please give your name and number to Sarah at the desk, and I'll let you know what happens here. Leave her your neighbor's address, too. I'm going to call the city animal control and report this as abuse. Your neighbor will be in trouble."

"I'd love to see him fined or something. His place is the dump of the neighborhood. I'd stay to see how the dog does, but I've got to get to work. Don't forget to let me know about him?" The man gave the dog one last look before leaving.

Jaylin's day had started out gloomy, and it looked as if it was going to get worse. She worked with Kristen for the next hour, cleaning the dog and figuring out what it needed. After they had him stabilized on an IV and cleaned out his wounds, he seemed a little more responsive. Just as she was beginning to believe he might make it, he stopped breathing.

"Damn it." Jaylin listened intently for any sign of a heartbeat. "He's gone." Jaylin took off her stethoscope and stood back, shaking her head.

Kristen walked around the table to Jaylin's side. She placed her hand on Jaylin's shoulder, and Jaylin tipped her head back, trying to hold back her tears.

They stood that way for a few minutes before Kristen said, "I'll take care of this. Why don't you get some air?"

Jaylin nodded and left the room. It was bad enough when an animal died from a disease or from an accident. But when one died from abuse, it crushed her. She went to her office and rested her head on her arms. She let her mind go blank.

❖

"Come on. I'll take you to lunch." Kristen had moved the dog's body to the large freezer used for holding animals until owners decided on burial or cremation and had cleaned up the surgery room and taken care of the paperwork, while she waited for Jaylin to call animal control. She'd felt as pissed as Jaylin at the cruelty they'd witnessed, but her heart ached at the tears Jaylin tried to hide. All she wanted to do was make her feel better.

"Yeah. I need to get away from here for a while," Jaylin said.

"I'd suggest burgers and beer, but we have to come back for your afternoon appointments."

"Let's go get a sandwich at Panera's."

"Sounds good," Kristen said.

Kristen drove to the cafe and took the opportunity to look at Jaylin for a moment before gently grazing her cheek with the backs of her fingers to wake her.

"I'm sorry. I fell asleep, didn't I?" Jaylin tipped her head side to side as she spoke, rubbing her eyes with the backs of her hands.

"It's been a tough morning. Let's go inside." She followed Jaylin inside and pulled out Jaylin's chair for her. "I've never eaten here before. Are their sandwiches good?"

"I like them. So, I know about a place that you don't, and I've only lived here a few weeks?" Jaylin smiled.

"I guess so. I'm glad you're settling in." Kristen folded her arms in front of her on the table.

"I am. I like it here. Well, this morning's work wasn't so pleasant, but I'm sure that will be the exception rather than the norm. Thanks for your help, by the way. I have a hard time keeping my cool when I see such blatant animal abuse. I just don't understand it."

"I agree. I don't get why people take responsibility for animals and then neglect them. I'll go order our sandwiches. What would you like?"

"A smoked turkey sandwich and an iced tea."

"You got it. Be right back." Kristen went to place their order and returned to their table. "They said it would only be a few minutes. You doing okay?"

"Yeah, I'll be fine, it's just that I haven't seen anything that severe in years," Jaylin said.

"Your expletive to describe the dog's owner was perfect. The fucker."

Jaylin laughed and Kristen sighed in relief. She liked hearing her laugh.

"I think animal control will be picking up Doggie Doe this afternoon," Jaylin said. She pinched the bridge of her nose. "I feel as if we've worked a full day already."

Kristen smiled. "Yeah, me, too."

"Well, I'm sure glad you were there to help me this morning. It was a sickening experience," Jaylin said. She took a bite of her sandwich.

"Yeah, but if that dog had lived, it would have been pretty cool. We would've been responsible for saving him." Kristen surprised herself by continuing. "It's interesting to me that I'm starting to enjoy working with animals smaller than a pony. I never thought I would. I guess I have you to thank for that, and for suggesting this sandwich." She spoke between bites. "It's good."

"I'm glad," Jaylin said.

Their ride back to the clinic was quiet. Jaylin put her head back on the seat and closed her eyes. Once again, Kristen gently touched Jaylin's cheek to wake her when they arrived at the clinic.

"Thank you," Jaylin said. She spoke softly as she tilted her head into Kristen's caress.

"For what?"

"For lunch, and for helping me."

"You're welcome. I told you I'd do my best to help you. We had a rough morning, but we can look forward to the afternoon." Kristen straightened in her seat and refrained from pulling Jaylin into her arms.

❖

Jaylin relaxed into a familiar pace, soothed by the rhythm of her gait and swinging arms. She couldn't settle down once she'd gotten home from the clinic, so she'd decided to take her dog for a walk. The day had continued to be busy, and after the way it had started, she'd been wound tight by the time she left. She breathed in the cool air and slowed to listen to the soft rustling of the leaves on the tree-lined path. She carried Railroad's leash in case they ran into any early evening strollers, but she knew she wouldn't need it. With a flick of her finger that a casual observer would have missed, Railroad fell in step, pasted to her left leg. Her rescued border collie mix was intelligent and eager to learn.

She stopped to lean on the bridge railing that stretched across a tiny stream. She watched the water rush over the rocky bottom and felt the tension of her day dissipate. Another flick of her hand, and her dog sat at her side watching intently for any further commands. Jaylin had loved living by the water in St. Clair. She found the river's consistency soothing. The flow only changed during the spring thaw in late February and early March, when the ice floes bumped and banged against each other in their race toward the lake. This wasn't the St. Clair River, but it would do.

Then there was Kristen. Jaylin turned away from the water and leaned against the rail. Kristen's attentiveness, and her own reaction to it, unsettled her. She'd felt heard by Kristen, but she'd learned the painful lesson of offering her trust to the wrong woman once before. Sally's name-calling, degrading, and lying had scared Jaylin, but when Sally had become violent, Jaylin's instinct for self-preservation had kicked in. She ate until she tipped the scales at over two hundred and fifty pounds. It wasn't the healthiest or most honest way to protect herself, but it had worked. Sally came home drunk from the bar one night, called her a big fat pig, slapped her in the face, and stormed out of their apartment.

That was then, and this was now. Her relationship with Sally had awakened desires in her that had more to do with trust and love than sex, but she'd discovered Sally's focus was control and emotional manipulation. She'd stayed with Sally even when the relationship had turned abusive, and that still frightened her. She'd convinced herself that Sally would change. That she could change her. She pushed away memories of the nights she'd spent crying herself to sleep while Sally lay passed out on the far side of their king-sized bed. At least she hadn't turned to drugs or alcohol to try to escape, and she credited her sponsor in the twelve-step Codependents Anonymous group for her growing self-awareness. CoDA helped her deal with the insecurities that kept her in that dysfunctional relationship, but she was still too leery to consider getting involved with anyone.

Jaylin began walking the day after Sally had left. She gradually built up the stamina to run and grew to enjoy the meditative state running provided. She ran for her life, away from the memories, and toward the woman she knew she could be. It took her a year to take off a hundred pounds, and she planned to stay in shape both physically and emotionally. No one was going to take that away from her. She'd never be taken advantage of again. Staying in total control meant keeping people at arm's length, even if that meant she was lonely sometimes. It was worth the price.

CHAPTER EIGHT

Jaylin went in search of Kristen, through the throngs of spectators milling about the horse arena. She'd said she had an Appaloosa, but all Jaylin could see were chestnut horses. Her phone chimed a text message just as she began to wonder if Kristen's event might be in another area.

They moved our stump race to the ring at the back of the fairgrounds. Just in case you're here. K

She texted a response and walked past the crowd to a smaller arena behind the barns. She noticed Zigzag immediately. He looked like one of the smaller horses in attendance, but he was the only Appaloosa she saw. He must be Kristen's. Even from a distance, she could tell he was solid muscle and striking. *Like his owner.*

Kristen waved and smiled, and Jaylin ignored the flickering in her gut. She walked to the fence surrounding the arena and Kristen waved as she approached, leading Zigzag.

"I'm glad you could make it. Did you have any trouble finding the fairgrounds?" Kristen asked. She wrapped an arm around Zigzag's neck as he stuck his head toward Jaylin.

"No trouble at all. It's a big place. This handsome guy must be Zigzag." Jaylin stroked his soft muzzle.

"Yep. This is my baby." Kristen patted him on the neck. "It looks as if they're getting ready to start. I'd better get back there. Can I buy you an iced tea or something after the event?"

"Sounds good. I'm going to grab a seat." Jaylin indicated the rapidly filling bleachers behind her.

"I'll catch up with you later then." Kristen grinned and mounted her horse.

Jaylin watched them trot to the other side of the arena doubting she'd ever seen anyone sexier astride a horse. She turned to search for a seat on the benches.

The match race involved three barrels set up on either side of a line on the ground with two horses and riders positioned beside each other facing opposite directions. The horse who got through the course first won the chance to race against the next winner. When a bell sounded the start of the race, they each sprinted around the barrels, mirroring one another's pattern. The crowd cheered as the smaller pinto, ridden by a pretty blonde with her ponytail flowing out from under her hat, hurtled out his side of the course seconds before a stocky quarter horse.

Kristen was up next. She and Zigzag were pitted against a lanky buckskin. Jaylin noted the buckskin's longer legs, but that could mean Zigzag had the advantage of a tighter turning radius.

The bell rang and Kristen was a blur as she and her horse negotiated the turns around each barrel. Jaylin was correct in her assumption. The taller horse was fast, but Zigzag was quicker and more agile. Kristen easily beat her opponent, and Jaylin clapped excitedly, overcome with unbidden pride.

Two more riders finished the course, and it was Kristen's turn again. Her opponent was the quick little pinto. Jaylin stood and cheered as Kristen and Zigzag charged around the barrels and exited a nose ahead of their competitor. Jaylin narrowed her eyes at the blond rider as she winked at Kristen and blew her a kiss before leaving the arena. *Who's that?* Jaylin shoved away thoughts of Kristen having a lover. She'd never indicated she was involved with anyone. *And it's not my business if she is.*

One more horse to beat. Jaylin watched the palomino quarter horse prance toward the course. She was a beauty, but Jaylin's money was on Zigzag. As they lined up, the tension in the crowd was palpable, and Jaylin sat on the edge of her seat while the horses took their starting positions. Jaylin wondered if Zigzag was tiring. The quarter horse got a fraction of a second head start on Zigzag, but that only seemed to spur him on. The muscles in his haunches bunched as he flexed his hind legs and propelled himself around the barrels. Horse and rider melded into one as they shot out of the course ahead of the palomino. Cheers erupted from the spectators, and Jaylin jumped to her feet and clapped wildly, her heart racing. Kristen grinned at her as she rode a victory lap around the ring. *Grinning at me, you little blonde.* Jaylin chastised her own pettiness at the thought as she made her way down to meet Kristen.

"That was fun. Thanks for letting me know about this." They sat at one of the concession stands with iced tea and lemonade after Kristen had taken care of Zigzag and accepted her blue ribbon.

"It's a fun event to ride in, too," Kristen said.

"How often do you participate in these, and is a ribbon all you win?" Jaylin looked over her plastic cup of iced tea, enjoying the sparkle in Kristen's eyes.

"That, and bragging rights. These events are just for fun for the locals. There's no money involved. They have some sort of event every weekend throughout the summer. It's not always a stump race. This was the first one I've tried. I usually just enter the barrel and keyhole races. Last year we raced in five."

"Did you win them all?"

"I've never cared much about winning. I do my best and try to beat my best score. If it turns out I defeat a competitor, so be it, but that's not my focus." Kristen finished her lemonade and rolled the empty cup between her hands, grinning but not making eye contact.

"So you did win them all."

"We did. Zigzag is good and he loves it."

"Hey, Kris. Nice riding." The blonde sauntered up and ran her hand down Kristen's arm before she leaned down to kiss Kristen lightly on the lips.

"Hi, Kelly. You did well out there yourself. Pogo looked great." Kristen shifted in her seat and turned to make introductions. "Jaylin, this is Kelly. Pogo is the pinto that raced today."

"It's good to meet you, Kelly." Jaylin hoped her lie didn't show on her face.

"You, too, Jaylin. Do you ride?"

"No. I just came to watch Kristen. We work together, and I wanted to see what this was all about." *Go away.*

"Well, I'm glad you came today. It was a good one to start the season. I have to trailer Pogo home. Will I see you next week, Kristen?"

"I don't know yet. I'll see how the week goes."

"I'll be looking for you." Kelly leaned toward Kristen to whisper in her ear, and Kristen squirmed, clearly uncomfortable. Kelly grinned and ran her finger down Kristen's cheek. She glanced up for a moment before she turned away. "Take care, Jaylin. Bye."

Jaylin watched her stroll away and took a deep breath. *Time to go.* "I think I'll head home, too. I need to let Railroad out."

"I'll walk you to your car," Kristen said. She pulled out Jaylin's chair as she stood.

"You don't have to. You probably want to get Zigzag home."

"He's not going anywhere. He looked half asleep after I rubbed him down and settled him in a stall."

Against her better judgment, Jaylin indulged in a pleasant walk across the fairgrounds with Kristen by her side. She resisted the inclination to take Kristen's hand and wondered at the feeling of rightness that simple desire produced. Had she really only known Kristen for a few weeks?

Kristen pointed to a few horses as they walked and recounted stories of their races, along with the name of each one and its owner. Jaylin smiled, enjoying Kristen's enthusiasm.

"Here's my car." Jaylin pressed her remote key lock and watched the lights flash as the car unlocked. Impulsively, she leaned toward Kristen but realized what she was doing and backed away. *God, I almost kissed her.*

Kristen didn't seem to notice and opened the car door for her. "I'll see you at work Monday."

Heat flared in her belly, and she deliberated a hug good-bye. She wanted a kiss, but she spoke instead. "Bye, Kristen. Thank you again for inviting me. I loved it."

"You're welcome. I enjoyed your company. Careful driving." Kristen gently closed the door, but with a moment's hesitation. *Could she have wanted a kiss, too?*

❖

Kristen parked in the back of the clinic and wasn't surprised to find Jaylin already at the little table. "Good morning," Kristen said. "So, do you live here now?" She enjoyed the warm smile her question provoked.

"I suppose it must seem so, but no. I do go home after work. Help yourself to some coffee."

"Thanks." Kristen filled the empty mug sitting in front of her from the carafe on the table. "I think I could move in, with service like this." She sipped her coffee and would have been content to sit there all day watching the morning sun glint off Jaylin's hair, but she was supposed to be working. "Are we going to be busy today?"

"No more fleas or maggots, but Sarah said we have a Great Dane puppy coming in this morning. The owner says, and I quote, 'It's stupid.'"

"Huh. How in the world can you tell if a dog is stupid?" Kristen couldn't remember ever learning how to diagnose learning disabilities in dogs. That seemed like a dog trainer's job.

"I have my suspicions, but we'll see. We also have an afternoon filled with heartworm checks. It's that time of year."

"I was pretty good at drawing blood, but it was a number of years ago." Kristen experienced a flutter of nerves that surprised her. She hadn't drawn blood from a dog since the year she graduated from the vet tech program.

"Thanks again for inviting me to your barrel race. I enjoyed it," Jaylin said.

"I'll be riding in one more at the fairgrounds before Memorial Day. That's where the annual parade starts. You'd probably enjoy it."

"Railroad's training school is planning an obedience demonstration after the parade. I might enroll her. Show her off a little."

The ringing of Jaylin's cell phone reminded Kristen it was time to go to work. She followed Jaylin inside to their first appointment.

"Good morning, Mrs. Reynolds. I'm Dr. Meyers, and this is my vet tech, Kristen. I understand you're having problems with your new puppy." Jaylin stood next to a beautiful harlequin Great Dane puppy nearly as tall as Kristen's pony. Kristen noticed Jaylin rest her hand gently on the dog's neck as she stood within its line of sight. *She suspects.*

Kristen watched the young female dart her bright eyes around the room, seemingly to memorize it. She'd seen this hyper awareness before in one of her dad's Appaloosas. This dog wasn't stupid. She couldn't hear.

"Please call me Amina. We can't get it to do anything we ask. It just ignores all our commands." Amina stood by the door. She looked about to dash out, leaving this huge burden behind.

"Does she have a name yet?"

Kristen suppressed a grin at Jaylin's diplomacy. Amina probably knew the gender of the dog but clearly didn't want any connection to "it."

"I just call her It," Amina said. She waved her hand as if trying to make the dog disappear. "She doesn't respond to anything we call her anyway."

"Would you please hold her attention there in front, Kristen? Just put your hands on either side of her face."

Jaylin looked at Kristen as she spoke, and Kristen could tell she already knew this puppy was deaf. She watched the young dog's tail wave as she cooed and stroked her. Jaylin stood behind the dog and clapped her hands loudly. The owner jumped, but the puppy continued her calm tail wagging. Not even a flinch.

"I believe your puppy may not be able to hear you. I think she's deaf." Jaylin pulled out a tuning fork from a drawer and took over Kristen's position.

Jaylin's sensitivity captivated Kristen. Jaylin knelt in front of her so it could see her as she held the device to each side of her head. The pup didn't even twitch an ear. However, she did give Jaylin a sloppy doggie kiss in the face that elicited chuckles from everyone in the room. Kristen thought maybe there was hope for Amina after all.

"This color of your Great Dane is called harlequin. Unfortunately, this color dog is prone to hereditary deafness."

Amina moved closer to her dog before speaking. "Really? I got her from a friend who was moving out of state. She told me the puppy was nine months old and healthy. Now I'm thinking she just wanted me to take her off her hands." Amina transformed before Kristen's eyes. Tears formed as she stroked It's back. "My ten-year-old son is attached to her. He's the only reason I didn't take her to the Humane Society. He calls her Roxie, so I guess that will be her official name." Amina paused as if in deep thought. "Harlequin." She pronounced the word as if it were a prayer. "Maybe I can convince my son to call her Quin." Kristen smiled as Amina pronounced the dog's new name slowly and distinctly while holding Roxie's gaze. Roxie would learn to read lips if Amina had her way.

"I'll give you the name of a reputable trainer who can help you train Roxie. She has a facility here in town. I think you have a sweet dog, and I've seen many deaf animals thrive in the proper environment."

"Thank you, Dr. Meyers. I appreciate your help. I thought there was something mentally wrong with her."

"I'm going to check her ears for any wax buildup or infection before you go, but she looks fit."

Jaylin took Roxie's temperature, looked in her ears, and listened to her heart. "Except for her lack of hearing, she seems healthy. Has she had all her vaccinations?"

"I'll check her papers and give you a call. You can let me know what she might need."

"Sounds good. Good luck with her." Jaylin gave the giant puppy a hug before holding the exam room door open for Amina.

"When did you realize that dog was deaf?" Kristen sat across from Jaylin at the outdoor table as they ate their lunch later.

"I pretty much knew when I first looked at her. We had a deaf dog in my last year at vet school. He was an interesting example of how adaptable they can be. We had to be careful he never wandered near the street, but he learned to read hand signals, and he reacted to vibrations in the floor. He could feel someone approaching. I think Roxie will be fine if her owners allow her, and themselves, time to adjust."

Kristen finished her sandwich and sat back with a bottle of water. "How many heartworm checks do we have coming in this afternoon?"

"Only three. The first one's due in an hour," Jaylin said.

"Good. We have a little time." Kristen turned her face to the early afternoon sun and closed her eyes.

"Tired?"

"No. Just relaxing."

"Thanks again for your help. You knew that dog was deaf, too, didn't you?" Jaylin took a sip of her iced tea and mimicked Kristen's pose.

"Yep. My dad had a horse that was deaf. She displayed the same sort of vigilance as Roxie." Kristen opened her eyes and turned toward Jaylin. Their eyes met and Kristen felt herself swirling into a hazel vortex.

She thought about how gentle Jaylin was with the animals. She'd worked with horses all her life and dealing with horse owners was very different from small animal owners, but Jaylin knew how to handle the animals as well as the owners, without being overbearing. In fact, she seemed to handle everything in just the right way. Jaylin's sensitivity and immediate sense of awareness of her patient's needs intrigued Kristen more each time she saw it. She squelched her thoughts of Jaylin using that awareness to *handle* her. She turned away and sucked in a settling breath.

CHAPTER NINE

Kristen left her dad and headed to the gun club where she shot one of her worst rounds of skeet in a long time. Her father had barely recognized her, and his latest doctor's report indicated his dementia had worsened. He still hadn't been diagnosed with any specific cause, but his doctor requested a brain scan in six months. He'd had one a year ago with no definitive results, and she remembered his severe agitation at going to the hospital for the procedure. She wasn't sure she wanted to put him through it again, especially since it wouldn't change anything.

She rubbed her eyes with her palms and tipped her head back, groaning. She'd spent the night tossing and turning. A year ago, she'd managed to shove memories of her one failed relationship deep into the recesses of her mind so she could move on with her life. She'd felt weak, vulnerable, and unable to be who Lynda needed, and would never again try to be someone she wasn't. It was past midnight when she'd finally forced the recollections of Lynda back where they belonged. She couldn't figure out why the buried memories were surfacing now.

She arrived at the clinic an hour early. She'd enjoyed having Jaylin watch her ride last week. She'd liked that Jaylin saw the real her when she was doing what she loved instead of what was expected of her. It made her feel seen in a way she hadn't in a very long time, and she liked it. Maybe too much. So when Jaylin had asked if she'd assist in the surgery today, she hadn't hesitated to say yes. They'd agreed that Kristen would only work three days a week unless Jaylin needed more help, and so far she hadn't asked for anything more. It didn't matter what the procedure was; she'd be there.

"Thanks for coming in early. I appreciate your help today," Jaylin said.

"No problem. I'm supposed to be here to help, although you don't seem to need my help with most things, so I'm honored that you asked. What's so special about this one?"

"Bob Miller is a long-time client of mine. He drove quite a distance to bring his new bulldog to me for neutering. I want to be sure everything goes smoothly. The puppy is healthy, and his blood work looks normal, so I don't think there'll be any issues, but I appreciate you assisting." Kristen followed Jaylin to the surgery room.

"If I remember my dog breeds correctly, bulldogs have that smooshed in face and can have trouble breathing. Am I right?"

"Correct." Jaylin's smile warmed Kristen in areas of her body she would prefer to ignore while at work.

"We're going to intubate him then?"

"Yeah. I want a nice open airway. I've pretty much got the surgery room ready. Bob will drop Bambi off at eight thirty. I'd like to get him finished before the clients start coming in at ten."

Kristen looked around the room before turning to Jaylin. "What do you need me to do?" She saw everything in place except their patient. The blush that crept across Jaylin's smooth cheeks kindled the heat simmering in Kristen's belly. She had to get control of her reactions to Jaylin.

"I'm sorry. I'm used to doing things myself. When Bambi gets here, you can help me get him sedated and prepped. I'd appreciate it if you'd keep an eye on his respiration and heart rate while I'm doing the procedure."

"Sounds good."

"Shall we relax outside while we wait for Bambi? I have some bagels in the kitchenette. It's a beautiful morning."

Jaylin positioned the chairs so the morning sunshine would warm their backs and not be in their eyes. God, her eyes. She had to keep herself in check. Kristen was there to help establish her presence at the clinic. That's all. She'd be gone soon, and Jaylin would be on her own. Nothing new. She'd been on her own all her adult life as well as most of her childhood, when she thought about it.

"This is nice. Thanks for suggesting it. I put a note on the door to have Bob come around back if he gets here early," Kristen said.

"Thanks, Kristen. I didn't even think of that."

"No problem. I like to be prepared. You never know what these small animal owners might do."

Jaylin smiled at the good-natured teasing. "Huh. At least they don't wake you in the middle of the night to come out because their horse has a belly ache."

"You should know, as a veterinarian, that a belly ache in a horse can indicate a potentially fatal condition. My father had a mare that died because the vet he called 'in the middle of the night' didn't show up for three hours. Bambi will be here soon." Kristen bounced to her feet and stomped back into the building.

So much for a good working relationship. She'd pushed some button that set Kristen off. She certainly hadn't meant to, and she hated the feeling of anxiety it sent coursing through her. She sprang from her chair and followed Kristen. "Wait, Kristen, tell me what I said wrong."

She found Kristen setting up the anesthesia, but she didn't respond. They completed the surgery in silence except for Kristen's occasional update as to Bambi's status. She kept her stethoscope on throughout the procedure and kept her eyes on their patient without sparing Jaylin a glance. When they were done, she walked out without a word.

"Bambi did fine, Bob…Yes, you can pick him up in the morning… Nine would be great…I'll see you then." Jaylin disconnected the call and slumped back in her office chair. Kristen had stayed long enough to see that Bambi was awake and stable before fleeing out the door. With anyone else, she might have shrugged it off and apologized the next time she saw them. But with Kristen, the need to make amends felt more urgent. She needed to make things right with her friend. *Friend?* She shook her head. Whatever it was, she had to fix it.

❖

Jaylin claimed a seat in the bleachers facing the arena. When she'd mentioned on her way out her intention to track down Kristen, Sarah had told her about Kristen's Gymkhana event. She'd hoped to be able to sit back, watch without calling attention to herself, and talk to Kristen after the event. If they were going to work together, even for only a short time, she wanted to try for affability, at least. Although there couldn't be anything romantic, she liked Kristen's company, both inside and outside the clinic, and she didn't want to let a stupid comment jeopardize that. She'd never heard of this type of competition and she wanted to learn all about it.

She watched as Kristen led Zigzag into the arena. She mounted and waved to the crowd as she positioned him in the starting area. The first event was a keyhole/barrel timed event where each horse and rider entered the little round area marked off with chalk, turned, and exited as fast as possible. Then they'd ride back into the arena and race around each of three barrels as fast as they could. The competition seemed complicated, and Jaylin wasn't sure if points were allocated or if it was a race. But Kristen looked great in her faded jeans, boots, and button down shirt. She concentrated on that.

As Jaylin watched the event, more of it made sense. She could make out the pattern that the horse had to follow. There were barrels that the horses had to pay attention to and a chalk line the rider had to make sure the horse never crossed. She cheered as Kristen rode Zigzag through the course with the fastest time. She hopped off the bleacher, intending to get an iced tea before looking for Kristen.

"What are you doing here?"

Jaylin jumped more at the harshness of the tone than the unexpected presence and was instantly on the defensive. "I came to watch this *public* event." Jaylin set her hands on her hips then quickly relaxed, realizing her reaction wasn't going to help the situation. "Sarah told me you were riding today, and I wanted to talk to you. To apologize for my comment yesterday. I was insensitive."

"Yes, you were." Kristen turned to walk away but Jaylin grabbed her wrist.

"Please. Of course I know how serious colic can be. I know all about gastric impaction and torsion. I'm sorry for the stupid joke. I was just teasing you, and I didn't think before I spoke." She let go when Kristen stared fixedly at her hand. She'd hoped for a response other than Kristen walking away. What she didn't expect was Kristen seizing both of her wrists and pinning her up against a post under the bleachers. She didn't resist. Wetness pooled between her legs, and a knot formed in her stomach. Before she could figure out what she wanted to do, Kristen kissed her. The kiss was the sweetest, most tender Jaylin had ever experienced. Possessive, yet yielding. Claiming, but questioning.

Her stomach knot unraveled, and she kissed Kristen back. Hard. She spun them around and pushed Kristen against the same post that had been at her own back. She held Kristen's wrists away from her body. She leaned back, but held Kristen in place. They were both breathing hard. Kristen stood in quiet supplication, her eyes closed. Realizing she still held Kristen's wrists tightly, she flashed back to Sally's possessiveness and flinched. She would accept love freely given, not take it. Jaylin released Kristen's arms and stepped back.

"I'm sorry. I didn't mean…"

Kristen wrapped her arms around Jaylin's waist and gently tugged her into another kiss. "No. Don't apologize. I've wanted to kiss you since the day I met you."

"But I thought…" Jaylin struggled with her feelings. What did she think? She felt how gently Kristen held her in her arms. Clearly, her worry came from her own issues, not something Kristen was feeling. She wasn't forcing her into anything, and that kiss…she'd never felt cherished from a kiss before.

"I don't know what you thought, but if it was that we can't do this, I agree. I didn't mean to make you uncomfortable." Kristen's breath tickled her neck. Kristen released her, and Jaylin moved back on wobbly legs.

Kristen turned and walked away after giving Jaylin a sad smile.

Jaylin fought to clear her lust filled mind. She wanted to say more, but Kristen was gone.

❖

"You won't believe what I did, Railroad." Jaylin sat on her back porch with her dog in her lap. "You're kinda big for a lapdog, you know." She smiled and made no move to push her off, and Railroad looked up at her as if hanging on every word. Jaylin took a sip of port wine and sighed, trying to push the heaviness from her chest. "I kissed Kristen. I mean I really kissed her." She'd never lost control like that before. When she and Sally were first together there was passion, but with Kristen, it seemed beyond passion, as though she wanted to devour her. She couldn't get enough. Kristen was tender and strong, yet gentle. She liked it a lot, and it scared her to death.

Jaylin had left the Gymkhana event after Kristen had walked away. She'd needed to find a way to get rid of the excess energy running through her, but the sip of wine warmed her in places that hadn't cooled off yet, and her body still thrummed with sexual tension. She wanted Kristen. She had to figure out why. What would Maggie say? *Am I making her into who I want her to be in my mind?* She's not Sally. She's gentle. *I don't deserve her.* Another sigh pushed its way through her constricted chest. She finished her glass of wine, guided Railroad off her lap, and headed to bed.

Jaylin tossed and turned as fragments of her dreams drifted through her memories. She'd come instantly when she'd snuggled under her down comforter and touched herself, with memories of Kristen's warm lips and gentle touch flowing through her consciousness. She was in Kristen's arms, their naked bodies sliding over each other. Her arms were pinned to the bed, and Kristen's firm nipples were pushed against hers. Her hot tongue circled her clit and teased her opening before her fingers parted her warm folds and slid inside. Then Jaylin was rubbing her center against Kristen's, combining their wetness. Another orgasm rocked her, completely beyond her control.

Jaylin woke to Railroad's soft whines. She glanced at her clock radio. Eight thirty. She rarely slept past seven, even on Sunday. She padded barefoot to the dining room, noticing the slickness between her thighs, and opened the sliding door for Railroad, her thoughts filled with Kristen. Snippets of her dreams and memories of their kisses triggered yet another round of wetness. At this rate, she'd be unable to walk by Monday. What was Kristen doing today? She could be riding Zigzag or shooting skeet.

Kristen's kiss was so tender, and her arms were warm, protective. She had to get herself under control. She'd be seeing Kristen tomorrow, and she had no idea what she would say to her. *We can't do this*, Kristen had said. She was right, of course. She barely knew Kristen and had no idea what her past held. If it contained anything like Jaylin's baggage, they were definitely better not going any further. *Too bad.* She let Railroad back inside and occupied herself with making breakfast. The ringing of her cell phone interrupted the serenity of the quiet backyard setting where she was sipping coffee and eating her oatmeal. Her emergency number. This was the first non-office hours call she'd gotten since she started working at the new clinic. She grabbed the phone, listened to the caller, and wrote down directions before heading out the door.

❖

Zigzag nickered at the rough currycomb and turned his head to look at Kristen. She realized how hard she was brushing and threw the brush to the ground. "Sorry, Zig. I've got this woman on my mind." Kristen laughed at the silly assumption that her horse knew what she was saying, but smoothed her hand over his back. "Ah well. It's over. It never began, actually, but damn, that was some kiss. I know she felt it, too. I have to forget about it, though. It can't go anywhere. I don't have time for anything more than friendship."

She reprimanded herself for her angry outburst. The memory of her father's pain at the loss of his favorite mare had triggered the temper she worked hard to contain. Jaylin had come to apologize, not to be pushed against a post and kissed. Now she'd have to be the one apologizing.

She picked up a dandy brush and gentled her brushing. "It's you and me, boy. Next week we practice for another stump race. I think you'll do well." Kristen alternated between a softer body brush and a grooming rag until Zigzag's coat shone, then she loaded him into her horse trailer and pulled it toward the exit. She glanced around as she passed the bleachers, half-expecting Jaylin to be standing where she left her. She concentrated on merging her F250 into the traffic when she left the fairgrounds and thought about what she would say to Jaylin the next time she saw her. She quivered at the memory of the kiss.

CHAPTER TEN

I ain't seen you so off since you started shootin' as a kid." Tim stroked the stubble on his chin. "You feelin' all right?"

Kristen nestled her shotgun into her hard case before turning to him. "Yeah. I'm distracted today. I could use a cup of your Italian roast, if you have some made."

"You know I always keep a fresh pot goin'. Especially when you're around."

Tim's crooked grin and solid presence grounded Kristen. She'd tossed and turned most of the night, beset with thoughts and dreams. First, she was kissing Jaylin, holding her firmly against her body, then Lynda, then Jaylin again. By the time she threw off her covers at four o'clock, her mind was a jumble of confusion. Jaylin had felt so perfect in her arms, yielding and reciprocal. She was soft, warm, and passionate. Lynda had been once, too. No, it didn't matter how good that kiss was. Jaylin was off-limits.

"Here you go." Tim set her coffee on the round table and they sat across from each other. "So what's got you so distracted? Is your dad okay?"

"Yeah, he's doing all right. At least, he's no worse. I'll be fine. Thanks for asking. How's the new member working out?" She'd known Tim for years, but she wasn't about to talk to him about her love life.

Tim rested his calloused hand on Kristen's. "You need to talk, you just let me know. And about the new guy…somethin' seems off about him. I can't put my finger on it, though." Tim rubbed his chin as he spoke.

"Yeah? I only met him for a minute outside a couple of weeks ago. He didn't introduce himself, but he talked as if he knew me somehow. Weird."

"Huh. He's real interested in the upcomin' club shoot. I'm positionin' you second, by the way. He's been askin' for that spot, but I told him he can't have it. He got all huffy with me. Like he had some special rights or somethin'. I'm beginin' to think he's got somethin' up his sleeve. Let me know what you think when you see him." Tim shook his head and stood. "See you later."

Kristen finished her coffee and headed to her car. It was time to see her father, and she hated the niggle of dread she felt at the prospect.

❖

Kristen noticed the Volvo as soon as she pulled into the care facility's parking lot. She looked closer at the XC70 on her way into the building. *Why would Jaylin be here?* Memories of their passionate kiss triggered fluttering in her stomach. She ignored the sensation. She was here to visit her father.

"Hey, Dad. How're you feeling today?" Kristen found her dad in the same spot she'd found him in every week for a month. Today, however, he was reclined in his chair instead of sitting with his feet on the floor. A quick assessment discovered the reason. "I see your ankles are swollen." She gave her father a kiss on his clean-shaven cheek and noted the scent of Old Spice. His favorite. He still hadn't responded to her question, and she wondered if he'd heard her or if his dementia had taken him away. "Are your feet bothering you today?" She hoped for a response. Any response. Fear stabbed at her heart. Maybe he'd slipped away from her for good this time.

"Are you here for that dog, too?"

Kristen leaned on the side of his chair in relief. "What dog would that be, Dad?"

"That woman down the hall. She has that little fluffy dog that sits in my lap sometimes." Kristen hadn't seen her father smile in so long that she was confused for a moment. The home allowed residents who were able to care for small dogs to have them, but she didn't know her father ever saw one. "It's been sick for a week. I'm a doctor, you know. I told that woman to call someone. The dog was throwing up and pooping all over. I think she finally called a..."

Kristen watched her father's eyes glaze over as he struggled to find the elusive word. "Veterinarian? Is that who she called?" *Maybe that's why Jaylin is here.*

"Yes, that's it. I think the nurses called. That woman was crying and carrying the little dog up and down the hallway all night. I couldn't help her. I couldn't find my black bag. I don't know where I put it. It had my stethoscope in it. Do you know where it is?"

"No. Sorry, Pop, I haven't seen it."

"I probably left it at the office. I do that a lot. Maybe you could go check on the little dog. You used to work with a veterinarian, didn't you? No. That was my daughter. She'll be coming to visit me soon. I need to rest now."

Her father closed his eyes, and Kristen fought back tears.

❖

"I'll be back tomorrow to check on Trixie, Mrs. James. I think she'll be fine. She must have had too many treats from all her friends in the building." Jaylin smiled at the tiny ball of fur curled up on her lamb's wool bed. "Keep her in your room for a few days, and make sure all she eats is the lamb and rice I gave you. I want to make sure her diarrhea clears up. She doesn't have a fever, but I'll send the blood sample I took to the lab today to check for an infection. Make sure she gets plenty of water. I don't want her dehydrated."

"Please call me Doris. Thank you for coming, Dr. Meyers. She was so sick, I thought I'd lose her. She's such a sweetheart. Everyone loves her." She darted her eyes back and forth from her dog to Jaylin.

"I can see you're anxious about her. If it makes you more comfortable I can take her to the clinic with me and keep an eye on her there."

"Oh, no, I couldn't abandon her." Doris clutched the front of her robe with both hands. "Please come back tomorrow and check on her. I promise I'll keep her here. I have to let Dr. Eckert know. He loves Trixie so."

Jaylin looked up from her task of repacking her emergency kit as Doris shuffled out the door. *Dr. Eckert?* She picked up her bag, took one more look at the little dog curled contentedly in her bed, and headed for the nurses' station.

She heard her voice before she saw Kristen standing at the counter. She considered ducking back into Doris's room but changed her mind. She was here for an emergency. Whatever, or whomever, Kristen was here for, was none of her business.

"Good afternoon." Jaylin stood off to Kristen's side, out of her personal space.

Kristen turned to focus on her, and Jaylin's stomach flickered. *Probably should have finished that bowl of oatmeal.* She saw the misty look in Kristen's eyes and her heart ached for her obvious pain.

"You have a way of showing up unexpectedly." Kristen's grin tempered her words, and Jaylin relaxed a little.

"The nurses called this morning. A dog in the building needed help." She shot back a grin of her own and struggled not to squirm under Kristen's scrutiny.

"Okay then. I'll see you at work tomorrow." Kristen didn't move away, and Jaylin hesitated.

"I just need to talk to the nurses before I go." She leaned against the wall next to the counter and waited.

"Go ahead," Kristen said. "I'll be back in a little while," she said to the nurse on duty. She gave Jaylin a quick smile before heading off down the hall.

❖

There *was* a sick dog in the building. Kristen hadn't completely dismissed what her father had told her, but she'd learned to question pretty much everything he said these days. She was surprised to see a visitor with her dad when she got back to his room.

"Hello. I'm Kristen. Dr. Eckert's daughter." She held out her hand in greeting and tried not to flinch when Doris hugged her. She smelled of unwashed clothes and stale White Shoulders perfume.

"I'm Doris. I live down the hall. It's nice to finally meet you. Your father talks about you all the time."

"He does?"

"Oh, yes." Doris lowered her voice to continue. "Well, when he's lucid he does."

"I see." Kristen moved around Doris to her father's side. "Hi, Dad. Did you have a good rest?"

"Kristen? Is that you? I knew you were coming today, but I thought later."

"Nope, I'm here now, Dad."

"Good. Did you meet Doris? She lives down the hall and has a little dog. She's sick, but Doris said a nice young doctor came to take care of her." Kristen hadn't heard her father talk so much in months. This dog and neighbor must be good for him.

Doris took her father's hand and squeezed before she spoke. "The doctor said her runs and throwing up were probably from too much junk food. She gave her some medicine, and Trixie's settled down in her bed now. I'm going back to keep an eye on her. You have a nice visit with Kristen."

Doris was leaving the room as Jaylin popped her head in. "I'm sorry to intrude, but the nurse told me you were in this unit. I wanted to give you some Imodium for your little girl. I left word with the nurses to call me if she gets worse."

Kristen stepped out from behind Doris. "Hello again, Dr. Meyers."

"Kristen? Sorry to interrupt, but I needed to give this to Doris."

Doris looked from one woman to the other. "Do you two know each other?"

"Yes." Jaylin spoke first. "Kristen and I work together. Here's Trixie's Imodium. I wrote down how much to give her on the bottle. I'll see you tomorrow."

"Wait. Please." Kristen refrained from grabbing Jaylin's wrist. She remembered where that led. "Could I talk to you for a minute in the hallway?"

"I'm heading home. Thank you again, Dr. Meyers," Doris said. Then she shuffled past them out the door.

"What did you want to talk about?" Jaylin asked when she and Kristen were alone in the hall.

"It's about Trixie. I think I know what made her sick. It may not be the only thing, but I believe my father might have given her Rolos."

"Rolos? That's a chocolate candy isn't it?"

"Yeah. Chocolate and caramel."

Jaylin ran her hand through her hair. "That would explain her symptoms. I suspected she got into something toxic. Chocolate would do it."

Kristen bent her head and massaged her forehead. "I'm sorry. If he did give her Rolos, he didn't know any better."

Jaylin rested her hand on Kristen's shoulder. "It's okay. I do believe the dog will be fine. I think she probably threw it all up. Doris panicked and asked the nurses to call. I was here within an hour of them calling."

Kristen raised her head and straightened, but didn't pull away from Jaylin's touch. "But Dad said she'd been sick for a week." She should have known that her father's week could easily have been a day or a few hours. She hesitated for a moment, trying to decide how far to let Jaylin into her life. "Yeah. Okay. Good. Do you want to meet him?"

"Your dad? I'd love to."

Kristen shivered as cold replaced the warmth of Jaylin's hand when she removed it. She took Jaylin's hand and led her into her father's room.

"Dad? Are you awake? I brought someone to meet you." Her father had moved from his chair and now lay on his bed staring at the ceiling. "Dad?" Kristen gently touched his shoulder and got no response. She turned to Jaylin. "Sorry. It appears he's in one of his stupors." She kissed his forehead and covered him with his comforter.

"How long has your dad been here?"

Kristen walked Jaylin out to her car, held open the door for her, and paused a moment before answering. "Two years. I tried to keep him at home and take care of him myself, but it got too hard. He began wandering away from the house. I hid the keys to his car, so he started hot-wiring it. Of all the things to remember how to do, right?" Kristen smiled at the memory. She'd admired his ingenuity. "When my mother died of cancer six years ago, Dad kind of gave up. It's like he couldn't bear to have memories of her dead, so his mind gave them all up." Kristen stroked the warm car window absently. "I hired a few homecare workers, but he was more than they could handle, too. I found this place and moved him as soon as there was an opening. Anyway, you don't need to sit here and listen to me lament my father's fate. I'm sure you have a better way to spend your Sunday." Kristen turned to head for her car. "Have a good one."

"Kristen? Thank you for telling me about the chocolate and for sharing about your father. I missed most of my breakfast, and I need to get something to eat. I passed a Big Boy on my way here. Would you like to grab a bite to eat?"

Kristen watched Jaylin's hazel eyes turn a shade darker before she stepped back and shook her head. "I have my gun in my car. I don't usually carry it around, and my Boxter would be too easy to break into. I have to take it home."

"I guess I'll see you tomorrow then." Jaylin hesitated a moment, and then got into her car and closed the door.

Before she could start it, Kristen was knocking on her driver's door window.

"Can I change my mind?" Kristen spoke loudly enough for Jaylin to hear through the closed window.

Jaylin rolled down the window. "Of course you can. I'll meet you there."

CHAPTER ELEVEN

Jaylin pulled into the parking lot and got out of her car to wait for Kristen.

"Do you mind if we sit by the window? I'd like to keep an eye on my car," Kristen said.

"Not at all." Now that they were in the restaurant, Jaylin's nerves threatened her power of speech. Should she bring up their kiss? She was about to tell Kristen this was a bad idea when Kristen's warm hand on her lower back grounded her.

"Is this all right?"

"Great." Jaylin smiled and relaxed. She could do this.

"Coffee?" the server asked.

"Yes." Jaylin and Kristen answered at the same time.

"Kristen. I want to say something. It's about the other day." Jaylin picked up her napkin and twisted it into a roll.

"We're going to talk about our kiss, aren't we?" Kristen asked.

"I think we should. Don't you?"

"I suppose so. Go ahead." Kristen leaned her elbows on the table.

"The first thing I want to say is I'm sorry."

"Sorry for what?"

Jaylin fidgeted in her seat before answering. "Sorry for forcing myself on you at the horse event. It won't happen again."

"The way I remember it, I kissed you first." Kristen took a sip of her coffee.

"Yeah, you did, but I should've stopped there. I didn't, and I apologize."

"Listen, Jaylin." Kristen ran her fingers gently over Jaylin's hand. "I don't play games. I think you know I'm attracted to you, and I believe you're attracted to me. I need to apologize as well. I don't normally lose my temper the way I did at the clinic that day. My father's favorite mare died due to the delay of that vet. He lost his prized line of Appaloosas with her. It's the reason I pursued my degree in veterinary technology and found Dr. Berglund. I'm a little touchy about it, so I'm sorry. Anyway, we're both adults. What happened between us was consensual. Can we leave it at that? It won't happen again. If that's what you want." Kristen pulled her hand back and picked up her fork.

Jaylin still wanted something from Kristen. She didn't know what, and she nearly choked on fear. "Yes. Yes, that's what I want."

"Let's eat our lunch, as friends. Would that work?" Kristen asked.

"That sounds right. I'd like to consider you a friend."

"Good. I would, too. I'm not looking for a relationship. So, Trixie will be okay, huh?" Kristen tipped her head and looked genuinely concerned.

"I think so. I'll follow up with Doris tomorrow, but Trixie seemed alert and ready to go exploring by the time I left. She even seemed to enjoy the little bit of lamb and rice I gave her." The tightness in Jaylin's chest eased as their conversation moved on to work and the clients scheduled for Monday.

They finished lunch and Jaylin headed home, questioning her decision.

❖

A prancing Railroad greeted Jaylin as soon as she walked in the door. She opened the sliding door and let her out into the yard before she grabbed a beer and joined her.

"Good girl, Road. Now we're going to practice your down and stay command." Jaylin had been working with her for an hour, and she hadn't missed or shown any resistance to any command Jaylin gave her. "You're getting good at this. I think we may have to accept the offer to participate in the Memorial Day parade. You deserve to show off a little." Jaylin released Railroad and stretched out on her patio lounge chair with her dog on her lap. "This is getting to be a habit." She laughed as Railroad wiggled to get more comfortable.

Jaylin took a swallow of her beer and allowed her mind to wander. She had an hour before she'd have to leave for her meeting. She could indulge in a little meditation, but her mind kept taking her back to lunch. Kristen said she wasn't interested in a relationship. Jaylin hadn't asked herself that question in years. She'd met Sally the first year out of college and never questioned the seriousness of their connection. She was just happy to have someone want her. She'd matured considerably since then, but she wasn't ready to be serious about anyone. Being lonely was nothing new to her.

Uninvited thoughts of Kristen at work or riding Zigzag, intense and focused, streamed through her consciousness. Smiling at her from across the table. Kissing her. *Don't go there. This is not meditation.* "I've got to get up, girl." Jaylin guided Railroad off her lap and went inside. She hadn't opened her computer since her e-mail from Sally. None of her clients had her e-mail address, and she usually just called Maria if she wanted to talk to her. She winced at the realization that she had no friends who would e-mail her. She took a deep breath and powered it on, praying Sally had only amused herself once, and she'd leave her alone.

There was another e-mail.

Hey, sugar. I was hoping we could hook up soon. I know what you like. I know what you want. Remember?

Jaylin slammed her laptop closed and headed out the door. Tomorrow she'd abandon that e-mail account. She wouldn't allow that woman to mess with her life, ever again.

❖

"What do you think Sally wants from you?" Maggie asked.

"I have no idea. I can't figure out why she'd be contacting me now after so long. I know I don't want to have anything to do with her." Jaylin paced, struggling to maintain emotional balance. She wouldn't let Sally get to her. She closed her eyes and tried to focus. For no reason she could imagine, Kristen's image infused her with a sense of tranquility.

"Let me ask you a more important question." Maggie placed her hands on Jaylin's shoulders, ending her pacing. "What just happened?"

Jaylin stopped herself from wrenching free of Maggie's gentle hold. Her war was with her own demons. She relaxed and grappled with her answer. "What do you mean, 'what just happened?'"

"I mean, you were dealing with your feelings about Sally. You were agitated and then, as though tripping a switch, you went all serene on me."

Jaylin tipped her head back and closed her eyes again. "I don't know. There's this woman I've been working with. She's worked her way under my skin, and it scares the hell out of me."

"Are you attracted to her?"

"Definitely."

"Has she done anything to lead you to believe you can't trust her?"

"No, but I keep thinking that she will."

Maggie smiled and hugged Jaylin. "I remember your struggles with Sally. We can't control other people. The only one we can control is our self."

"I know, I know." Jaylin ran a hand through her hair and resumed her pacing.

"Jay, stop." Maggie took Jaylin's hand and guided her to a table where they sat down. "Let's sit and figure this out."

They settled in their chairs, and Maggie continued. "So, you're attracted to this woman, and you think she's attracted to you?"

Jaylin thought back to the kiss and the intensity of Kristen's reaction. "I believe she is."

"What's her name?"

"Kristen."

"There's something about Kristen that you're attracted to, and that scares you. Is that right?"

"Yes."

"She's not Sally," Maggie said. Her gaze was direct but not challenging.

"She's nothing like Sally. She's gentle. She's caring and respectful. Yeah. Nothing like Sally." Jaylin wondered where this conversation was going.

"So, you're attracted to a woman who treats you with respect and caring?"

"I guess I am."

"And that scares you."

"I guess it does." Jaylin watched Maggie sit back in her chair and study her. "What?"

"I know how hard you've worked to get past your obsession with Sally. She was bad for you, but you believed that was all you deserved. Someone has come along who treats you decently, and you don't know what to do."

Jaylin sighed. "I suppose you're right. I don't know. I won't be treated the way Sally treated me again, but I'm scared." Jaylin rested her forehead on her hands lying on the table. "I'm scared," she said, admitting the depth to which she was truly terrified.

Maggie's smile was sad as she spoke and gently rested her hand on Jaylin's back. "You deserve to be treated with respect, my friend. You said Kristen's gentle. Could she be someone you can trust?"

"I don't know. There's more, actually. She's not interested in a serious relationship."

"Are you?" Maggie asked.

Jaylin sighed and sat up straight. "I wish I knew."

❖

"Good morning."

Jaylin must have gotten in early. She always seemed a step ahead of Kristen. When she'd worked for Bill, she regularly arrived an hour before him.

"Good morning. Are you sure you go home after work?" Kristen smiled, and Jaylin laughed.

"I'm sure. I think my dog would come looking for me if I didn't show up. We have a full schedule of patients, but I was hoping we could talk this morning. Maybe about ten thirty, after our first patient?"

"Sure." Their attraction was undeniable. Kristen felt the leftover sexual tension from their kiss like the proverbial elephant in the room. Jaylin wanted to talk. Maybe it was about relationship stuff. She knew she wanted to kiss Jaylin again, but it wasn't going to happen.

CHAPTER TWELVE

Jaylin waited for Kristen at the garden table. What would she say? She needed to figure out what she wanted and what she was willing to give. She wasn't sure if she could continue to ignore her growing feelings.

"You all right?" Kristen sat across from Jaylin.

"I'm fine. Thanks for taking time to talk," Jaylin said.

"We already talked about the kiss. Is there more you need to say?"

"Probably a lot." Jaylin wrapped her arms around herself. "But I don't know where to start."

"Is everything okay? I thought we agreed to be friends."

"Yes, and that's what I want. To consider you a friend, but I can't stop thinking about kissing you. And more."

"I see." Kristen leaned back in her chair. She looked sad.

"I'm sorry. I've made some bad choices in my life, and getting involved with someone scares me."

"I've made bad choices, too. I'm sorry I pushed myself on you that day. I won't say I'm sorry for the kiss though. It was magnificent, and I think about 'more' with you, too, but as we agreed, it won't happen again," Kristen said. "I can't get involved with anyone either. Is it too difficult for you to work with me?"

"I don't know, Kristen. I'm not sure what I want, or what I can give. I only know that I can't stop thinking about you. I can't stop wanting you, and I don't know what to do about it." Jaylin stood and leaned on the back of her chair.

"I can talk to Bill." Kristen pushed her chair back. "Maybe it would be best if I left. I'm sure he has an extra tech to help you out if you need it, but from what I've seen, you're pretty self-sufficient. That should ease the pressure on both of us." Kristen stood to leave.

"Wait, Kristen, please. Sit back down." Jaylin reached out to stop her.

Kristen remained standing, her gaze locked on Jaylin. What she saw nearly buckled her knees. Raw desire, fear, sadness, and longing. She wanted to pull her into her arms, kiss her fears away, and keep her safe. She couldn't do that. There were no promises in this world, at least none she could make. She sat down anyway. "What?"

Jaylin dropped her hand. "I think I just needed to get that out. Every day I wrestle with voices telling me I'm not good enough, that I'll never be worthy of love. I grew up with nothing. As nothing. Now that I've made a life for myself, I'm struggling to acknowledge my accomplishment and allow myself to believe in my own self-worth. I feel so much when I'm with you. I can't seem to sort out all those feelings, but I know that I want to. I'd like to start by calling you my friend. I believe I'm worthy of friendship."

Kristen reached for Jaylin's hand. When Jaylin took it, she pulled her out of her chair and onto her lap. "You are worthy of so much more than friendship. I'm going to kiss you now. I don't want you to think it's anything more than a friendly kiss. I don't expect anything from you, and I'm not promising you anything. It's just a kiss."

Kristen cupped Jaylin's face in her hands and tenderly placed her lips on Jaylin's. Her intention to graze her mouth turned into a passionate exploration when Jaylin covered her hands with her own and leaned into her. Their tongues collided in an effort to bind their passions. Kristen pulled back a breath and Jaylin pressed herself harder against her before gently pushing herself away. They were breathing hard and she held Jaylin until they both could speak.

"Damn."

"Yeah. I'm not going to say I'm sorry for that, but I meant what I said. It was just a friendly kiss." Kristen grinned at the absurdity of her statement.

"Kristen." Jaylin moved out of her embrace. "You make me wish I could do *casual*, because I really want you right now, but I know I can't. My heart tends to ride along with my libido, and I can't trust myself with that."

"I know, and I don't want you to be uncomfortable. Should I talk to Bill about leaving?" Kristen considered Jaylin's remark about doing "casual." A feeling bordering on panic squeezed her chest when she realized she could never do "casual" with Jaylin. There was something too vulnerable about her, something Kristen felt the need to keep safe, and that meant casual would never be an option.

"Maybe it would be best if we don't work together anymore."

Jaylin looked so forlorn Kristen almost grabbed her and kissed her again. She took another step backward.

"I agree. Take care of yourself, Jaylin." Kristen brushed the back of her fingers down Jaylin's cheek and went back into the building to gather her things. It had been nice while it lasted.

❖

"Ain't you workin' today?" Tim placed a cup of hot coffee on the table in front of Kristen.

"No. I was only working on a temporary basis. I'm free again." Was that what she wanted? She missed Jaylin, and it had only been a few days. She missed the invitation to sit at the table in the back of the clinic. It surprised her that she missed the animals, or perhaps it was watching Jaylin with the animals. She missed her sensitivity and confidence. Their agreement not to work together made her sad, but it would make it easier for Jaylin. Would it be easier for her? They could try going to lunch or dinner as friends occasionally. That would be better than nothing.

"I'm glad you're here. The new member will be here today. His name's Rupert Winningham. Let me know what you think if you meet him."

"He seemed a little odd that time I met him, but he's got money if he can afford a Fabbri." Something besides his oddness waggled in the recesses of her memory, as if she'd heard his name before.

"Oh, he's got money. He comes from a long line of Winninghams. They own a lot of property 'round here, and I was glad to have him join the club, 'cause of the name and all. But I don't like him."

"I'll watch out for him. I plan to shoot four rounds today, so I'll be here for a while."

"Thanks, and don't forget about the club shoot in a couple weeks." Tim proceeded to the table next to her to talk to another shooter.

Kristen retrieved her shotgun and strode to the skeet stations. She was surprised to see Rupert already awaiting his turn. He looked different with his skeet vest and shooting glasses, but the slicked back hair was the same.

"Hello. My name's Kristen Eckert. You must be the new member. Welcome to the club." Kristen extended her right hand while resting her over-and-under over her left shoulder.

"Hello again," he replied. "I see you're ready to shoot today. How about we go a round?"

Kristen lowered her ignored outstretched hand and considered her response. "You go ahead." She stepped aside and contemplated returning to the clubhouse, but she had as much right to take her turn shooting as he did. She stepped away from the station and waited. Rupert pulled out a large flask from his vest and drank heavily from it before slipping it back into his pocket, winking at her, and loading his shotgun. Maybe the flask held hot chocolate. She doubted it.

Rupert shot well on the first station. Kristen noted his smooth swing and accurate aim. No doubt, he had the financial means to shoot whenever and wherever he desired. She briefly wondered why he chose this gun club, but her mother had loved this place, and she was a member of the U.S. Olympic skeet team before she got sick.

She stepped to the first station and noted that Rupert hung back to watch her. She had nothing to prove, but he stirred something in her that made her ground herself and focus extra intently.

"Pull." She smoked all four targets on station one and stepped back to wait for Rupert to shoot at station two. He pulled his flask out again before loading his shotgun. No wink this time.

His aim on station two was as accurate as the first station, but Kristen noted that he only chipped the doubles. Chipped or pulverized, they counted as hits.

She repositioned her shooting glasses and leaned into her shotgun. "Pull," she yelled a fraction of a second before the target flew into her line of sight. Another target demolished. Her rhythm was good, and she felt loose. His turn.

Rupert didn't pull out his flask for station three. Stations three, four, and five were single shots, and shooters often fell into a sense of complacency without having to shoot doubles. He rolled his shoulders and called for the bird. His first shot nicked the target, enough to break off a piece. The second shot split the target. His grin bordered on feral. He pulled out the flask again and offered it to Kristen.

"I don't know what's in that flask, but I presume Tim told you that alcohol isn't allowed on the property. Guns and alcohol don't mix."

"Yeah, yeah. I got the list of rules and regulations. A little nip to keep you warm on a spring morning can't hurt." Rupert took another swig from the flask and stashed it back in his vest pocket before moving to the next station. The following stations were more of the same. Kristen was dead-on with her shots, and Rupert barely took a chip out of the targets.

"You gonna give up now, hotshot?" Rupert asked.

"What do you mean?" Kristen had worked hard to ignore the obnoxious man as she concentrated on her shooting.

"It's the last station."

"Yeah, so?"

"We can wager on the outcome."

Kristin watched Rupert take another draft of his flask. "Why don't you just finish your round?" She stepped a few extra steps away from the station.

Rupert loaded his gun and swayed slightly as he stepped to station eight. He positioned his over-and-under and called for the target. His swing was sloppy and his shot went behind the bird by a foot. "Fuck!"

Kristen stood back and kept an eye on him. She could hear his expletive even with her earplugs. He wasn't falling down drunk, but gone were his smoothness and accuracy.

Rupert set his stance for the second target and got a piece of it as it whisked past.

Kristen finished her last station without missing and turned to walk back to the clubhouse.

"See ya next week."

Kristen ignored his sneer and kept walking. She made a mental note to talk to Tim about this newcomer and pick a different day to shoot. She waved at Tim as she settled at one of the round tables.

"Hi, Kristen. Did you see Rupert out there?"

"I sure did. He's a showoff. I'm not sure I trust the guy," Kristen said. "There's something really off about him."

"Well, if you don't trust him, I'm gonna keep my eye on him. Thanks." Tim started to walk away from the table.

"Oh, Tim. I'm not sure if it's anything, but you might want to ask him about a flask he carries in his vest," Kristen said.

"A flask, huh? Thanks. I'll check it out." Tim waved and went in search of Rupert.

As she got ready to head home, a place that felt strangely lonely lately, Kristen's thoughts turned back to Jaylin. How could she miss her already, and what was she going to do about it?

CHAPTER THIRTEEN

Jaylin pulled into the end parking spot of the cemetery and clipped the unnecessary leash on Railroad. She strolled to her brother's grave and sat in front of his grave marker. "I feel as though I'm sitting in your lap, little brother." Jaylin lay on the grass and pulled her dog close to her side. She imagined she could feel the security of her brother's arm cradling her.

She wasn't sure how long she was there until she noticed the lengthening shadows signaling the onset of sunset. "Guess we should go." She didn't move.

"Do you remember when we used to lie on the ground, and I'd make up stories about the clouds?" Jaylin watched the white swirls drift past across the early evening sky. "They were our secret refuge places. No one could touch us there."

Jaylin rested her left hand on the grass as if trying to feel her brother's presence. She and her brother had been shuffled from foster home to foster home and abused constantly. Plenty of horrors accompanied her childhood memories, so the ones she had of quiet moments with her brother, like watching the clouds, were extra special. Her past had shaped her relationships, and she'd chosen Sally and predictably slipped back into the victim role. But she wasn't a victim anymore. Whatever direction her relationship with Kristen took, she needed to stand on her own two feet. She chastised herself for giving up without trying. She was an adult. She could try for friendship, and let things take their natural course from there. That's what normal people did, right? She hoped Kristen would be willing to keep trying.

Jaylin stood and guided Railroad back to her car. It was time to stand tall.

❖

"Good morning, Sarah. Am I booked for the day?"

"No, you have a few open spots. Your first appointment is coming in at ten o'clock."

"Thanks. I'll be in my office until then."

"By the way, Jaylin, Bill wanted me to tell you that Kristen won't be back. He has a couple of other technicians to help you if you need them."

"Thank you. Shall I let you know if I need them?"

"Holler and I'll send someone." Sarah grinned and gestured with her hand as if she were waving a magic wand.

Jaylin laughed and squelched her disappointment. What did she think? She and Kristen had agreed it was best if they didn't work together. She would have to live with her decision and figure out how to stifle her desire. She was halfway to her clinic when her cell phone chimed. The emergency number.

"Yes, this is Dr. Meyers...I see. Okay. I'll be there in about thirty minutes."

Jaylin grabbed her emergency pack and let Sarah know where she was headed as she flew out the front door.

❖

"Thank you for coming so quickly, Doctor. Trixie was so much better. She was eating normally, so I've been letting her go visiting again. I do keep a close eye on her though," Doris said. "She started vomiting this morning and refused her breakfast. She's been curled up in her bed since I had the nurses call you."

Jaylin gently lifted the tiny dog and set her on Doris's bed so she could examine her. "Did you happen to keep any of what she vomited?"

Doris thought for a moment and grinned. "I did. I'm not sure why. Something must have told me that it might be a good thing to do. But you can see for yourself. It's in the bathroom."

Jaylin followed Doris as she shuffled across the room.

"I cleaned it up with some paper towels and threw them in this basket." Doris held up a small wastebasket filled with paper towels.

Jaylin didn't need a lab report to tell her the contents of the little dog's stomach included chocolate. "It looks like she got into some chocolate, Doris. Did you let all your neighbors know she's never to have chocolate?"

"Oh, yes. I'm not sure Dr. Eckert understood me, though. He even forgets who I am sometimes."

"I'll go talk to him before I leave, but I'd like to take Trixie with me today to keep an eye on her. Now that I know that it's chocolate, I'll put her on IV fluids and give her some medicine. It will help keep her from getting any sicker."

"Oh my." Doris wrung her hands and walked around in circles.

"Do you want to come with me? I have a comfortable office where you could wait. I'll be giving Trixie some activated charcoal every few hours. Her vomit looks as if she ate milk chocolate. That's good. Dark chocolate is much worse for dogs." Jaylin gently rested her hand on Doris's shoulder. "I'll take good care of Trixie."

"Yes, Doctor, take her to the doggie hospital. We haven't been separated since I got her as a puppy. She's a purebred Pomeranian, you know. Will you bring her home tonight if she's well?"

"I will if she's well enough. Are you sure you don't want to come with me?"

"No. Thank you. I couldn't stand to see my Trixie hooked up to whatever you have to hook her up to."

"Do you have a little crate for her?"

"Yes. The nurses are kind enough to take her for her shots every year. They can give it to you."

Jaylin packed her emergency kit and took one more look at the four-pound ball of fur intently staring at her. She regretted having to take her away from Doris, even for a few hours, but she was so tiny she couldn't take a chance on leaving her. "I'll be right back," she said and left to get the crate.

She peeked around the open door of Kristen's dad's room, but he was sleeping peacefully, and she didn't want to wake him. Maybe he'd be more lucid when Kristen came by to see him. She returned to Doris's room, and once she got Trixie settled, though the dog hardly moved, she gave Doris a hug and more reassurance before heading out to the car. Just as she was putting the crate in the car, she heard a familiar voice.

"Here we are again."

Jaylin set Trixie's crate into her Volvo and turned to face Kristen. "I guess we are. I got a call this morning that Trixie was sick again. I'm taking her to the clinic for the day to keep an eye on her. It seems she got into some chocolate, and I don't want to take any chances. She probably weighs all of about four pounds."

"I quit bringing Dad Rolos, and I asked the nurses to keep an eye on him, but I wouldn't be surprised if other residents had chocolate." Kristen shook her head. "I'll ask the nurses to post signs around the building to remind the residents to be careful."

"Thanks. I've got to get back to the clinic. I have a ten o'clock appointment I might be able to keep." Jaylin walked around to her driver's door. "Say hello to your dad. I stopped in to see him, but he was sleeping." Jaylin hesitated. "Are you okay?"

"What? Yeah. Yeah, I'm fine I…I miss you." *Jesus. What am I saying?* It had only been a few days since she'd seen Jaylin.

"I miss you, too. Maybe we could have lunch one day. As friends. I mean, we're both adults and neither of us wants to get involved."

"I'd like that, but are you sure you'd be comfortable with it?"

"Well, I've been thinking about it, and I'd like to try if you will." Jaylin glanced at her watch.

"Okay. Get Trixie out of here. Come out to the fairgrounds Saturday, and I'll buy you lunch after my race."

"I'll plan on it. See you Saturday." Jaylin got in her car and headed back to work.

Kristen stood outside her father's door for a few minutes, collecting her thoughts. She'd made a date with Jaylin "as friends." What if she wanted to kiss her again? *We're not sixteen. Surely we can manage our hormones.* Her feelings for Jaylin weren't diminishing, but the fact that Jaylin felt similarly made it clear they shouldn't work together. Jaylin was willing to try for friendship without any romantic involvement. She could, too. She shook off her wandering thoughts and turned her attention to her dad.

She found him in his usual position, asleep in front of the soundless TV. She covered him with his quilt and sat beside him for a while, contemplating the complexity of emotions. She'd begun losing him years ago after she'd lost her mother, and she'd discovered working with Jaylin fulfilled a need to be productive that she hadn't known she had. She was losing that now, too. She shuttered her mind to negative thoughts in an attempt to protect her heart from the invading loneliness.

❖

"I'll be out at the backyard table if you need me," Jaylin told Sarah before pouring a cup of coffee, retrieving her laptop, and heading out the back door. She needed a moment to regroup after the last particularly difficult case. A seventeen-year-old high school boy had brought his sixteen-year-old shepherd mix in for possible euthanasia. Jaylin believed in exhausting every possibility for sick animals, but sometimes her efforts weren't enough. This was one of those times. The dog had lived past his life expectancy, even for a mixed breed. She wasn't sure how she'd managed not to break down as the young man cried for five minutes on her shoulder. After he'd composed himself, she'd asked him if his parents or someone had come with him. He'd said no, that, "Rocket had been his dog since he was a kid and this was his responsibility." The high school senior had taken on the duty, alone, to be with his lifelong friend at the end of his life. Jaylin relaxed into the plastic chair, and shook off the sadness. She'd never be able to do her job if she let every tough case get to her. She concentrated on Trixie.

Trixie had responded well to treatment, and she planned to take her to Doris after her last appointment. She looked at her watch and went back inside.

"Good afternoon. My name's Dr. Meyers. This must be Bailey."

The short, heavyset woman set a medium sized crate on the exam table and unlatched the door. "It's nice to meet you. Yep, this is Bailey and I'm Jill. I'm not sure what's wrong with him. He was fine this morning and after I got the kids off to school, I noticed he didn't seem quite his normal self. He's only a year and a half and usually wants to run around the backyard most of the day. Today he didn't even want his morning doggie treat. He's just not himself."

Jaylin reached into the crate to urge Bailey out. His tail thumped against the floor of the crate, but he didn't budge. "See if he'll come out for you," she said.

Jill tipped the crate and a listless small beagle tumbled out.

"Let's take a look at you." Jaylin listened to his heart, gently palpated his belly, and took his temperature. "Is he up-to-date on his vaccinations?" she asked.

"Oh, yes. He had all his puppy shots and his rabies six months ago." Jill ran her hand over Bailey's back and scratched his ears.

"He doesn't have a fever, but he sure seems subdued. His belly looks a little bloated. Did you change his diet recently or did he get into anything that you're aware of?"

"No, nothing I know about. He's been a healthy, happy puppy since we got him at twelve weeks old." Jill looked worried.

Jaylin checked Bailey's mouth, nose, and ears. "Has he had a bowel movement today?"

"No. He didn't even want to go outside to pee this morning. Is he all right? My kids will be devastated if something happens to him." Jill hugged Bailey and frowned.

"I think I'd like to take a couple of x-rays. You can wait in the waiting room. It won't take me long." Jaylin reached for Bailey and Jill stopped her.

"Can I stay here?"

"If you want to, but I'm sure you'd be more comfortable in the waiting room."

"Please. I'd rather stay." Jill was pleading.

"Of course. I'll be as quick as I can."

Jaylin returned within twenty minutes to where Jill was anxiously waiting.

"It looks as though Bailey got a hold of someone's sock." She held up the x-ray for Jill to see. "This spot here"—Jaylin pointed—"I think is a small sock."

Jill tilted her head and touched the film with her finger. "Wow. Will it pass through?"

Jaylin set the image on the counter and prodded Bailey's abdomen. "I've seen larger dogs pass several socks within a day. I can give him a mild laxative and see if that works, but if it doesn't come out in his stool by tomorrow, we may need to consider surgery."

Jill's smile turned into snickering and then full-blown laughter. "He ate a sock? Oh my goodness."

Jaylin smiled with her. "Puppies are notorious for eating clothing. I can keep him here and monitor him. If he expels the sock by morning you can come and pick him up."

Jill stroked Bailey's head and Jaylin could see her struggling with the decision. "Do you want to call someone? Your husband?"

"No. He would just tell me to do what I think is best. What's the danger of me taking him home?"

"If you keep a close eye on him and make sure he has a bowel movement, he won't be in any danger. But it needs to be within the next twenty-four hours."

"Give him the laxative, and I'll bring him back tomorrow night if he hasn't passed the sock. Will that be okay?"

"Sure. Let me know how he does."

Jaylin cringed as the memory of Kristen's angry outburst reminded her of the dangers of delayed treatment for an impacted bowel. She wrote a note as a reminder to follow up on the young dog.

Jaylin walked Jill to the waiting room and let Sarah know she was taking Trixie home. She couldn't help but hope she'd run into Kristen.

CHAPTER FOURTEEN

Kristen watched Debby and Shadow as they maneuvered through the muddy keyhole track. The day had been rainy and chilly, so she'd decided not to work Zigzag. She had a week before the Memorial Day parade, and her only plans were to ride him down Main Street and show him off.

"Good job, Deb. You and Shadow are doing well." Kristen grabbed Shadow's bridle as Debby hopped off and splashed down in the mud.

"Thanks, but he's the star. Are you not riding today?"

"No. I thought I'd give Zig a break. I have plans to ride him in the Memorial Day parade. Are you going to ride in it?"

"I wouldn't miss it. Shadow loves to show off his parade saddle."

"Cool. I have a special treat planned for Zig. Do you want to come over this afternoon and see it? I'll grill some burgers."

"I'm not going to turn down an offer for your grilled burgers. I need to hose off Shadow and brush him down first."

"Sounds good. I'll see you in an hour or so."

An hour later, Kristen carefully positioned the handmade beef burgers on the grill.

"You're pretty good at that." Debby pointed to the grill with the bottom of her beer bottle.

"Thanks. Dad taught me everything he knew. These won't take long, and then I'll show you my surprise."

"A surprise, huh? What's it about?"

"You'll see. I have something special planned for the parade this year."

"Speaking of special, what happened to you introducing me to the sexy doctor?"

"I don't work with her anymore. I told you that. She showed up at the stump race, but it was the week you weren't there." Kristen carefully flipped the sizzling burgers and stepped away from the smoke.

"So? Does that mean you can't introduce me?"

"No. I can, Deb. I haven't seen her for a while. Last time we talked, she was clear that she wasn't interested in getting involved with anyone, though."

"Did you ask her out or something?"

"No. We were just talking, and she said that." Kristen wasn't going to admit to kissing Jaylin to Debby.

"Will she be at the Memorial Day parade?"

"I don't know. Probably. I think she said something about being there with her dog."

"Geez. Did you two have a fight or something? Don't you talk to her at all?"

"I haven't talked to her lately, okay?" Kristen waved her spatula in the air in frustration.

"Okay, okay. So, would you go to the club with me Saturday night? I'm tired of going alone. You don't have to do anything but keep me company. I want to do some dancing. What do you think?"

"No, thanks. I'm riding in the stump race Saturday. I think I'll just rest up for Memorial Day after that." Kristen didn't want to tell Debby about meeting Jaylin Saturday. What if she didn't show up? *And why do I hang on to the irrational feeling that we could have more than friendship?* If Jaylin wanted to go out with Debby, that was her decision. It wasn't up to Kristen to make the choice for her. She shook off her musing and pulled one of Jaylin's business cards out of her wallet. "Here." She handed it to Debby and turned to the grill.

"Thanks." Debby watched Kristen flip the burgers. "Maybe Jaylin'll go dancing with me Saturday night. I'll tell her you're my friend, okay?"

"Sure, but like I said, she isn't interested in getting involved with anyone."

"It's just dancing, Kris." She tilted her head and smiled. "You're all right with it, aren't you?"

"Of course." Kristen moved the foil wrapped vegetables off the grill and plopped them on a plate. *It's Jaylin's choice.*

"Good. You'd tell me if you weren't, wouldn't you?" Debby rested her hand on Kristen's shoulder.

Kristen took a deep breath. "Yeah, I would. I'll admit I like Jaylin a lot, but she deserves to meet someone totally available to her, and she might love to dance."

"You let me know if you change your mind, and I'll back off. Are we going to eat sometime today?" Debby looked stern, but her small smile gave her away.

"I'm on it." Kristen lifted the burgers off the grill and placed them on hamburger buns. "Let's eat and I'll show you my parade plans."

❖

"Hi, Dad. How're you feeling today?" Kristen had been sitting by her father's bed for ten minutes, hoping he'd awaken for her visit. He finally did, but she could see him struggle to figure out who she was. "It's Kristen. Your daughter. I came to visit you."

"Kristen? I have a daughter named Kristen. Do you know her?"

Her father's lucid days were becoming fewer. Kristen had hoped to take her dad to the Memorial Day parade. Now she wasn't sure if it would be wise.

"It's me, Dad. I'm your daughter, Kristen."

"I know who you are. I'm glad to see you, honey. Is your mom with you?"

Kristen cringed. "No, she's not."

"She works too much. She's a nurse, you know. At that big hospital downtown."

"Would you like to sit in your chair for a while?"

"Yes. That would be nice. I can't seem to get around as easily as I used to. Maybe you could give me a hand."

"Of course, Dad." Kristen guided him by the arm as he pushed off his bed and shuffled to the chair. "Where are your slippers?"

"I don't have any. I lost them in the last big snowstorm. My daughter bought me some warm socks for Christmas last year. I hide them under my mattress, at the head of the bed." Her father whispered the last few words as if someone was listening to their conversation.

"Good. They'll be safe there." Kristen retrieved his socks from exactly where he told her they were and put them on his feet. "There. Feel better?"

"Yes. Thank you. Did you hear about that little dog down the hall?"

Kristen's stomach flipped. Was Trixie sick again? "No. What happened?"

"She had another attack."

Did he mean that last one a few weeks ago, or the first one? "What sort of attack, Dad?"

"That pretty young veterinarian had to take her away for a day. Doris told me she gave her an IV. That's serious. I know we always hooked our patients to an IV when they were having surgery. She must have been pretty sick. That doctor is very nice. She stopped by to say hello before she left."

"I'm glad she did. She didn't tell you what was wrong with Trixie, did she?"

"No, she didn't." He stopped and stared at the wall in a pose Kristen recognized as his way of trying to reclaim a lost memory. "She told me that little dogs should never have chocolate. Did you know that? I've never heard of such a thing, but I promised her I'd never give the dog any. I don't think I have any left." He stuffed his hands between the sides of his chair and the seat cushion searching for the candy and came up with nothing. "No. I must have eaten it all."

"I'll bring you some shortbread cookies tomorrow, Dad."

"Thank you, honey. Make sure it's after dinner. The nurses tell my doctor if I don't finish my meals."

"I'll come by about seven."

"Bring your mother with you. I can't remember the last time we had dinner together, but I think it was last Sunday. We had a pot roast with mashed potatoes. She's such a good cook."

Her father's eyelids drooped and he slumped sideways. She gently leaned him back into his recliner, covered him with his afghan, and tucked it in around him.

Kristen allowed her tears to stream down her face. She vividly remembered the last meal her father and mother had shared, and it was pot roast. Her mother had been too sick from her chemo treatment to cook, so Kristen had made the meal. That was seven years ago.

She wiped her face and blew her nose before leaving.

❖

"Good morning, Sarah." Jaylin leaned on the counter and set a bag of warm bagels on the desk behind it. "I stopped at Panera Bread in town and picked up some bagels."

"Ooooh!" Sarah cooed. "I love Panera's bagels. Is there one of the cinnamon ones in here?" She riffled through the bag as she asked.

Jaylin laughed, pleased that she could do something to show her appreciation for Sarah's help with the new clinic. "Yep. They're my favorite, too. I wanted to do a little something to thank you for your help these past few weeks."

"No problem, Dr. Meyers. It hasn't been a hardship. I enjoy scheduling things. Before I forget, a Mrs. James called yesterday and left a message on voice mail."

Jaylin's stomach knotted at the thought of the tiny dog getting into more chocolate. "Nobody called me about an emergency. What did she say?"

Sarah looked up from the bag of bread. "Sorry. I should've clarified. I'm just excited about breakfast. I have access to all the voice mail messages at home, so I check them daily. Her message wasn't an emergency. Her exact words were, 'Trixie misses her Dr. Meyers. Come and visit when you have a chance.' I guess you made an impression on her."

Jaylin smiled. "Trixie was the little dog that got into chocolate. I'll have to stop by and see her." Maybe she'd run into Kristen. Jaylin reflected on the last time she'd seen Kristen there. She'd invited Jaylin to her stump race and lunch as "friends." At night, under the covers, "friends" turned into so much more. As long as that's where she kept it, there was no harm. She flushed slightly at the previous night's delicious images, and forced herself to focus on Sarah.

"We had one more call that wasn't an emergency. It was from Jill, with Bailey. She wanted you to know that her daughter's sock is now in the garbage with the poop bags, and Bailey is running around the yard again. Why would she put a sock in the garbage?"

Jaylin laughed. "Bailey ate a sock, and it was stuck in his intestines. That's why Jill brought him in."

Sarah shook her head. "Dogs! Thanks for the bagels, Doc. I'll talk to you later." Sarah grabbed the phone on the third ring and opened the appointment program on her computer.

Jaylin went to her office and sat at her desk. She took a bite out of a fresh bagel and considered the appropriateness of calling Kristen. She seized her cell phone and dialed before she could change her mind.

Hi. This is Kristen. Leave a message.

"Hi, Kristen. This is Jaylin. I just wanted to say hi. I'm looking forward to the race on Saturday and to seeing you." She hung up and sighed. The message was utterly awkward and totally insufficient. She wanted to say more, but what she couldn't really fathom. Hopefully, she'd be more articulate come Saturday.

Jaylin went to prepare for her first patient.

"Good morning, Janet. I'm Dr. Meyers. Who do we have here?" Jaylin looked at the obviously pregnant Yorkshire terrier and smiled.

"This is Mable. I don't know what's wrong with her. I haven't been overfeeding her, honestly, but she's gained so much weight that I didn't know what to do, so I called Dr. Berglund because he takes care of our minis, and my neighbor told me that he takes care of dogs now, too, and I didn't know what to do." Janet stood holding the little dog like a child holds her teddy bear.

"Let's look at Mable. Would you set her on the table, so I can examine her?" Jaylin hoped Janet would take a breath so she wouldn't have two patients in her exam room.

Janet carefully placed the tiny dog on the table but held on to her with both hands.

Jaylin rested her stethoscope on Mable's chest and positioned it between Janet's fingers on Mable's enlarged belly. She had a hard time believing the owner didn't know her dog was pregnant, but she was a small dog with lots of hair.

"It looks as if Mable's going to be a mom. She's pregnant."

Janet released her hold on Mable as if she were on fire and stepped away from the table. Jaylin rested her hand on the tiny dog so she wouldn't scoot away. "Are you all right, Janet? Your dog looks healthy. She'll probably only have one or two puppies."

"Oh, God. My Mable was raped." Janet sank to the floor and covered her eyes as she cried.

"Janet?" Jaylin picked up Mable and sat on the floor next to her. She held Mable in her lap. "Janet. Mable is fine."

"You don't understand, Dr. Meyers. This isn't a planned pregnancy. Mable isn't a year old yet. She can't have puppies until she's a year old." Janet's tears stopped as quickly as they had begun.

"Dogs go into heat and start their periods as early as six months of age, sometimes. Do you have a male dog in the house?" Jaylin asked.

"My husband has a little boy, Mickey, but he isn't a year old either."

"Boy dogs can impregnate girl dogs as early as six months. Maybe it would be a good idea to neuter Mickey. Is he also a Yorkie?" Jaylin wasn't sure she was getting through to Janet. She sat staring at her dog as if she were an alien being. "Janet?"

Janet got up from the floor and took a deep breath. "Yes. I'm fine. Mickey is Mable's brother. Thank you, Dr. Meyers. I'll take my little girl home now."

Jaylin scrambled to her feet and gently placed the pregnant dog in Janet's hands. "Do you want some information—"

"I don't want anything. I'm going home to tell that no-good husband of mine that his dog got Mable pregnant. Her own brother! I'll stop and see Sarah on my way out to take care of any charges for this visit. Thank you again."

"You're welcome. Let me know if you need anything." Jaylin leaned on the counter and watched Janet whisper tenderly to Mable as she carried her out. This would go down as one of her oddest client stories. She wished Kristen could have been here to see this one. She'd prided herself on her diplomacy throughout the years of her veterinary practice, but some days it was hard not to laugh at the outrageousness of some clients.

CHAPTER FIFTEEN

Jaylin scanned the parking lot before parking her car. She didn't see Kristen's Boxter, but she was there to see Trixie and Doris. She wanted to see Kristen, but she didn't want her to think she was following her. She hadn't heard anything from her after she had left her a message earlier in the day.

"Hello, Doris." Jaylin spoke quietly. Doris dozed while sitting propped up on her bed with Trixie in her lap.

Doris snapped awake with surprising speed. "Dr. Meyers! It's so nice to see you again. Especially since it's a social call instead of an emergency. Look how good she looks." Doris held the squirming little dog over her head to display her healthy tiny body.

"Yes. I'd say she looks quite robust."

"Robust, yes, quite robust." Doris sat straighter against the pillows propped behind her and grinned. "Thank you for all you did for her. You probably saved her life."

"You're welcome. No more chocolate, I see." Jaylin held out her hands. "May I look her over?"

"Of course." Doris passed the pocket-sized dog over.

Jaylin looked into her clear eyes, and setting her down on the bed, palpated her belly. Trixie wagged her tail furiously and tried to twirl in circles. Jaylin pulled out her stethoscope from her emergency kit and listened to the solid beating of the tiny heart. "Everything sounds great in there," she said.

"Thank you, Doctor. Dr. Eckert's daughter asked the nurses to put signs in the hallways warning us not to feed her anything. Especially not chocolate. That was nice of her, don't you think?"

"Yes. She's a nice person." Jaylin could tell Doris was fighting to keep her eyes open. "I hate to leave so soon, but I have another patient to check on tonight. I doubt he'll be as robust as Trixie."

"Robust. Yes." Trixie circled twice before settling back on Doris's lap and both their eyes seemed to drift shut at the same time.

Jaylin slipped quietly out of the room and made her way to Dr. Eckert's room on the way out.

"Good evening, Dr. Eckert." Jaylin stepped into the room. He was sitting in his recliner watching a flat screen TV with the sound off. She watched Alex Trebek mouthing questions to contestants for a minute before moving into the room to see if the doctor was awake. "Hello, Dr. Eckert. I'm Jaylin. I met you a few weeks ago. I'm the vet—"

"I know who you are. Is that little dog sick again? I didn't give it anything. I promised my daughter I wouldn't, and I haven't."

"Good. That's good. She's a little thing so it doesn't take much to make her sick. She's doing fine now. How are you feeling?"

"Did my wife come with you today? She's a nurse, you know. At that big hospital downtown."

Jaylin scrambled to remember what Kristen had said about her mother. *Died six years ago.* "No, she didn't come with me today."

A look of sorrow fleetingly passed over his face and quickly disappeared. "She works too damn much."

Slowly his head nodded forward and he closed his eyes. Jaylin wasn't sure if she should offer to help move him to his bed. *Best left to the nurses. I don't want to intrude.* She stopped on her way out to mention it to them. Somehow, doing a little something for Kristen's father made her feel just a bit closer to Kristen. It was disconcerting just how much that meant to her these days.

❖

The early evening shadows of the trees lengthened, giving the impression of fingers caressing the gravesites. Jaylin stood at Roy's final resting place, bothered by her sudden impulse to pray. She hadn't prayed since she was seventeen, and those earnest prayers had never been answered. She wasn't going to bother now, even with the sudden impulse.

"Hi, brother." Jaylin sat on the ground, leaned back on her hands, and stretched out her legs. She flopped her feet side to side, following the movement with her eyes. She shifted and crossed her legs. "I'll have to remember to bring my folding chair next visit."

She wished she could share so much with Roy. *So many years lost. So many tears.* Her thoughts flowed aimlessly, with Kristen at the forefront of most of them. Would she and Roy have gotten along? Maybe she could bring Kristen here for a picnic. *Yeah, a picnic in a cemetery. That's romantic.* As odd as that sounded, some small voice told her that Kristen probably would enjoy it.

She walked to her car, bewildered by the unbidden phrases playing through her mind: *Keep him safe. Keep him happy.* She could only hope, if Roy had been in pain, that it had died when he did.

She rested her forehead on her steering wheel for a moment, trying to shake off the deep melancholy stealing through her. Her phone pinged, indicating a text message just as she backed out of the parking spot.

Burgers and beer? A just-friends dinner? K

Jaylin replied, her mood lifting instantly. *Be there in fifteen minutes.*

❖

Jaylin couldn't find an open spot when she pulled into the bar's parking lot. She finally replaced one of the many pickup trucks and hurried into the bar. Kristen sat in a booth next to a window toward the front of the room. She looked a bit subdued but sexy as hell in her T-shirt and jeans. She leaned back in her chair and Jaylin's breath hitched at her grin and quick appraisal. She steadied her breathing and slid into the seat across from Kristen.

"Hi. Sorry it took me longer than I figured to get here. There was a lot of evening traffic."

"No problem. I've been nursing a beer. How are you?"

"Good. I'm good." *Better now.*

"How's everything at the clinic?" Kristen waved at the server.

"We're getting busy. I've had one of Bill's techs helping out when I need her."

"I'm glad Bill had someone to help you." Kristen picked at the label on her beer bottle as she spoke.

Jaylin wondered if their conversation would be this strained all evening. *Maybe this was a mistake after all. Maybe it's too late.* The thought made her feel slightly dizzy. "I miss you, Kristen." Jaylin wished she had a bottle of beer to fiddle with the way Kristen was doing.

"I miss working with you, too, Jaylin." Kristen continued her label peeling, her brow furrowed.

Before Jaylin could speak, the server set a bottle of beer on the table, and she gratefully took a drink. She wondered if she should clarify her meaning. She missed Kristen, not just working with her. But then, Kristen's choice of words was telling.

"I'm struggling a little," Kristen said.

Jaylin set her bottle down and reached for Kristen's left hand, but Kristen pulled it away. "What is it, Kristen? What's wrong? I thought we were friends."

"Yeah." Kristen rubbed the side of her face.

She looked so lost. Jaylin reached for her hand again. This time Kristen took it and ran her thumb over Jaylin's knuckles. Jaylin closed her eyes and reveled in the soothing sensation.

"We both admitted to making bad choices and not wanting to get involved with anyone romantically, and I'm trying to respect that. I'm struggling because I want to be your friend, but I can't stop thinking about kissing you."

Jaylin opened her eyes and gently withdrew her hand. She'd wanted to know what Kristen felt, but now she almost wished she didn't.

"I'm sorry, Kristen. I want us to be friends, but I don't want you to hurt. I was involved with a woman who turned out to be abusive. I allowed myself to be used by her, and I learned that I'm not very good at taking care of myself in relationships. I'm working on figuring it all out, but I'm not there yet." Jaylin blew out a breath. "I don't know what to do."

"I had a girlfriend, too. I was young and had no idea what a relationship was supposed to be. I knew I was a lesbian, and I figured Lynda and I would make a life together and that was that. It didn't take long for me to realize we had very different goals in life, and I could never be enough for her. Now, I'm not sure I can fit a relationship into my life." Kristen sat back in her chair looking pensive. "What if we make a pact? No more kissing. We're friends and we can do things together and enjoy each other's company without kissing. Sound okay?"

"Yeah. I think that'll work. No kissing allowed." Jaylin smiled.

"No kissing of any kind allowed." Kristen grinned.

"Perfect. Let's eat our burgers while they're hot. I think better on a full stomach." Jaylin picked up her burger and took a bite.

"Has the practice been getting busier?" Kristen asked.

"A lot busier. I'm pretty much booked up every day now. I think Bill's name is what brings most clients in, but I'd like to think I'm keeping them coming back."

"That's great. I'm sure you are why they'll come back. You're very good with the patients as well as their owners."

"Thanks, Kristen. I appreciate your confidence. I know I love my job." Jaylin smiled and finished her beer. "How's your dad? I stopped in to say hi to him, and he recognized me."

"He's as good as he can be. His doctor says he's in good shape physically. He still talks about how you saved Trixie."

Jaylin shook her head and twirled her empty beer bottle. "I hope I never have to see Trixie again for an emergency, but I'm glad I got to meet her and Doris, and your dad."

"Me, too." Kristen bit her lip. "I'm glad you joined me tonight."

"I'm glad you asked me to. I think we'll be able to make this work." *Maybe if I just don't touch her?*

❖

Kristen pondered her dilemma as she drove to her father's nursing home. Jaylin stressed that friendship was all they could have, but she still wanted to kiss Jaylin. She wanted to hold her hand, feel her soft lips on her neck, and cuddle in bed. She'd never before had longings for someone that caused such uncertainty. She'd have to decide if her heart would allow merely friendship with Jaylin, but if it didn't, she had no idea what to do about it.

"Hi, Dad." Kristen entered her dad's room quietly. She found him in his usual position, reclined in his pajamas, watching the silent TV.

She wondered for what seemed like the hundredth time, what it was that caused her father to need a soundless television. When she first moved him to the home, she had turned on the TV expecting him to enjoy his favorite shows, but he'd waved his hands, obviously agitated, and insisted she mute it. His doctor speculated that it could be that the stimulation added to the confusion in his mind. She kissed him on his clean-shaven cheek.

"Is that you, Kristen? Did you bring your mother?"

"No. I'm by myself tonight."

"She's a nurse at that hospital…" Kristen watch his eyes glaze as he stared at the wall. "She's probably working."

"She works way too damn much," Kristen said. "How are you feeling, Dad?"

"That pretty young vet took care of that little dog again. She said the dog was too little to have too much of something or other. It made her sick."

"She was sick again?" Had the residents ignored the signs she had posted?

"I don't think so. She didn't bring your mom with her either. I think she was working."

"It was nice of Dr. Meyers to stop and say hello." Kristen made a mental note to thank Jaylin when she saw her on Saturday. "I'll check on Trixie before I leave. I wanted to ask you if you'd like to go to the Memorial Day parade again this year. What do you think?"

"I love that parade. I used to march carrying my M16. Damn thing used to jam when I needed it most. Will I have to march?"

"No, Dad. You can sit in a parade car and wave. Just like you did last year. Remember?"

"Will that nice young veterinarian be there?"

"Do you mean Jaylin?"

"I think so, yes, I think that was her name."

"I don't know, Dad. Probably."

"Good. I'll go then."

Kristen shook her head. *What the hell? He's fallen for her, too.*

She allowed herself a moment to reflect on what it would be like to have Jaylin as a life partner. She was good with her dad, and he obviously liked her. Jaylin's "no kissing allowed" words echoed in her memory, and she refastened the lock on her heart.

"I'll be back in a little while." Kristen patted her father's hand before leaving to check on Trixie and her warning notices.

All the signs Kristen had posted regarding the danger of feeding chocolate to Trixie were still clearly visible along the nursing home's hallways. She knocked lightly on the doorframe of Doris's room before calling out to her.

"Hello. Doris? It's Kristen. Dr. Eckert's daughter."

"Kristen. Come in, come in." Doris was propped on her bed with Trixie sitting at full alert, tail wagging furiously. "It's so nice to see you, dear." Her smile faded, and she frowned. "Is your father all right?"

"Yes. He's fine. I didn't mean to worry you. I stopped by to see how Trixie was feeling." Kristen moved to stand at the side of Doris's bed.

Doris smiled as she lifted the tiny dog into the air. "Dr. Meyers said she was 'robust.' Doesn't she look robust?"

Kristen grinned at the term. The puny canine could have been a stuffed animal in Doris's hands. "Yes, Doris. She looks quite robust to me, too."

Doris set Trixie on her lap and leaned over as far as she could to kiss Trixie's head. It must have been a gesture often repeated because the little dog raised herself on her hind legs, and as soon as Doris's lips left her head, turned and licked her under the chin.

Maybe having a dog wouldn't be so bad. The thought of that kind of unconditional love made her swallow against a sudden lump in her throat. "I'm glad she's doing well. I worried that the residents hadn't paid attention to the signs I put up."

"I believe they do. I talked to several of them. They all feel terrible about Trixie getting sick. I appreciate that you took the time to make those signs."

"Well, good. You and Trixie take care. I'm going to say good-bye to my dad," Kristen said.

"Good-bye, dear. Come visit again. Trixie likes visitors." Doris leaned back onto her pillows and closed her eyes.

Kristen closed the door behind her and went back to her father's room. He was sound asleep, and she pulled the comforter over him before kissing his forehead. *Age comes to us all.* The thought of being alone when her time came made her feel glum. Without siblings or a child of her own, she would truly be on her own.

Unbidden, she thought of Jaylin's smiling face. *No. Alone is better than betrayal or whatever other pain it brings.* She headed home to snuggle up with a book and a beer.

CHAPTER SIXTEEN

Jaylin arrived at the fairgrounds as the main barrel race competition was starting. The place was just as crowded as the last time she was there for the rodeo events. She strolled to the main arena and looked for Zigzag. She didn't see him, but the blonde with the pinto horse was waiting in line for the next match. *Kelly.* She prickled at the memory of her kissing Kristen and whispering something in her ear. *I'm not kissing her. She can kiss whomever she wants. Damn it.*

She strode to the other arena where she'd found Kristen the first time she was there. She noticed the striking palomino she'd seen before but didn't find Zigzag and Kristen. She pulled out her cell phone and sent Kristen a text.

Jaylin turned toward the main arena and saw Kristen as soon as she reached the bleachers. She looked amazing as she and Zigzag raced around the barrels. Jaylin settled on one of the benches to watch the contest. This was a timed event, so Zigzag didn't have to beat the other horses, he had to beat the best time. She watched as Kelly rode her pinto through the course. She was fast. Jaylin could see the concentration on her face as she spurred her horse around the last barrel. She waved and flashed a huge grin to the cheering crowd as her winning time lit up the electronic scoreboard.

Jaylin wished Kristen and Zigzag had won, but she knew Kristen would be happy for the winner. *The pretty blond winner.*

Jaylin's phone chimed a text message just as she was preparing to hop off the bleachers and search for Kristen.

I'm glad you made it. I'll meet you at the lemonade stand. K

Jaylin smiled at the thought that Kristen might have noticed her in the stands, watching. Their dinner the night before had been a little strained at first, but she felt comfortable with their no kissing pact. She was optimistic that they could be friends and put their mutual attraction aside. It was all she could offer and Kristen had said the same thing.

Jaylin lost herself in thoughts of Kristen. She threw herself into everything she did. She hadn't been happy about working with animals other than horses, but she'd thrown herself into the task without complaining. She rode Zigzag with complete intensity. She probably did the same with her skeet shooting. As a lover, that was probably just as true. She quickly shoved the thought aside, although she'd had a tiny taste of her passionate kisses, and the thought of being the focus of that passion stole Jaylin's breath.

She reached the concession area and looked for an empty table. She began making her way toward a seat when she felt Kristen's warm arm circle her waist. She unconsciously leaned into her and allowed herself to be led to the available seats.

"I'm glad to see you." Kristen's warm breath rustled her hair as she whispered in her ear.

Kristen smelled like fresh air and horses. She snuggled closer before realizing what she was doing and stiffened. She stepped away, sat at the table, and pulled herself together.

"You looked good out there. I was sorry that you didn't win though," Jaylin said.

"Thanks. Pogo was the faster horse today. Kelly's been working hard with him. She's planning to take him down to Texas for the rodeo championships." Kristen sat next to Jaylin and rested her arm across the back of her chair.

"Well, I rooted for Zigzag. Shall I get us a couple of lemonades?"

"You sit. Enjoy people watching. I'll get them." Kristen rose and trailed her fingers over Jaylin's hand before heading to the concession stand.

❖

What am I doing? Kristen chastised herself for her indulgent touching. She'd been so happy to see Jaylin, she'd instinctively wrapped her arm around her. At least she'd refrained from kissing her, which had been her first impulse. She mentally shook herself, carried the tray to the table, and took the seat across from Jaylin.

"I grabbed us a couple of burgers, too. I'm starving."

"Thanks. That sounds great." Jaylin grabbed her burger and took a bite.

Kristen watched Jaylin gracefully wipe catsup from the side of her mouth and wished like hell it was her own finger doing it. *Or my tongue.* She took a long drink of lemonade.

"What time Monday will you be doing the dog obedience show?" Kristen asked.

"It'll be after the parade. Road's trainer plans to start about three o'clock. I've never been to Novi's parade, but I understand the ending time varies year to year." Jaylin sipped her lemonade, and Kristen tore her gaze away from her lips wrapped around the end of the straw.

She shifted in her seat before speaking, trying to ease the pulsing between her legs. "The parade lasts longer than it did a few years ago. I'll be riding toward the front, behind the veterans' parade vehicles. Dad will be riding in the second car." Kristen tripped over her last words and quit speaking when she caught the gold sparkle in Jaylin's eyes.

"I'm glad your dad feels up to going to the parade. Do you need any help with him?" Jaylin reached for her hand but withdrew it before touching her.

"No, but thanks for asking. He'll be in a car with my friend's brother, and I won't be far behind them."

"I have a couple of friends coming from St. Clair to join me. We'll be sitting somewhere along the parade route," Jaylin said. "I expect a special wave."

"I'll find you." Kristen grinned and finished her hamburger. The words felt somehow prophetic. *Geez. What's going on with me?*

"There you are. I was wondering where you rushed off to after the race. I didn't get my congratulatory kiss." Kelly ran her hand up and down Kristen's back as she spoke. "Oh, hi. Jaylin, right? You here to watch again?"

Kristen saw Jaylin's eyes narrow and her back stiffen, and she slowly shifted away from Kelly's touch.

"It's good to see you again, Kelly. Yeah, I came to cheer for Kristen and Zigzag." Jaylin smiled sweetly and sipped her lemonade.

"You and Pogo looked great today, Kelly. I think you'll do well in Texas," Kristen said.

"Thanks, cutie. I wish you could go with us. I could use a cheering section." Kelly pointedly ignored Jaylin as she spoke.

Kristen stood and grabbed Kelly's hand to lead her away. "Be right back," she said. She hoped Jaylin would still be there when she returned.

"Kelly. This isn't a good time. Can I call you later?"

"I think I see what's going on here." Kelly sighed and smiled.

"Nothing is going on. It's just...complicated." Kristen couldn't think of a good reason, but she didn't want Kelly's attention when she was with Jaylin. It felt wrong. *But she may be going out with Debby tonight anyway.*

"Sure. I'll talk to you later." Kelly kissed her lightly on the lips and walked away.

❖

"She seems to like you a lot," Jaylin said. She'd picked apart her Styrofoam cup while she waited for Kristen to finish with her *blonde*. She pushed the pile away and sat back in her chair. She had no claim on Kristen, by her choice as well as Kristen's. She'd have to suppress her inappropriate jealous urges. *But damn, I really dislike that woman touching Kristen.* She wondered about Kristen's "bad choices." Kelly didn't seem to be one of them.

"We've been riding together for several years. She's a friend."

Jaylin studied Kristen from across the table. She was Kristen's friend, too, and now she wondered what that meant. *Why does her "friend" Kelly get to kiss her, and I don't?*

Kristen fidgeted with her empty cup and avoided Jaylin's gaze. Jaylin couldn't stand her discomfort, so she allowed herself to do what she'd wanted to all afternoon. She took Kristen's hand in hers.

"I'm glad she's your friend. She seems pretty taken with you, though."

Kristen visibly relaxed and squeezed her hand. "Like I said, we've known each other a number of years."

"You don't have to pretend, Kristen. I know we both admitted to making poor choices with lovers in the past, but if you and Kelly are trying, I'm happy for you."

"What? No. Honestly, Kelly and I are not 'trying' for anything. Do you want another lemonade, or are you going to reconstruct that one?" Kristen pointed to the pile of white chips on the table.

Jaylin released Kristen's hand and laughed. "No. I think a new cup is in order." She let go of the niggling discomfort at Kristen's explanation of her "friendship" with Kelly. For now.

Kristen went to retrieve their drinks and set a fresh cup of lemonade on the table. "Here you go."

Jaylin brushed her debris onto a napkin and threw it away. "I had fun today. Thanks for inviting me. I enjoy watching you and Zigzag race around those barrels." Jaylin stretched her legs out in front of her.

"I'm delighted you came to watch." Kristen's eyes sparkled as she spoke. "I'm going to take Zig home pretty soon. Would you like to follow me home? I can grill a couple of steaks, unless you have other plans."

Jaylin mentally counted the hours she'd be gone. "No other plans, and I'd like that, but I'll have to be home by six. I don't usually leave Railroad longer than six hours at a time."

"Let's hit the road then." Kristen stood and reached for Jaylin's hand.

The simple gesture felt heavy with meaning, but she hesitated only a second before taking it. Friends could hold hands, couldn't they? *She kisses her friend Kelly. Does she hold her hand, too?*

Once Jaylin was in her car waiting for Kristen to pull out of the lot, she began to question the wisdom of her decision. They were friends, but this day was beginning to feel too much like a date. She considered her options. She could change her mind and use Railroad as an excuse, or she could use this as an experiment to see if they could really be just friends. She chose the latter. She wanted to know what Kristen's home looked like. She wanted the extra insight, even if it made her more irresistible. *Or maybe I won't like what I see, and it will cure me of this infatuation.* Somehow, she doubted it.

CHAPTER SEVENTEEN

Jaylin stopped at the entrance of what looked almost like a two-lane deer path leading into a forest of pines and hardwoods. Kristen had pulled ahead, out of sight, but she was sure this was where she'd turned. She continued onto the road and proceeded down the narrow lane. She'd driven about half a mile when the woods opened into a meadow of wild flowers resembling a patchwork quilt. She continued along the tree-lined path until it transformed into a gravel driveway. As she rounded a curve and wondered how Kristen traversed this in the dead of winter, the gravel driveway spilled out onto a scene out of one of her romance novels.

She slowed to a stop and took in the expanse of land. A large, freshly painted red barn sat to the north of the most beautiful Cape Cod style home she'd ever seen. Blue shutters framed the four windows behind the expansive front porch and accented soft, cream-colored siding. Two gabled dormers on the second floor were positioned exact distances apart above the front door. Three huge blue spruce trees stood guard on the south side of the house and two smaller versions flanked the north edge. Various perennials defended the front porch and the winding flagstone path leading to it. Yards of hardy rye grass blanketed the ground surrounding the house. A large pond with a solar powered fountain spraying water in the center, completed the serene picture.

Jaylin pulled up behind Kristen's truck and trailer. She took her time as she got out of her vehicle and walked to the front door. She resisted the urge to settle into one of the cushioned Adirondack chairs and put her feet up.

"No trouble finding the place? Sorry I lost you." Kristen stood in the open doorway, leaning against the frame with her arms crossed.

Jaylin had been so lost in her reverie, she hadn't noticed Kristen open the door. Her nipples tightened and warmth spread through her. Her body was clearly at odds with her mind when it came to the "friends" thing. "No. No trouble. It's beautiful out here."

"Yes. Beautiful." Kristen didn't take her eyes off Jaylin. "Come on in." Kristen stepped aside for Jaylin to enter the house. "I just finished unloading Zigzag and fired up the grill."

"It's equally lovely inside." Jaylin gazed around the entryway as she followed Kristen down a short hall that opened into the kitchen. Beyond the kitchen, a family room with large door walls looked over a large deck on which the grill smoked lightly. She stepped outside and walked to the railing.

A split rail fence delineated a huge area behind the house. It included the barn and a feeding area filled with fresh hay and a large water trough. Beyond the barn, a grazing area stretched to the edge of the woods. Zigzag stood next to the fence nearest to the house with his head lowered. He might have been asleep. A Welsh pony stood near him grazing.

"Wow." Jaylin stood in awe.

"What?" Kristen asked holding a barbeque fork in the air.

Jaylin turned to look at Kristen and laughed at her expression of concern.

"This." She waved her hand toward the expanse of land. "It's fantastic."

"Thank you. I'm used to it, I guess. I've lived here most of my life. Would you like something to drink? I have beer, water, and iced tea."

"I'll have water, but I'll get it. You want one?"

"Please. Plenty of bottles in the fridge."

Jaylin went into the kitchen and admired the oak cabinets. The house was neat and tidy. Like Kristen. She rummaged for the water and carried it outside to the deck. "This awning is perfect for a west facing deck. I bet it gets hot out here in the summer." She handed a bottle of water to Kristen as she spoke.

"Thank you." Kristen took a sip. "My parents had this place built in the early seventies, before I was born, so I grew up here. They were both too busy to spend much time back here, but I loved it. I added the awning after my mother died and Dad started his decline." She looked out toward her horse, now contentedly grazing. "I needed a space where I could sit, watch the sunset, and chill out."

"So you've never lived anywhere else? Bill said you graduated from MCC. That's quite a drive from here."

"I lived in New Baltimore for a few years. I liked it there, but I missed the horses." Kristen fidgeted with her cooking utensil. "Then I met a woman. My one and only relationship, and we moved to an apartment in Novi."

"What happened?"

"It didn't work out. We were just too different, and it took me a few years to realize I couldn't be who she wanted me to be. What about your 'bad choices?'"

"My one relationship became abusive, and now I'm too scared to try again."

"Well, here's to learning from past mistakes." Kristen lifted her water bottle, offering a toast.

Jaylin raised her bottle, and they both took a drink before she relaxed into the floating motion of a glider located in the shaded area of the deck.

Front porch or back deck, Jaylin never wanted to leave. This was a problem.

"Can I help with anything?" She offered as a distraction more than an interest in helping with the meal.

"Nope. I've got it covered. You relax." Kristen leaned and placed a gentle kiss on Jaylin's lips.

Jaylin straightened and pushed herself out of the glider. "We agreed to no kissing."

"Damn. I'm sorry, it was an automatic response, and it won't happen again."

The sounds of Zigzag and the smaller horse eating their way through a pile of hay, and birds calling in the distance were the only sounds to break the tense silence that descended between them.

Kristen concentrated on grilling steaks. She had squash, zucchini, and Vidalia onions wrapped in foil and ready to cook on the grill. Everything was set for dinner, except her. Jaylin looked so damned hot. Meeting in public had helped her maintain distance, so maybe it was a mistake to invite Jaylin to the safety of her home, where it was private.

Intimate. She could still feel the heat of Jaylin's gaze as it had traveled down her body when she'd arrived.

Jaylin appeared to be completely comfortable in Kristen's kitchen getting them drinks and relaxing into Kristen's favorite seat on the glider. Lynda had refused to move in with Kristen, claiming the quiet disturbed her. She'd preferred being closer to the club and to movie theaters, places they didn't have to completely interact. Jaylin, however, seemed content to settle in. *She must have turned down a date with Debby by now, but what does that mean?*

"Is medium rare all right for you?"

"Medium well for me please," Jaylin said.

"Medium well it is. The vegetables are almost done. I thought it would be nice to eat outside."

"Sure." Jaylin stood. "I'll get the dishes."

"Oops. Thanks. They're—"

"I'll find them." Jaylin headed into the kitchen.

This felt way too good. Kristen pulled everything off the grill and set the foil bundles on the table while she waited for Jaylin to return with plates and silverware.

"Thanks for getting the plates. I was wrapped up with the grilling and forgot about them."

"No problem. It gave me a chance to look at that beautiful kitchen of yours. I don't do much cooking, but I can appreciate a well-equipped kitchen."

Jaylin held the plates as Kristen placed a steak on each of them.

"I need to say something." Jaylin sat at the table and started cutting into her steak. "I have too many issues to work out for myself before I can even consider getting involved with anyone. Your kisses make me forget that."

"You're right. I'm not holding to our agreement very well." Kristen sighed and shook her head. "I wouldn't blame you if you left."

"Are you kidding? And miss out on this incredible looking meal? This steak is excellent. Perfectly done. We can do this." Jaylin's last words were almost a whisper.

"Yeah. We can. Let's eat," Kristen said. "My dad loved to barbeque. I learned it all from him. Speaking of my dad, I have a question for you, Dr. Meyers."

Jaylin smiled. "Yes?"

"Robust?" Kristen smirked and tilted her head.

Jaylin burst out laughing. "It sounded like something James Herriot would say, don't you think? Doris loved it."

Kristen joined in the laughter. "She did love it. I stopped in to say hello, and she couldn't stop talking about it."

"I hope Trixie stays healthy. Doris is so attached to her," Jaylin said. "Animals are such great companions for the elderly. I can't imagine how she'll cope if anything happens to Trixie."

"Yeah. Those two even had me considering getting a dog."

"They're great company. I don't know why I never had one before Railroad." Jaylin took the last bite of her steak and leaned back in her chair. "I'm stuffed."

"Me, too. If you're done eating, I can take you on a little tour."

"Sounds good." Jaylin stood, grabbed her plate and Kristen's, and all the silverware.

Kristen picked up the salad bowl and the rest of the empty dishes and followed her into the kitchen as if they'd done it a hundred times before. She allowed herself to enjoy the moment without giving in to the notion that it could be permanent.

"Do you have any coffee?" Jaylin asked.

"Sure do. I have one of those Keurig coffee makers. It won't take long."

Five minutes later, Kristen carried their cups outside and they leaned on the railing, shoulders touching.

"It's peaceful out here," Jaylin said.

"Yes, it is." She smiled at Jaylin. "I'm glad you accepted my invitation for dinner."

Jaylin grinned. "I am, too."

"Come on. I'll show you the barn." Kristen grabbed Jaylin's hand and pulled her down the steps.

"I see Zigzag lives as comfortably as you do," Jaylin said. She took a deep breath. "I love the smell of barns. Fresh hay, horses, leather tack." She ran her fingers over the brass latches on the four wooden stall doors. "And is that an automatic watering system?" She pointed to the wall at the back of the stall.

"Yep. I got tired of hauling the hose out here."

"This is great. Do you do all the maintenance? No helpers?"

"Dad had a high school kid come in and help when his two Appaloosa mares were bred every two years. I do it myself now." Kristen watched Jaylin study the barn. Lynda had hated the "dirty" floor and "stinky" animals.

"You okay?" Jaylin asked.

"Yeah. I guess this barn is so full of memories that I get a little caught up in them sometimes."

"I hope they're mostly good memories," Jaylin said.

"Mostly."

They wandered quietly through the barn, this silence nothing like the tense one from earlier. Kristen pointed out a thing or two from her time with her dad, and Jaylin asked a few questions about items she didn't recognize. It was companionable, sweet. Right.

"Come on. I have a couch in my barn office." Kristen checked her watch. "It's only four thirty. You don't need to leave yet, do you?" She led her past the stalls to a room at the end of the barn.

"No, I'm good for a while. You have a barn office?"

"Uh huh. I have Wi-Fi for me and a dish on the roof so Zigzag can watch reruns of *Mr. Ed*." Kristen pulled out two bottles of water from a small refrigerator and handed one to Jaylin.

"*Mr. Ed* indeed." Jaylin shook her head and grinned. "This is nice." She sat on the leather couch and looked around the room. An oak desk sat against a wall across from a window that overlooked the paddock where Zigzag grazed and a bookshelf filled to overflowing rested against the wall next to it.

"Thanks. Dad used to conduct all of his Appaloosa breeding business from here. I still have the records from all of his horses. I can't seem to bring myself to get rid of them, although I don't want to get back into breeding horses. I've been living comfortably on what my mom left me when she passed away, but now, I'm not sure what I want from life anymore." Kristen ran her hand across the top of the desk, and a deep sadness crossed over her face.

Jaylin willed herself to stay seated. She wanted to pull her into her arms and erase the pain. "I'm sorry about your dad. What kind of doctor is he?"

"He was a heart surgeon. I remember him being gone a lot when I was a child. He was either doing emergency surgery in the middle of the night or seeing patients during the day. I looked forward to the weekends when he'd mostly be home and we'd spend all day with the horses."

"Did your mom work with the horses, too?" Jaylin sat on the couch and watched as Kristen lost herself in memories.

"She loved to ride, and she supported my father in his breeding business, but she was wrapped up in her Olympic skeet shooting." Kristen sighed and wiped her hand over her face, as though to scrub away the memories.

"You told me your mom died of cancer, but did she work before that?" Jaylin didn't want to dredge up painful memories for Kristen, but the yearning to know her, all of her, urged her to ask.

"She was a surgical nurse. That's how she met my dad. She worked until after I was born, then she stayed home to raise me and concentrate on her skeet shooting. Hey. Here I am going on about me." Kristen looked at her watch. "I'm glad you agreed to spend the day with me."

"I'm glad you asked me. I think this friend thing is going to work out." Jaylin stood and started for the door.

"What are your plans for tomorrow?" Kristen asked.

The question surprised Jaylin, and she hesitated. "I'm taking Railroad to a park I discovered last weekend. It has a path through the woods where we can run. And I have my CoDA meeting Sunday nights."

"You'll have to tell me what CoDA is next time we get together. I've never heard of it."

Together they walked to Jaylin's car, and Jaylin felt the heaviness of expectation as they ended their day together.

"Thanks for dinner. It was great. Next time it's my turn. I'll admit that I have no cooking skills, so I hope you like carryout." Jaylin smiled.

"I don't need a home cooked meal to enjoy your company. Carryout would be fine. Have a good day tomorrow. I'll see you on Monday at the parade, right?" Kristen said.

"Absolutely. See you there."

There was a moment, the briefest hesitation, before Jaylin ducked her head and smiled before she got in the car. Kristen stuffed her hands in her pockets and shrugged. Clearly, she'd felt it too. But they'd agreed. It was better this way.

Jaylin thought about her day with Kristen as she drove home. They'd both managed to relax and enjoy each other's company.

She considered their friendship-only agreement and questioned her desire to hold to it since her heart seemed to be giving her a different message. Kristen's description of her childhood reminded Jaylin of their differences. There were no gun clubs or horses in her past, and the only decent foster home she remembered was her last one. They'd let her live in their basement until she finished high school. She'd had to struggle her whole life to make ends meet, and her idea of living comfortably was obviously very different from Kristen's. *She probably doesn't even need to work.* Jaylin drove home ignoring the reservations warning her to keep her distance.

CHAPTER EIGHTEEN

Sunday night, Jaylin sat in her car for five minutes before heading into the building. The CoDA meeting was already well in session, so she took a seat in the rear of the room. Maggie sat toward the front with her back to Jaylin. In the years she'd attended the Codependents Anonymous meetings, she'd avoided standing at the front of the room and talking. Tonight she felt compelled to tell her story, and the feeling had nearly kept her from attending.

When the stories waned, and there was a lull in the sharing, she stood and raised her hand. The facilitator smiled and waved Jaylin to the lectern.

Standing at the front of the room, Jaylin clutched the sides of the podium to hide her nervousness. "My name is Jaylin, and I'm glad to be here. I felt the need to speak tonight." Jaylin looked out over the room. "A few years ago, I came to CoDA at the suggestion of my therapist. With the help of my sponsor, I got to a place where I felt able to enter into a relationship." Jaylin met Maggie's eyes and smiled. "I didn't think I was all healed and healthy, but I went out with a couple of women and found one that seemed compatible." Jaylin chuckled and shook her head. "I need to rephrase that. I found one that I could glob on to, become emotionally dependent on, and fix."

Memories of Sally washed over her. "The important point I wanted to share tonight is that I was wrong. I wasn't ready. I didn't even know who I was, much less what I needed or deserved. When I finally realized that I was in a terribly dysfunctional relationship that had become abusive, I withdrew. I felt degradation and disrespect was normal, and I need to change that. This codependency stuff is real. I realize I was powerless over my lover, and the only one I can change is myself.

I look forward to being present in my relationships and honestly sharing who I am without fear or shame." Jaylin stepped away from the podium. "Thank you all for being here tonight and taking time to listen to my story." Jaylin walked to her seat followed by applause, and a thumbs-up gesture from Maggie.

"Can we talk after the meeting?" Jaylin asked Maggie as she walked past her.

"Of course," Maggie said.

At the end of the meeting, Jaylin settled herself at a table with a bottle of water and waited for Maggie.

"What's up?" Maggie asked and sat across from her.

"I'm struggling with my feelings for Kristen." Jaylin stared into her water bottle as if she could find answers in the clear liquid.

"That's good," Maggie replied.

"What's good about it? I say I'm struggling and you say that's good?"

"Think about it. You're allowing yourself to feel something. You may not know what it is, but at least you're feeling." Maggie paused for a moment before continuing. "When you spoke tonight, I was impressed with your insight and honesty. You got involved with Sally, probably, because she made you feel things. You'd been in the protective, non-feeling mode for so long that you latched on to any feelings, good or bad. Maybe the bad ones felt most normal for you, and Sally took advantage of that." Maggie shifted in her chair and leaned forward, her tone serious. "When it comes to Kristen, you don't trust that she's safe, and if she is, that you deserve her. And you're worried that when she gets to know you, she'll leave."

"I'm not so sure I like all this feeling stuff. I wouldn't mind going back to being numb." Jaylin groaned.

Maggie chuckled. "Yeah, but I know you. You're a brave woman who wants a life. You wouldn't be here if you didn't. I know that I used the words 'she made you feel,' but I think you know that nobody makes you feel anything. You're responsible for what you feel. You feel whatever you feel, and you allow others to feel whatever they're feeling. Your feelings are your own responsibility."

"Damn, Maggie. I see why you're a sponsor."

Jaylin hoped all her courageous words would be enough to bring healing to her many wounds. She didn't want to go through life alone. It was true. No one could make her feel anything, so maybe it was time for her to take charge of her own feelings.

CHAPTER NINETEEN

Kristen helped her dad settle into the parade car. A World War II vet would be in the front seat, and her dad and Debby's brother would be in the backseat. She was glad the weather was lovely enough for the Lincoln convertible to keep the top down. She'd slathered her dad with sunscreen and made sure he had his sunglasses. She kissed his cheek, stepped backward and waved. "I'll see you at the end of the parade." She reflected on a time he'd call her back for inspection before she hopped on one of the horses and galloped around the paddock. He'd made sure she'd put on her riding boots and tightened the cinch. Now it was her turn to keep him safe.

Her father sat up straight and saluted. She blew him a kiss and walked over to where Debby was waiting with their horses.

"I appreciate your brother watching out for Dad."

"He's happy to do it." Debby gave Shadow's mane one last combing. "He's looking forward to spending some time with other veterans. He doesn't talk much about his experience in Iraq, so I think this will be good for him."

Kristen double-checked the tightness of the cinch on her parade saddle as a knot balled up in her stomach. "I'm not sure Dad will be much company for him. When I picked him up this morning, he was confused about where he was going and why he was wearing his 101st Airborne military uniform. His eyes lit up when he saw the horses and flags though."

Kristen grabbed the jacket she had thrown behind her saddle and slipped into it before mounting.

"Whoa, Kris. That jacket is unbelievable. You, my friend, are going to have every woman, lesbian or straight, chasing after you today." Debby swung herself into her parade saddle and gawked at Kristen. "I might be first in line."

"Thanks. I couldn't let Zig have all the attention. I bought this when I got my saddle." The Nez Perce black leather, fringed jacket had the same red, yellow, and blue beading as her saddle. "You can probably drop behind in that line. You like short leather skirts and stilettos, remember?" Kristen grinned. "You'll never see those on me."

"Yeah, but damn, you look hot. And I can use my imagination."

Kristen laughed and shook her head. "Let's go show off." Kristen wondered if Jaylin would agree with Debby.

❖

The area fenced off for the dog obedience events was at the opposite end of the grounds from where the parade was starting. Jaylin could hear and smell the horses, but the band members and Cub Scout groups scurrying to get in position blocked her view. Kristen was here somewhere, and Jaylin couldn't wait to see her, though she tried to ignore just how excited she was about that prospect. She took Railroad in search of a good vantage point along the parade route. She set up three folding chairs, sat down, and sent a text to Maria.

The crowd clapped and cheered as a twenty-foot high float with a ten-foot-by-ten-foot American flag made completely of red, white, and blue crepe paper flowers, inched by. Next in line were four convertibles filled with flag waving American veterans of various wars. Jaylin recognized Dr. Eckert and waved. He looked comfortable and alert, although he didn't wave back. She hoped he was lucid enough to enjoy the event.

The arrival of her two friends interrupted her search for Kristen.

"This is great," Dana said as Maria sat in one of Jaylin's chairs and set a small cooler next to them. She retrieved a bottle of water from the cooler and offered one each to Jaylin and Maria. "It's been a long time since I've been to a parade."

"I guess this one has been going on for years. I love the bands." Jaylin motioned at the high school band passing by.

"I love anything musical. Thanks for inviting us, Jaylin," Maria said.

"I'm glad you could make it. Railroad looks forward to showing off later. You didn't bring Frankie, huh?"

"No. I wasn't sure how he'd react to a large crowd. He's fine at home, probably curled up in his bed."

The eruption of applause interrupted their conversation. Jaylin looked to the parade, and her mouth went dry. Kristen and Zigzag had captured the attention of the crowd. She was hatless, her hair in a tight braid with its red highlights shimmering in the morning sunshine. Jaylin was captivated by the stunning beaded saddle, bridle, and matching leather fringed jacket. She wore those sexy faded jeans she'd worn at the keyhole event, with soft looking beaded moccasins.

"Wow. That's magnificent," Maria said.

"Yeah. I've never seen a saddle like that," Dana said.

Jaylin sat spellbound. Kristen was resplendent. Kristen tilted her head slightly, as if hearing Jaylin's thoughts, and turned to gaze directly at her. Kristen's blue eyes sparkled as her grin spread. She waved, and Jaylin stood and clapped with enthusiasm. She mouthed, *beautiful*, and Kristen winked.

"Do you know that woman?" Maria asked.

Good question. "Her name is Kristen. We worked together for a few weeks when I first moved here."

"She's nice looking."

"Nice looking? She's way hot," Dana said. She pulled Maria into a one-armed hug and grinned.

Jaylin sat in her chair and laughed at her good-natured banter. "I agree with you both. She's nice looking, and she's way hot."

They watched the last few horses and riders make their way along the parade route, but Jaylin's thoughts were on Kristen. Her wink may as well have been a caress, based on her body's reaction. She still felt the warmth and slight buzz between her legs. She sighed. *What the hell am I going to do?* She hoped they could find time to talk after the parade.

"You like her, don't you?" Maria asked.

"She's a good person. I do like her," Jaylin said.

"Uh huh. I meant you seem *taken* with her. As if you'd want more than friendship."

"God. I don't know. It's complicated."

"Important relationships are. Let me know if you want to talk." Maria squeezed Jaylin's arm and offered a knowing smile.

They watched the Cub Scout troops march past, waving flags and carrying a banner with their troop number in bold letters. Another band followed, and the crowd sang along to "The Star-Spangled Banner" and "America the Beautiful." Jaylin heard Maria's voice harmonizing with the mass of people. An antique fire truck, driven by the local firefighters, rode past blasting its siren and occasionally spraying water into the air. A line of children clapped, and adults kept them from running into the street after it. A float sponsored by a local bank followed the fire truck with red, white, and blue LED lights forming dazzling American flags covering the entire thing. "You're a Grand Old Flag," blared from speakers on either side, and the crowd cheered as it rolled past.

"Mind if I join you?"

Jaylin jumped at the soft breath on her ear. "Kristen. Of course." Jaylin shifted her chair closer to Maria to make room for Kristen's folding chair.

"Are you done already? The parade isn't over yet," Jaylin said. Anticipation fluttered in her belly.

"Yeah. We were at the front of the line, so I put Zig in the barn and came out to find you."

Jaylin realized she was staring when a light cough got her attention. "I'm sorry." Jaylin fumbled through introductions. Maria shook her hand politely, and Dana gave Kristen a mischievous grin. Maria nudged Dana unsubtly in the ribs.

"I can't stay long. I have to get Dad. He was content to visit with the other veterans, but I could tell he was getting tired. I was hoping we could talk, but later would be better, if that's okay?" Kristen settled into her chair and rested her arm along the back of Jaylin's.

Jaylin resisted the temptation to lean into her. "Yeah, that would be fine. I'm glad you found me." The words felt laden with meaning, and she pushed the feeling away.

They watched the last of the parade and Kristen stood. "I need to head back. I'll stop by the dog obedience area after I collect my dad. See you all later. Nice to meet you." Just before walking away, she leaned down and placed a feather light kiss on Jaylin's lips. "Later," she whispered.

"That's it. I want to know all about Ms. 'It's complicated.'" Maria turned to face Jaylin and Dana waited with a grin, too.

Jaylin was stunned. She hadn't expected the kiss, and her whole body simmered. "As I said. It's complicated." She was sure she was stammering.

Maria and Dana shared a glance before Maria spoke. "Okay. Let's go see Railroad work. You can tell us all about Kristen at dinner afterward."

❖

"Come on, Dad. I've got your wheelchair ready. We'll go watch the dog obedience for a few minutes before I take you home." Kristen could tell the event had taken a lot out of her father. Debby's brother told her that her dad had nodded off several times toward the end of the parade, but she wanted to say good-bye to Jaylin.

"Will that nice young veterinarian be there?" her dad asked.

Kristen shook her head in wonder. Of all the things he could remember, what about Jaylin made her one of them? "Yes, Dad. She's waiting for us not too far from here."

The fenced off area where the obedience exhibition was located had attracted a large number of spectators, but they parted quickly when they saw Kristen's uniformed, wheelchair-bound father. Kristen spotted Dana and Maria sitting along the fenced area. She wheeled her father to their seats and introduced her dad. "May I sit with you?"

"Of course." Maria pointed to Jaylin's empty chair. "Have a seat."

"Thanks. Are you comfortable there, Dad?" Kristen positioned her father in the shade next to them.

"I'm fine, honey. Did your mother come today?"

Kristen's heart ached. "No. Not today, Dad."

"She's probably working. She's a nurse at that hospital downtown. She works too damn much." Kristen watched her father's eyes flutter closed after speaking, and he quickly drifted to sleep.

"I'll have to get him home soon," Kristen said.

"We'll let Jaylin know you were here if you have to go. You did come to see Jaylin and Railroad didn't you?" Dana asked. "She told us that you worked together?"

"I filled in as Jaylin's vet tech for a while when she first moved here. I wanted to see the wonder dog in action. So, how do you two know Jaylin?"

"We live in Marine City, which is near St. Clair. She invited us to the parade so we drove out here this morning. We're going to grab a bite to eat at Panera Bread later and then head home. Would you join us?" Maria asked.

"I have to take my dad to the residence and then trailer my horse home. After that, I'll swing by the restaurant and see if you guys are still there."

"Sounds good," Dana said.

"Is that the nice veterinarian?" her father suddenly asked.

"Yes, it is, Pop." Kristen couldn't believe her father was alert enough to recognize Jaylin. Especially from so far away, while running full speed with a border collie mix glued to her left leg.

"She took care of Doris's little dog, you know."

"Yes, she did. Her dog's name is Railroad. She's doing obedience with her." Kristen had no idea if her father knew what she was telling him, but she had to try. He'd been more alert today than he'd been in a long time, but she knew just how fleeting that could be.

"Oh." His eyes glazed and Kristen could tell he was trying to figure out what he was seeing.

She watched as Railroad perfectly executed every command Jaylin gave her. "She is good, isn't she?"

"Yeah. Very good," Dana said. "I've seen many obedience trials, and it's rare that a dog dedicates itself so thoroughly to its owner. Jaylin must work with her a lot."

"Do you do dog obedience, too?" Kristen asked.

"No. I run a dog grooming school in Marine City. I groom at quite a few dog shows, and a lot of those have obedience events."

Kristen watched intently as Jaylin put Railroad through her commands. Her gentleness and concentration inspired pride and an emotion she couldn't quite identify but one that scared her. She looked over at her dad and his attentiveness surprised her.

"What do you think, Dad? She's pretty good isn't she?"

"Yes. I like that dog. It's bigger than the one Doris has."

"She is bigger than Trixie. I bet Jaylin would bring her to visit if you asked her."

"Maybe she could bring your mother with her, too. She always wanted a dog."

Kristen was dumbfounded by her father's statement.

"She probably can't bring Mom with her, but I'm sure she'd bring her dog to visit you." Her dad nodded off again, and her heart swelled with love for him. She turned to Jaylin's friends. "I think I need to get Dad home. Tell Jaylin she looked great out there. I'll try to make it to Panera later." Kristen stood and rested her hand on her father's shoulder.

"Will do. See you later," Dana said.

Kristen headed back to her truck with her father, who occasionally woke long enough to look around. She could see the confusion on his face, but before she could console him, he'd drifted off again. She managed to get him in the truck, and her heart broke as she saw him trying to figure out his surroundings, although he didn't ask any questions. Fate was so cruel.

She headed toward her dad's home and soothed herself with images of Jaylin's gorgeous body maneuvering through the obedience course.

CHAPTER TWENTY

"Did I see Kristen here earlier?" Jaylin finished with Railroad's events and joined her friends on the sidelines.

"Yeah," Maria replied. "She took her dad and her horse home and said she'd join us later at Panera."

"That'd be great. Are we ready to head over there?" Jaylin hid her disappointment at missing Kristen, but she realized it must have been a long day for Kristen's father. She turned to wave good-bye to her fellow obedience participants.

"Can we stop by your new clinic on the way? I'd love to see it," Maria asked.

"Sure. It's not out of the way."

Jaylin gave Dana and Maria a tour of her clinic and they sat outside for a few minutes watching the birds at the feeder.

"I like it," Dana said.

"Yeah. It's cozy." Maria raised her face to the sun, her eyes closed.

"Thanks. I like it here. So far, the clients have all been receptive and Bill told me he's gotten positive feedback, so I guess I'm doing all right."

"Now I'll be able to tell Frankie that I found his Dr. Jay. He wasn't happy with the new vet that bought your practice," Maria said.

"What happened?" Jaylin tensed, worried that the doctor she'd entrusted her clinic to wasn't good.

"I didn't mean there was anything wrong with him. Sorry. It's just that Frankie is used to you. He trusts you."

Jaylin laughed with relief. "Well, then. You tell him I miss him, too. You did get the letter I sent you with my new address didn't you?"

"Yes, and now that I know where you are, I'm going to bring him here. It only took us about forty-five minutes to get here. That's not so bad."

"Thank you, Maria. I appreciate that you'd make that trip. I'd love to take care of Frankie, of course. If you have time when you bring him, plan to join me for lunch. I'm here on Mondays, and you don't usually work Mondays, right?"

"Right. Sounds good. I'll plan on it. So, shall we go eat?"

Jaylin smiled as they gathered their things. She thought about how much she'd wanted to date Maria, once upon a time. Now she knew they wouldn't have been a good match, and she was glad to have both Maria and Dana as friends. Kristen, however, felt like an incredibly good match. *If only.* Dana and Maria followed her to the café, and although it was busy, they managed to find a booth next to a window overlooking a wooded area.

"They have good food. I come here for lunch sometimes."

Dana's face was practically pressed against the glass as she gaped at the various freshly baked desserts and breads.

Jaylin could tell Maria was nearly bursting in anticipation of hearing about Kristen. They placed their order and Jaylin started talking, not bothering to wait for the impending questions.

"I met Kristen when I was first offered the position in the new clinic. She and I didn't hit it off right away, but we worked things out and managed to work together for several weeks."

"I'd say you worked things out pretty well, based on that tender kiss this afternoon," Maria said.

Jaylin unconsciously touched her lips. They still seemed to hold Kristen's warmth. "Yeah. She's tender, gentle, and kind, and just plain sexy." Jaylin sighed, knowing she'd revealed more than she'd intended.

Maria smiled and took Jaylin's hand. "I'm happy for you. You deserve someone who is 'gentle, and kind, and just plain sexy.'"

"Enough about me. How are you two doing and what's new in St. Clair?" Jaylin picked up her glass of iced tea and took a sip, hoping they'd let her change the topic.

Jaylin laughed at some of Dana's grooming tales and she shared a few stories about her patients. Maria told stories about clients from her beauty shop and her friends in the choir. Jaylin realized how much she missed having friends.

"How's Justin doing?" Jaylin had met Maria's son a year ago when he was a freshman in the same college from which she'd graduated.

"He's doing well. He's in his second year and still loves school and still plans to finish veterinary medicine. I told him you sold your clinic and moved, and he's looking forward to coming to check out your new place."

"Any time. I'm sure Dr. Berglund would be happy to show him the large animal side of the practice, too," Jaylin said.

"He'll be visiting us over the Fourth of July weekend. It'd be great if you could join us. We're planning a little barbeque at Pastor Wright's in Port Huron. Bring Kristen."

Jaylin allowed herself to believe that would be possible. Only for a moment.

Jaylin sipped her iced tea for fifteen minutes after her friends left and tried to swallow her disappointment. Maybe Kristen thought it was too late to stop. Maybe her dad held her up. He had looked tired. But Kristen would have called if she couldn't make it, wouldn't she? The whispered "later" after that gentle kiss had convinced her that Kristen would show up. She touched her lips again. They tingled with the memory, and she smiled.

She sat in her car for another ten minutes watching the parking lot. *This is ridiculous.* She pulled up Kristen's number and waited as it dialed.

Hi. This is Kristen. Leave a message.

"Hi, Kristen. It's Jaylin. I wanted to let you know that I'm leaving Panera. I'm sorry I missed you. Hope everything is okay."

Jaylin disconnected the call, took one more look at the parking lot, and started her car.

She was about to pull out of the lot when she saw Kristen's little Boxter slide into a spot in the front of the building.

"Damn fool." Jaylin grinned as she got back out of her car. "Hey. I didn't think you were going to make it."

"I'm sorry I'm late. I'm so glad you're still here. Are Dana and Maria gone?"

"Yeah. They had a forty-five minute drive home. I'm glad you made it, though. Have you eaten?"

"No, but I'm not hungry. You're probably ready to go home." Kristen rolled her neck from side to side, obviously trying to work out kinks.

"You look tired. Come on. We'll get you something to eat. I'll have a cup of tea." Jaylin cupped Kristen's elbow and led her into the restaurant.

"That sounds good."

Jaylin faltered for a minute as she realized the reversal of support. Kristen was always the one to take her arm or to perch her hand on her back. She was glad to support her for a change. "What's going on?"

Kristen plopped into a chair.

"You all right?" Jaylin asked.

"Yeah. I'm just tired. Dad wouldn't shut up when I got him home. It was like I'd given him a shot of adrenaline, so I couldn't leave him. You've made quite an impression on him, Dr. Meyers." Kristen smiled.

"Me? What do you mean?" Jaylin ordered a sandwich and two cups of tea.

"He kept going on about the nice young veterinarian with the dog that 'runs fast.'"

"Huh. I'm glad he enjoyed the obedience show. I kind of thought he would doze off."

"Nope. I'm glad I took him. He ended up having a good time, I think. He also went on and on about the veterans riding in the car with him. I haven't seen him so animated in a long time." Kristen took a bite of her sandwich and shook her head. "I wish I could bring him home."

Jaylin grasped Kristen's hand. "It must be hard, but he's well cared for, with twenty-four-hour nursing care. You did the right thing by moving him there."

"Yeah. I still have to convince myself sometimes, I guess. I feel as if I'm failing him somehow."

Jaylin could understand the feeling of failure. As hard as she'd tried, she hadn't been able to find her brother until after he was dead. She'd never had a parent she cared about, however. She squeezed Kristen's hand, let go, and drank her tea.

Kristen ate quickly, her attention on her food. Finally, she pushed her plate away and sighed happily.

"Thanks for the sandwich. I needed it." Kristen smiled at Jaylin, who seemed like she was miles away. "Where'd you go?"

"You just got me thinking about the fact that I don't have a parent. It doesn't usually bother me." Jaylin looked puzzled.

"I don't want to bring up a painful subject, but you told me once you grew up in foster care. So, you were never close to your foster parents?" Kristen shifted in her seat, realizing how self-absorbed she'd been. She pushed aside her fears and concentrated on Jaylin. The least she could do was listen to her.

"Nope. Never." Jaylin leaned forward and rested her arms on the table. "I already told you I never knew my mother. She left my one-year-old brother and me when I was three. By the time I was five, we were in our third foster home. That's when…"Jaylin blinked away tears and shifted back in her seat "They took my baby brother away. The family had four boys already and wanted a girl. I was miserable for three years. I didn't know where they'd taken, Roy, my brother. That, and their oldest son reached puberty that year." Jaylin lowered her head and Kristen covered her hand with her own.

"You don't have to tell me more." Rage blazed through Kristen at the thought of Jaylin hurting so much.

"It's fine. I haven't talked about all this in a long time. I spent another year with that family. It was a year filled with fear and panic. I was terrified of being alone with that kid. He'd grab my hand and rub it against his genitals. At least he never took his pants off. I think he was afraid I'd hurt him." Jaylin smiled. "I'd like to think that I would have. I was only eight years old, but I knew something was wrong about it. I didn't know exactly what though. Fortunately, my foster parents decided I wasn't such a cute little girl anymore, and returned me to the system. I was traded in for a younger model." Jaylin shook her head and snorted.

"So, did you ever see your brother after that?"

"No. I tried to find out where they'd taken him, but nobody would tell me. I spent the rest of my childhood living on memories of him, and hoping we'd eventually be together one day. But I never saw him again."

Kristen raised Jaylin's trembling hand to her lips. "I'm sorry you had to go through all that. Thank you for telling me."

Jaylin cupped Kristen's face with her hand. "Thanks for listening. Can we get the hell out of here? I'm sick of listening to myself, so you must be fed up with it."

Kristen frowned. How could Jaylin think she'd feel that way? Was she such a bad friend that it seemed she wouldn't stop to listen? She knew that she couldn't change Jaylin's past, but she feared her capability to support her. Maybe listening was enough.

"I'm not fed up with anything. I'll listen anytime you need to talk," Kristen said. She pulled Jaylin into a hug.

"Thank you."

"Let's go." Kristen grabbed Jaylin's hand and led her out of Panera.

"I didn't realize it was so late. I've been blabbing away at you, and you were tired when you got here."

"Not to worry." Kristen relaxed as they got closer to their vehicles. She released Jaylin's hand and opened her driver's door.

"Thank you again." Jaylin turned and leaned against the car with the driver's door open.

"Anytime." Kristen struggled with her desire to kiss Jaylin, who must be feeling raw and vulnerable. She didn't need her making a move, but she wasn't sure how else to show her support. She gently kissed her cheek. "Good night. Drive carefully."

"Thanks, Kristen."

"Oh, hey. I wanted to let you know about an event at my gun club. It's called a club shoot. It's a skeet shooting competition for members of our club. There'll be a dinner served afterward. I'd like it if you'd come as my guest." Kristen shifted from foot to foot, waiting for Jaylin to reply. She seemed to hesitate for ages, and Kristen was just about to tell her not to worry about it when she finally answered.

"I'd love to watch you shoot, Kristen, but I've never been to a gun club before. Is it fancy?"

"Fancy? As in dressy, fancy?"

"Yeah." Jaylin looked confused.

Kristen couldn't hold back. She lightly skimmed Jaylin's lips with her own and murmured against them. "No. Jeans and a T-shirt. Nothing fancy."

"Hmm. No kissing." Jaylin melted into Kristen's arms and wrapped her arms around her neck.

"Okay." Kristen deepened the kiss and pulled Jaylin against her.

Jaylin pulled back and took a deep breath. "Oh, my. This feels way too good."

She wrapped her arms around her waist, and rested her chin on Jaylin's shoulder. A sense of peace engulfed her, and she sighed at the feeling of rightness. "Yeah, it feels like it was meant to be, but I'm not sticking to our agreement very well."

"Huh. And I am?" Jaylin snuggled closer.

"Do you think we need to revise it? Like, only limited kissing?" Kristen nuzzled her neck.

Jaylin stepped out of her embrace and reached for her car door. "I'm really sorry, Kristen. I'm giving off mixed messages, but I can't seem to stop myself. It's been a long day, it's late, and we're both tired. I'll text you my e-mail address so you can send me the details of the gun club event."

"Okay. We'll talk again. Be careful driving." Kristen headed to her car. *Why can't I control myself around her?*

CHAPTER TWENTY-ONE

Jaylin drank her coffee as she waited for Maggie to finish talking to a newcomer.

"Sorry I took so long." Maggie pulled out a chair and sat across from her. "What's up? You're not usually here on Wednesday."

"I'm a little frightened." Jaylin ran a hand through her hair. "I got another e-mail from Sally."

Maggie reached over and squeezed Jaylin's hand. "What did she say?"

"That she wanted to hook up again. She wants to meet at some bar downtown. God, Maggie, I thought she was gone." Jaylin paced next to the table.

"You can probably get a restraining order against her," Maggie said.

"I suppose. She's playing games with me. She used to do that all the time. She'd tell me how important I was to her and then refuse to speak to me for days. She'd grunt and expect me to know what she wanted. When she started slapping me and telling me I liked it, I knew something had to change." Jaylin stopped pacing and sat down again.

"She's probably pissed because she can't control you anymore."

"Maybe that's it, but I'm not sure what to do, and it's been a long time. I'd have thought she'd moved on to someone else by now. Maybe she's between women and bored, so she's testing the waters. I don't know. I'm going to have to confront her and tell her to leave me alone. And then there's Kristen."

"What's up with Kristen?"

"We talked a few days ago and she told me she was struggling with her feelings for me but wanted to try to remain friends. Neither of us knew what to do about it. I don't want to hurt her, or myself. God, I'm a mess." Jaylin rested her chin on her hands.

"I can see how anxious you are. Take a deep breath. Try to relax. It's hard to find answers while consumed with apprehension." Maggie settled back in her chair and eyed Jaylin. "Do you want to know what I think?"

"Always. Why stop now?" Jaylin grinned. She allowed the serenity of Maggie's presence to wash over her.

"I think that there's a part of you who trusts Kristen, or wants to, anyway. She hasn't done anything to make you believe you can't trust her, and you're waiting for the shoe to drop. Am I right?"

"Yep."

"So, you won't trust her because idiot Sally abused you and you let her. Right?"

Jaylin sighed before replying. "Right again."

Maggie hesitated before continuing. "I'm not trying to put words in your mouth. You know that, don't you?"

"Sure." Jaylin rolled her empty coffee cup between her hands. "I know you're trying to help me sort through my feelings. Make sense of them."

Maggie looked at Jaylin and tilted her head. "Then just start talking."

"Okay, so she's not like Sally. Nothing like Sally, but she could be. She could decide that her needs are more important than anyone else's. She could decide that control by humiliation is what I need. Sally was all lovey-dovey and respectful when we first got together."

Maggie shook her head and shrugged one shoulder. "What if she did? What if you decided to trust Kristen, and she turned out to be untrustworthy?"

Jaylin covered her face with her hands and rubbed her eyes. "Damn it. It's me I don't trust. I don't trust that I'd be able to take care of myself, so I'm too afraid to try."

Maggie rested her hand on Jaylin's arm. "These lessons keep coming, don't they?"

"Yeah. You know, even if I decide I can trust Kristen, it doesn't mean she won't leave me when she totally gets to know me."

Maggie squeezed Jaylin's hand. "You want guarantees. And there aren't any. You're going to have to decide whether or not you're willing to take a risk. And only you know that."

Jaylin rested her head on her forearms after Maggie left. Questions beat at her and answers were nowhere in sight.

CHAPTER TWENTY-TWO

Jaylin made her way to a table between the bar and the door. She'd arrived earlier than their agreed upon time so she could see when Sally came in. She wiped her sweaty palms on her jeans and took a deep breath as she watched the entrance. She'd responded to Sally's e-mail and agreed to meet her at a nearby club with the intention of letting her know she didn't want anything to do with her. It felt important to do it in person, to face her demon head-on, rather than by e-mail, which clearly wasn't working. Her stomach rolled and her heart raced when she saw Sally strut into the building.

"There you are. I knew you'd come. I still own you." Sally snickered as she sat down.

"Listen, Sally. We aren't meant for each other. You need to find someone who can give you what you want. I just wanted to tell you face-to-face, so there's no question about the way I feel." Jaylin clasped her hands on the table to keep them from shaking. She glanced around, relieved to see several couples dancing and several more lined up at the bar. She would probably have help if she needed it. *I can do this.*

"I know you, Jay. I can give you what you like." Sally's scowl sent a shiver of fear down Jaylin's spine. That initial reaction of interest brought on by her e-mail was gone and had been replaced with revulsion. And strength.

"No, Sally. You don't, and you can't. I don't trust you. I want you to quit sending me e-mails and leave me alone. We're over." Jaylin stood and walked toward the door, feeling as though she'd shed a persona, and a person she no longer had any use for. It was invigorating. Kristen's image flashed in her mind, and she held fast to the resolve it evoked. Before she could reach the door, she was on her knees, her right arm twisted behind her, and the metal bite of handcuffs icy on her wrist.

"You can't just walk away. You'll go when I tell you to go," Sally whispered in her ear. She yanked Jaylin's arm harder.

"What the hell are you doing, Sally? Let go of me." Jaylin pushed herself to her feet and spun around, forcing Sally to release her arm. Panic threatened to overwhelm her and adrenaline shot through her. Sally pushed her forward and Jaylin turned in time to see a tall brunette step next to them.

"Excuse me, but do you need help?" the tall stranger asked Jaylin, ignoring Sally.

"Stay out of this. It's none of your business." Sally spat at the woman and twisted Jaylin's arm.

Jaylin raised her foot, slid her shoe down Sally's shin, and stomped forcefully on the top of her foot. Sally released her hold on Jaylin's arm and limped to a chair. *Who knew that lesson in foster care would come in handy?*

The tall woman grinned and shook her head. "Nice move. My name's Debby. It looks as if you have this situation under control, but let me know if you need me." Debby returned to the bar.

"Thanks," Jaylin said. Something about Debby looked familiar, but she turned her attention to Sally. "Take this thing off me." She held out her arm with the handcuffs dangling next to Sally's nose.

Sally glared at her and rubbed her shin before fumbling with a key and releasing the cuffs. She stood and hung the cuffs on her belt. "You don't deserve me. I'm leaving you. You blew your chance." Sally grumbled as she unsuccessfully struggled not to hobble out of the bar.

Jaylin slumped into a chair and rested her head in her hands. Her heart was racing, her pulse jumping, and her stomach felt like there were hamsters doing backflips in it. *I did it. I stood up to her. And she left.* Elation was quickly replacing fear. When she felt settled, she went to look for Debby.

"I wanted to thank you again for offering to step in to help me. My name's Jaylin." She held out her hand to Debby.

"You're welcome, Dr. Meyers. It didn't look as if you were enjoying that woman's attention. And you sure as hell let her know where to go." Debby's smile was warm, her brown eyes gentle.

"You look familiar, and you seem to know who I am. Why is that?" Jaylin took a step back, unnerved.

"I'm a friend of Kristen's. I saw you at Dr. Berglund's once when I was there talking to him about my horse."

Jaylin studied Debby for a second and smiled. "I remember you now. I was talking to Sarah at the clinic and you were leaving. I remember thinking you have a nice smile. Thank you again for offering your help today. That woman is my ex, Sally, and a real idiot."

"I was happy to help, but I'm glad you didn't need anything. I'm a bit of a wimp."

"It turns out, maybe Sally's the wimp. Thanks again. I'm getting out of here." Jaylin squeezed Debby's arm once before heading for the exit.

Jaylin sat in her car for a few minutes to settle her shakiness. She'd done well. She'd told Sally they were through and Sally decided it was her idea. Jaylin rested and allowed the relief to wash over her. She couldn't wait to tell Maggie.

She drove home replaying the incident. She could have just sent an e-mail telling Sally to back off, but she knew doing it in person would be more convincing. And she'd been right. She arrived at home feeling more relieved than she had in a long time.

She settled into her patio chair and held her cup of tea to the side to allow Railroad to settle on her lap. The sun was setting, and exhaustion had replaced the euphoria of ridding herself of Sally. She allowed herself to enjoy the elation about the positive way she accomplished it and to feel the relief of standing up for herself. She'd declared that she deserved to be treated with respect. And for the first time, she thought she might believe it.

Her thoughts turned to Kristen and her invitation to her gun club. She looked forward to spending time with her, but a gun club sounded pretentious. *I'll wear my new black jeans and a silk blouse.* Maybe she'd take a T-shirt and a pair of jeans, just in case, and she could change in the car when she saw what other people were arriving in. She reviewed her wardrobe in her mind. She mixed and matched for twenty minutes until she returned to her original decision of black jeans, sea-foam green silk shirt, and her brown leather jacket. She'd take a backpack with a change of blue jeans and a MSU T-shirt. *Shoes? Sneakers, loafers, or boots?*

"Geez, Road, it's just a gun club. It can't be that fancy, can it? Oh, maybe it has a website. Come on." Jaylin rose as Railroad slid off her lap and went inside to boot up her computer. Maybe there would be photos of Kristen. *Not that I'm becoming obsessed or anything.* She grinned and launched the website.

CHAPTER TWENTY-THREE

"Hey, Tim." Kristen sat at one of the round tables in the gun club. "Is lasagna on the menu tonight?"

"Sure is. You stayin'?"

"I sure am."

"Comin' right up."

Kristen settled in her seat across from the window and watched the shooters outside. She cringed when she saw Rupert at the last station, nipping on his flask. She'd been able to avoid him all week while practicing for the shoot, but it looked like her luck was about to run out. The spicy scent of his expensive, excessive cologne preceded Rupert to her area of the room.

"I thought that was you, hotshot. Looks as if I'm on time for dinner." Rupert pulled out a chair opposite Kristen and chuckled from across the table at her.

"I'd prefer to eat alone, Rupert. I'm sure there are plenty of empty seats at other tables."

"I kinda like this one. I got more to say to you."

Kristen hoped Tim would direct Rupert away from her table when he brought her coffee, but he just set it down with a nod. "So what more do you have to say to me?"

"I know who you are."

"What's that supposed to mean? I introduced myself to you weeks ago." Kristen wished he'd take his stinky self away from her table. She doubted she'd be able to enjoy her dinner with him sitting across from her.

"I knew your mom. She thought she was hot shit. Just like you." Rupert narrowed his beady eyes.

"What the hell are you talking about? My dinner will be out in a minute, and I don't like cold food. I don't have time for your lies."

Rupert's smirk sent a chill down Kristen's spine as he settled into his chair as though he was prepared to stay all night. "I'm not lying. You was just a skinny little kid the year I was the one supposed to go to Barcelona, the year I was up against your mom for a place on the Olympic team. I was always the better shooter, but she got lucky. Now you think you're gonna beat me, too."

"Rupert, I'd like to be left alone to enjoy my meal."

"Don't believe me, huh?"

"No." Kristen was losing her patience. She wished Tim would hurry with her meal.

Rupert leaned forward and rested his stubby hands on the table. "Rosalyn Eckert, United States Olympic Skeet Team, nineteen seventy-eight to nineteen ninety-two, and the women's events from two thousand to two thousand five. She died in two thousand eight. Have I got that correct, hotshot?" Rupert scowled at Kristen.

Kristen stared at Rupert. He could have been in his twenties in 1992, during the Barcelona Olympics. Most of her memories of her mother's competition for the Olympic team were sketchy, but she remembered that her mother had mentioned someone she'd beaten that year by only two shots. He'd been upset and had resorted to calling her names and complaining to the Olympic committee. His name was Rupert. That's why his name seemed familiar.

"I can tell you believe me now." Rupert's hostile grin exposed his bleached teeth. He snuck a drink from his flask and quickly hid it in his vest pocket.

"I think you should leave now. Tim won't be happy about that flask in your pocket." Kristen sat completely still. She wouldn't let him know he'd rattled her.

"You won't beat me. Remember that." Rupert stood and teetered toward the door.

Now that she realized why his name seemed familiar, she wondered about his presence at the gun club. Was the only reason he was here to beat her? Why hadn't he been there in the years since her mother's death? She didn't care to invest any energy in trying to figure him out. So, he'd competed against her mother. Plenty of people had. She decided to think about seeing Jaylin again instead.

❖

Jaylin parked in the gravel lot next to the gun club, as far away from the sound of shots as she could, before she pulled out her phone and sent Kristen a text letting her know she was there. The log building wasn't elaborate or pretentious, and the barred windows indicated a level of security that didn't surprise her. She admired the manicured lawn surrounding the cobblestone path leading to the steel door. The pots of geraniums and begonias lining the walkway surprised her.

"Can I help you, ma'am?" Tim asked, stepping in front of Jaylin as she entered the building.

"I'm looking for Kristen Eckert, I'm a friend of hers." Jaylin studied the rough looking man blocking her way. She hadn't known what to expect, but this guy fit her idea of someone who would work at a gun club.

"This here's a private club. You can't waltz in here askin' for people."

Jaylin shrank under the weathered man's brazen appraisal. "As I said, I'm a friend. I came to see her shoot today."

"What kinda friend don't let her friend know she's comin' to see her so she can meet her at the door? How do I know you ain't lookin' for trouble?" Tim narrowed his eyes and stared at her.

Kristen's privacy was certainly well protected. "Listen. I'm not trying to cause trouble. I'm looking for my friend, and she invited me."

"You're gonna have to prove that to me." He stood with his arms crossed and legs spread.

"I have her phone number." Jaylin pulled out her cell phone and showed Tim the readout.

"You could have looked that number up and put it in that fancy phone." He straightened still blocking her path.

"I know her father's name. Would that work?" This was the last attempt. If he didn't move after this, she'd call Kristen.

He squinted at her and Jaylin could almost hear his mind whirring.

"Never mind. Can you leave her a message at least? Please?"

The impolite man gestured with his chin toward the desk, where he handed her a felt-tip pen and a pad of paper. "You write down a message. *If* Kristen is around. I'll give it to her."

❖

Kristen watched Tim acting like a rooster protecting his flock. She waited for another second before working her way to where Jaylin looked ready to punch Tim. Knowing the ex-marine as she did, Kristen didn't want to take a chance of that happening.

"Did I hear someone's looking for me?" She couldn't have suppressed her smile at seeing Jaylin if she'd tried.

Jaylin looked up and relief flooded her face. "Thank God. This *gentleman* wouldn't let me in to find you." Kristen laughed aloud at the annoyance in Jaylin's voice.

"It's okay, Tim. This is my friend, Jaylin. Jaylin, this is the owner of the gun club, Tim Roland."

"Pleased to meet ya." Tim smiled and offered his hand.

Jaylin looked baffled, but she shook his hand in greeting. *The owner?*

"I invited Jaylin today to watch the club shoot. Sorry I didn't see you come in, Jaylin. I just saw your text or I'd have met you at the door. And I'm sorry, Tim. I should have let you know she was coming. I wasn't thinking." She turned to Jaylin. "Come on. I was just about to have a cup of coffee before I start. Will you join me?" Kristen knew she was grinning ear to ear.

"I'd love to," Jaylin answered, then proclaimed much louder, "I'm going to have coffee with my friend, Kristen." She glared at Tim and took Kristen's hand.

"He's a sweet man when you get to know him," Kristen said.

"Yeah. Well, that'll take some convincing."

Kristen led them to her favorite table by the windows. She pulled a chair out for Jaylin, then sat across from her.

"We have an hour before the shoot starts. I'm glad you made it," Kristen said. "You look great. I love that color green on you. It reflects your beautiful eyes." Kristen kept her eyes above chest level, though it took all her self-control to do so. Jaylin had left the top button of the soft looking silk shirt unbuttoned, and a hint of cleavage peeked through.

"Thank you. I wasn't sure what to wear to a gun club. All my jeans and T-shirts are thread-bare."

Before they could continue, Tim appeared and filled their coffee cups.

Jaylin took a sip. "Mm. This is excellent coffee."

"Tim makes the best Italian roast I've ever tasted. He won't disclose his secret, although everyone asks him. The food is good, too. He has a chef who comes in on weekends. You'll see. Can you stay for dinner after the shoot? I don't think it will be too late."

Kristen watched Jaylin scrutinize the room.

"I'd like that, if it's not too late." She looked around. "I didn't know what to expect, but it's cleaner than I would have thought," she said. "And bigger. The view is nice. Is that where you shoot?" Jaylin pointed to the skeet stations outside.

"Yep. We can walk out there and I'll explain how it works, if you're interested."

"Will we go before the shooting starts?"

"We have to. Only the registered shooters are allowed by the stations once the competition begins. It's safe and well regulated. You can sit and watch from this table if you want to."

After a brief tour of the stations, and explanations about the way the competition was judged, she led Jaylin to the watching area and headed back to get ready.

Kristen set herself on the first station and yelled for the target. She wasn't nervous. This was just a club shoot, which helped Tim keep the club qualified for the regional shoots. She thought of Jaylin watching the event and lost her concentration for a second, but she settled into a rhythm and willed herself to focus on the targets. By the second round, she was loose and warmed up. She anticipated a good final score, maybe even high overall. She had to admit, shooting that well was even more gratifying, with Jaylin watching.

The shooters were set up in groups of four, so Kristen knew she'd eventually have to shoot with Rupert. Rupert joined her group on their fourth round.

"Hey, hotshot. Looks as if we're neck and neck, but don't get cocky." Rupert shot first and cleanly broke all his targets. Kristen noted that he didn't have his flask with him, or at least he hadn't pulled it out yet. It would have meant automatic disqualification.

They continued the round and neither of them missed a target. Both were on track for a perfect score and ahead of the closest competitor by two shots. Kristen stepped up to the next station, positioned her gun, and shouted, "Pull." A flash of light crossed the sight line of the barrel of her gun a second before she pulled the trigger. She hesitated for less than a fraction of a second but it was enough. She missed the target.

Kristen stepped off the station. She checked the light clouds overhead that obscured the direct sunlight. She saw no metal objects anywhere or planes that might reflect the sun. She set her stance and focused. She broke the next targets cleanly and moved away from the station to allow the next shooter to take their turn. Rupert strode past her and flashed a crooked grin. He spoke quietly enough that none of the other shooters could hear him as he passed her. "Too bad, hotshot."

Rupert didn't miss a single shot for the rest of the round and he ended up taking the high overall prize with a score of a perfect one hundred.

"Congratulations," Kristen said. She didn't linger for any further conversation but headed to the clubhouse, where Jaylin was waiting for her.

❖

"You looked good out there. At least, in my totally inexperienced opinion." Jaylin grinned.

"Thanks." Kristen wiped down her gun and set it in the gun rack. She was clearly disappointed, but she tried not to let it show.

"Tim is bringing you a cup of coffee. Come on." Jaylin took her hand and led her to their table. She was inexplicably happy to see her. She'd watched the participants as they shot their rounds and tried to remember the mini lesson Kristen had given her. They all looked pretty much the same to her, and she'd quickly become bored, until she noticed the ugly man with slicked back hair. He hadn't taken his eyes off Kristen unless he was shooting. At first, Jaylin thought maybe he had a thing for her, but then she spotted his hateful sneer.

"Who's that guy with the greasy hair? He's creepy," Jaylin said.

"His name's Rupert, and I agree. He's creepy."

Tim set their coffee cups on the table and confirmed that they'd be staying for dinner. "It'll be about half an hour before dinner's served," he said. "Good shootin' today Kristen. What happened there at station seven?"

"You know, I'm not sure, Tim. There was a flash of light, a reflection from something maybe, that caught me off guard. I shot a ninety-nine though. That's not so bad." Kristen picked up her coffee and relaxed in her chair.

"Yeah. As I said, good shootin'." Tim retreated to the kitchen to oversee dinner preparations.

Jaylin looked at Kristen over her cup. "Do you think Rupert had anything to do with that 'flash of light'?"

Kristen looked surprised, either because Jaylin had asked the question, or because she hadn't thought of it. Jaylin wondered which.

"I can't prove that. Did you see him do something?"

"Only that he kept reaching into his vest pocket. I didn't see what he was looking for."

"It doesn't matter. I've missed before and I'll miss a shot or two again," Kristen said.

Jaylin shrugged. "I don't get it. You'd think he'd be happy to win on his own merits, not have to cheat to beat you."

"Yeah. It's not as if he needs the money. He just needs to win, I suppose," Kristen said. "But then, we don't know that he did anything wrong, either."

Tim delivered their meal and Jaylin enjoyed the fantasy of membership in a private club, dining on veal parmesan and prime rib with her…what? Friend? Person she was dating? She forced away those thoughts and relaxed. She'd enjoy Kristen's company and the good food and worry about their differences later.

CHAPTER TWENTY-FOUR

The early June morning was cool, but Jaylin's shirt stuck to her back and sweat trickled between her breasts as she ran. Her calf muscles burned, but she pushed herself harder, feeling the need to escape. What was she running from? She had nothing to fear from Kristen.

No, it was the things she felt for Kristen. Things that tugged at her heart. *Feelings.* Maggie said this was good. So why did it scare her so much? She wanted someone who respected her boundaries and who wanted her. Did she want to live the rest of her life in fear? Her past, especially her past mistakes, did not define her. If she didn't try again, how could she learn? How would she know if she was capable of love? Was it better to be alone forever? She had to find a way to make room in her heart for trust. *So what the hell am I running from? Am I running before she does?*

Jaylin walked the final half mile to her house. Railroad was waiting for her when she trudged back inside.

"Hey, you. Let's go do some training after breakfast."

Jaylin sat in her lounge chair with her coffee and contemplated her dilemma. She had to shut her brain down. She was getting a headache from the chaos tumbling around in her mind. Jaylin finished her coffee and oatmeal and concentrated on introducing Railroad to jumps and tunnels. She had to trust that at some point she'd know what step to take next. For the moment, as uncertain as she was, she knew she needed to wait it out. *Maybe.*

❖

Jaylin sat half listening to the various discussions going on around her. She jumped at the feel of Maggie's hand on her shoulder.

"You're jumpy tonight," Maggie said.

"Hi, Maggie. Yeah, but I'm fine. I'm working on figuring things out."

"Ah. Are you making headway?"

"Not much." Jaylin stretched her muscles, slightly sore from her energetic run, and leaned her forearms on the table.

"So, how is Kristen? Is she your dilemma?"

"Yep." Jaylin sighed and raised her eyes to Maggie. "Being with her, kissing her, her kissing me, is wonderful. It all scares me to death."

Maggie took a deep breath and expelled it. "Since you used the word wonderful, I'm presuming she didn't ask you to do anything you didn't want to do. Hence the feelings you're afraid of."

"God, Maggie. I don't know. I'm still so unsure of myself."

"It sounds as though you've come to a place where you believe Kristen will respect you. Am I right?"

"Yes. I do believe that." Jaylin smiled, remembering the tenderness of Kristen's touch and her gentle kisses.

"So, do you think you don't deserve her respect?"

"I don't know. I managed to let Sally know I didn't want anything to do with her. I got rid of her because she didn't respect me, so I think I'm at a place where I believe I deserve respect."

"Great. When did that happen?"

"Last week I met her at that bar downtown. I let her believe that leaving me was her idea instead of mine. I'm glad to be rid of her." Jaylin grinned, remembering the stunned look on Sally's face when she'd stomped on her foot.

"Good job. I'm proud of you." Maggie walked around the table to pull Jaylin into a hug. "You realize that's a big deal, don't you?" She held Jaylin at arm's length.

"Yeah. I do. I rather surprised myself with it all. I was nervous as hell, but I did it anyway. Now I just have to figure out where all that courage came from and what to do about Kristen." Jaylin sighed and settled back into her seat.

"You told me Kristen isn't interested in a serious relationship, but with all the kissing you talk about, it sounds as though maybe she is." Maggie took the seat next to Jaylin.

"We acknowledged our attraction to each other, but we agreed to be friends and not go any further. We're not teenagers. We can control ourselves. At least, we try."

"Huh. Is it a problem for you? Just being friends?"

"I think it might be. I have feelings for her that go beyond friendship, and they scare the crap out of me. I'm less worried about being good enough than the certainty it won't work out. That it's preordained she'll leave me."

"Sounds like awareness to me. You're aware of your fears and insecurities."

"Oh, I'm aware of them. I'm not sure why I'm letting them keep me from exploring what Kristen and I might have together, though." Jaylin frowned and shook her head.

"Can you accept them?"

"Accept them? Do I have a choice?" Jaylin struggled unsuccessfully to keep the bitterness and resentment out of her question.

"Always," Maggie said.

"I suppose if I accept them, it makes them real. I want them to go away. I want them to not be true."

Maggie placed her hand over Jaylin's. "People change because they're in pain. Pain is defined in as many ways as there are people who feel it. It sounds to me as if you're hurting. You hurt because you fear your insecurities, but you want Kristen." Maggie released Jaylin's hand. "Maybe if you're brave enough to try something more serious with Kristen, the two of you could grow and change together. You could learn to trust each other, as well as yourselves. In my experience, if you don't try, you'll never know."

❖

Jaylin prepared for her next patient. Sarah indicated that it was another obese dog, and Jaylin hoped it wasn't another pregnancy. She sat in her office and considered her options with Kristen. They'd spoken a few times on the phone since the shooting event, but as if by some unspoken agreement, they hadn't made plans to see each other. Jaylin could feel their distancing, and it made her sad. Or was it only her? Was she protecting herself from the inevitable?

Sarah's text interrupted her thoughts, and within five minutes, a gray haired woman entered the exam room with a rotund Chihuahua. "Good afternoon, Mrs. Lynley. Who do we have here?" Jaylin observed the hefty dog in his owner's arms from across the exam table. He, and it was a *he*, didn't look happy. He bared his tiny teeth and curled his lips. She had no doubt he would love to take a chunk out of her hand if he got the chance. His growling began as soon as his owner set him on the table.

"Oh, don't mind Pepe's growls. He does that to everyone except me. So, you're the new vet here, huh?"

"Yes." Jaylin kept one eye on the disgruntled patient as she spoke. "My name is Dr. Meyers. I've been here a couple of months. What did you bring Pepe in for today?"

"My daughter told me to bring him here. She thinks he's too fat. Do you think he's too fat?" Mrs. Lynley lifted the little dog's front legs to display his protruding belly.

Jaylin carefully placed her stethoscope on Pepe's chest and listened intently for a minute, trying to hear over the little dog's growling and snapping, and then slowly moved it away. "It looks as if he could stand to lose some weight. He'll feel much better if he does."

"My daughter said the same thing. She thinks he's miserable because he's so big."

"She may be right. Overweight dogs can get sore joints, and all their organs have to work extra hard. What kind of dog food are you feeding Pepe?"

Mrs. Lynley sighed and shrugged. "That's another thing my daughter said. That he shouldn't be eating people food. I give Pepe the same thing I eat. I figured if it was good enough for me, it should be good enough for him." She sighed again.

"I have to agree with your daughter again, Mrs. Lynley. I'll give you a sample of some healthy reduced calorie food you can try, and I have some literature I'll send home with you to read. Dogs have different nutritional needs than we do. I believe Pepe will lose weight and feel better if you put him on a healthy diet for dogs, and it may even change his temperament a little."

"I suppose I better try it. He won't be happy, I assure you of that."

"Just try easing him into the change slowly. Start mixing some of the healthy dog food in with whatever you're feeding him now. Try mixing it half-and-half for a week or two then cut that in half for a couple more weeks. See how he does. You can bring him in anytime and we can monitor his progress." Jaylin had inched her hand slowly toward Pepe while he was distracted and managed to feel his bloated belly. He twisted his head to regard her as if surprised.

"I'll give it a try, Dr. Meyers. I haven't seen anyone except me be able to touch him since he was a puppy. I guess if he trusts you, I will as well. Thank you."

"You're welcome, Mrs. Lynley. As I said, bring him back anytime if you need anything."

Jaylin walked Mrs. Lynley out to Sarah's desk and gave her a few sample bags of reduced calorie dog food. "Good luck. It was nice to meet you and Pepe." *I need to tell Kristen about this one.*

"That was a huge Chihuahua," Sarah whispered.

Jaylin laughed. "Yes, it was. I'll be in my office waiting for Judy," she said. "Just send her to the exam room when she gets here."

"Will do. I can't wait to see her new puppy."

Jaylin smiled. She never tired of the puppies. "Me too." Jaylin went to wipe down the exam room table, and her next patient came in within minutes.

"Good afternoon, Judy. Let's take a look at this little cutie." She bent to eye level and grinned as the puppy wagged her tiny tail. "Does she have a name yet?"

"Hi, Dr. Meyers. I named her Annie. Actually, my Irish grandmother named her. She took one look at her blue eyes and called her Annie."

Jaylin held Annie close to her body and listened to her heart. "Everything sounds normal. I'm guessing Annie is about eight or nine weeks old. Those blue eyes may change to brown in a couple of weeks. Will your grandmother want you to change her name?"

Judy laughed and held Annie while Jaylin took her temperature. "No, I think Annie will be her name. Gram had a dog named Annie years ago that looked like this one."

"Did you say you rescued her from a puppy mill?" Jaylin frowned at the readout on the thermometer.

"Actually, I got her from a woman in Ohio who had several litters she'd rescued. She came home from work one day and found a garbage bag full of newborn puppies on her doorstep. She nursed the ones that survived the best she could, but she didn't have room for all of them in her house, so she put the older ones outside in a pen. I had a different one picked out to adopt, but Annie kept following me around and beseeching me with those soulful eyes. She was covered in mud and feces, had fleas, and, I believe, she was surviving on the droppings of the other dogs. She was the tiniest of the puppies outside, so she was usually shoved aside at feeding time. I'm sure she'll need to be treated for worms." Judy stroked Annie's tiny body as she spoke.

"Well, it sounds like Annie sure lucked out. She probably wouldn't have survived long in those conditions. Her temperature is elevated, but that might be from worms." Jaylin separated Annie's hair and looked for signs of fleas.

"The first thing I did when I brought her home was bathe her. I found a flea powder that was safe for puppies, so I powdered her up with it and set off flea bombs in my house."

Jaylin lifted the little dog and set her on the scale. "I'll give you some samples of vitamins and puppy food. She's probably safe from heartworm, but her bloated belly looks like she's full of other ones. Have you seen any blood in her stool?"

"No. In fact, I brought a sample with me." Judy pulled a plastic bag out of her purse and handed it to Jaylin.

"Thank you. I'll give you a call tomorrow with the test results." Jaylin set Annie back on the table and cupped her tiny head in her hands as she spoke. "You are going to grow into a strong, healthy, beautiful dog."

Judy smiled and gently transferred Annie to her carrier. "Thank you, Dr. Meyers. I agree."

Jaylin pondered the fate of the young dog as she sipped her tea in her office. Annie was an abandoned, mistreated newborn, unwanted and dismissed. Now she had a safe home and a promising future. Annie hadn't shied away when she'd been examined; in fact, she'd wagged her tail and accepted Jaylin's touch trustingly. Did she sense that she was being helped? *She didn't allow her difficult past to stop her from trying for a loving home.* Jaylin sighed. Maybe she could learn from a puppy's courage.

Jaylin hung up her lab coat and frowned at the pervasive sense of sadness that overtook her. She missed Kristen, but she could feel herself detaching, shielding herself.

She stopped to fill the bird feeder on her way to her car. She heard the ping of a text message as she slid into her driver's seat.

I'm riding in the stump race at the far end of the fairgrounds Saturday. I hope you can make it. I'll buy you lemonade. K

Would it be easier if she just ignored the text? Could she? She started her car and headed home, a place that felt altogether too big and empty these days.

CHAPTER TWENTY-FIVE

Kristen relaxed into the lightweight riding saddle and let Zigzag amble along the path through the woods of her ten-acre property. She reached down to pat his muscular neck. This was her refuge, her escape to quietude. Surrounded by the trees, birds, deer, and squirrels, she could let her mind wander.

She followed the path to a small clearing surrounded by white pines. "Let's visit the earth awhile." She slid out of the saddle, pulled a small apple out of the pouch she wore, and fed it to Zigzag. She pulled out a bottle of water for herself and watched her horse chew the apple, such a small thing, so thoroughly enjoyed. She spread out the blanket she'd brought along and settled under one of the pine trees. She immersed herself in the serenity of the scent of decaying leaves, pine needles, and the fleeting sounds of birds distancing themselves from the interloper. The sunshine filtered through the branches, casting slivers of light across the ground.

"I don't know what to think of this Jaylin situation." Zigzag stood to the right of her with his reins hanging over her shoulder, his eyelids closed. Kristen smiled at his indifference as she idly twirled the ends of the reins.

Jaylin only wanted friendship, and that's all Kristen wanted as well. She didn't have time for anything serious. And she could tell Jaylin had been bored at the skeet-shooting event. They'd enjoyed a nice dinner, but she'd sensed Jaylin withdrawing, and she hadn't heard from her regarding the text she'd sent her days ago. They had agreed to ignore their mutual attraction, and then they had spent several days together. Maybe it was too much. *Or maybe she's just doing what we said we'd do.*

She'd worked with Jaylin, and she'd seen her interact with Bill and the patients and their owners. She'd sat at the little table outside of the clinic, and they'd shared bits and pieces of their lives. Jaylin was intelligent, tender, and sensitive, and felt perfect in her arms.

Maybe Jaylin didn't want to try for friendship anymore. Maybe it was too difficult. She could tell Jaylin's disclosure about her childhood had been hard for her. Kristen couldn't imagine growing up without parents and having to fend for yourself. *It's no wonder she's so self-sufficient and independent.*

How did Jaylin spend her free time? Did she drink coffee and read the paper in bed on Sunday mornings? She wanted to know the answers and she wasn't sure what that meant. Maybe Jaylin would show up Saturday. She hoped so. She'd send her an e-mail and wait for her answer. Until then, she'd remind herself that Jaylin was only a friend, as often as she needed to. Kristen pulled her phone out and scrolled to Kelly's number.

❖

"Would you like something to drink?" Kelly asked. She'd wound her arms around Kristen's neck as soon as she'd walked into her house.

"A beer would be nice, thanks." She pulled away and held Kelly's gaze. She noted Kelly's light blue eyes. *Not hazel flecked with gold.*

"Let's sit out on the patio by the hot tub," Kelly said. She retrieved two beers from the fridge. "Did you bring your suit?"

Kristen took a swallow of her beer and sat on one of the cushioned patio chairs. She scanned the expanse of fenced yard where Pogo grazed. "I didn't even think of it."

"Good. The water jets feel much nicer without one." Kelly set her beer down, straddled Kristen's lap, and began unbuttoning her shirt.

Kristen hesitated a moment before giving in to Kelly's seduction. She cupped her chin and kissed her thoroughly.

Kelly pulled out of their kiss to finish unfastening her top. "Let's get in the tub. I have plans for you."

They both stood, shed their clothes, and Kristen pulled Kelly tightly against her body. She pushed her thigh between Kelly's legs, eliciting a moan. "Oh, yes. I'm so glad you called today. I've missed you."

Kelly pushed her breasts against hers but drew away far enough to slide her hands between them and circle her nipples with her thumbs. Images flashed through her mind of Jaylin's beautiful hands. She wanted *those* hands on her breasts, teasing her nipples. A flood of heat spread through her. *This isn't right.* She liked Kelly, and she was a friend. She couldn't make love to her while thinking of Jaylin. This was pathetic. She eased away from Kelly's touch and gently clasped her hands between her own.

Before she could speak, Kelly grabbed Kristen's hand and shoved it between her legs. "Feel what you do to me."

Kelly was warm and wet. Why shouldn't she indulge? Kelly wanted her. Needed her. Jaylin didn't want anything more than friendship. They weren't even supposed to kiss. She fingered Kelly's clit, spreading her wetness with the barest of touches until Kelly was writhing in her arms, pushing against her hand. "Oh, God, Kristen, yes!" Kelly cried out.

Kristen teased her opening with her middle finger and took her mouth with the ferocity of someone drowning. She backed Kelly against the edge of the raised Jacuzzi and slowly eased her finger into her. She massaged her clit with her thumb until she felt Kelly tighten around her finger. She slid her finger deeper and nuzzled her neck.

Kelly squeezed Kristen's nipple with one hand and rammed Kristen's hand against herself while riding her finger and rocking her hips.

"Do you want to get into the hot tub?" Kristen whispered and nibbled Kelly's earlobe.

"If you stop now I'll run you over with my horse."

"We can't have that." Kristen fondled Kelly's breast and continued her ministrations.

"OhmyGod. I'm coming." Kelly clutched her shoulders and shuddered in her arms.

Kristen held her tightly and kissed her lightly on the mouth. "Am I safe from a stampeding Pogo now?"

Kelly rested her head on Kristen's shoulder and chuckled. "Absolutely. Have I mentioned how glad I am you came over today?"

Kristen eased her hand away from Kelly's heat and led her to a lounge chair. She held Kelly close until the cool air began to chill their overheated bodies.

"We should probably get dressed. It's getting chilly lying here," Kristen said.

Kelly sighed against Kristen's chest and mumbled incoherently.

Kristen gently moved Kelly off her and collected her clothes. She found a blanket inside Kelly's house and covered her before brushing a kiss on her lips and leaving. She carried Kelly's scent on her fingers. She wished it were Jaylin's. That thought excited her more than anything she and Kelly had just done.

She went home and took care of her own desires, all the while thinking of Jaylin's hazel eyes and smile, rather than the woman she'd just been with.

❖

"Whoa. Take it easy, Kris. I know Zigzag is fast. You don't have to prove that to me." Debby and Kristen had been taking turns practicing the keyhole event, and Kristen was pushing her gelding hard. She pulled on his reins and slid out of the saddle.

"Sorry, Deb. I'm a little off today. I don't need to take it out on my boy here." She patted him on the neck while she walked him around the ring to cool down.

Debby dismounted and pulled Shadow along to walk beside Kristen and Zigzag. "So, what's up?"

"I don't know, Deb." Kristen stopped walking and petted Zigzag's soft nose. "Kelly and I hooked up, but I kept wishing it were Jaylin. That she was the one I was teasing to orgasm. I'm all turned around about her."

"Last time we talked, you said you two were friends. That neither of you wanted anything more. Did that change?"

"No. That's still our agreement. We're ignoring our mutual attraction and pursuing a friendship." Kristen resumed leading Zigzag around the ring.

Debby pulled Shadow to keep up. "Why? I mean, if you're attracted to one another, why not go for it?"

"I don't know, Deb. Sometimes I think so, but I don't have time for a relationship. I've got to take care of Dad, and the house, and Zigzag, and...I just don't know." Kristen stopped walking and hugged Zigzag.

"Maybe it would be good to talk to her about it. Maybe she's struggling, too." Debby placed a hand on Kristen's shoulder.

"We did talk about it, and I know it's hard on her. We can't seem to keep our hands off each other when we're together, but we both have issues we're dealing with that seem to keep us apart. Somehow, mine don't seem so insurmountable when I'm with Jaylin, but I'm petrified that I won't have enough time for her, or that it'll turn out like the disaster with Lynda. I'm hoping she'll come to the stump race Saturday. I haven't seen her since the skeet shoot last weekend. Which, by the way, she didn't seem very interested in."

"My friend, you don't have to be into everything the other person is into. News flash, that makes people different from one another. Talk to her. I don't like seeing you so stressed." Debby followed Kristen to the barn, tethered Shadow, and picked up a currycomb. "And another thing. I never asked Jaylin out, and now I'm glad I didn't. I think you two would make a great couple if you get past yourselves." She turned away to brush Shadow, humming some silly children's rhyme about kissing in trees.

"All right, all right." Kristen rubbed the back of her neck and rolled her head. "I feel her pulling away, and I'm not sure what to do about it."

Kristen pulled her cell phone out of its case and sent another text to Jaylin. *Just to remind her.* She added a second note about a *friendly* glass of lemonade. Kristen feared her feelings were already way beyond friendship, and she had no idea how to change that, or if she wanted to.

❖

It was still early evening when Kristen arrived at her dad's care facility and the parking lot was full, an occurrence she couldn't remember ever happening before. She wondered what was going on and why she didn't know about it as she hurried into the building. She stopped at her father's room and, finding it empty, rushed to the nurses' station.

"Kristen, we're glad you made it. Dr. Meyers is just starting her demonstration. We thought you'd be here earlier. Your dad's at the end of the North hall, on the right."

"What's going on? What demonstration?" Kristen peered down the hall, where laughter and cheering were coming from the large dining area.

"We didn't call you because, since it was your dad's idea, we thought you knew about it. Dr. Meyers brought her dog here for a short obedience demonstration."

"Thanks. I guess I'll go check it out." Kristen sighed, recognizing another sign of Jaylin's detachment. She hadn't mentioned a word about this.

Kristen found her dad where the nurses had parked him in his wheelchair. Doris sat next to him in her matching chair with Trixie sitting on full alert in her lap. Jaylin stood in the middle of the large room encircled by the residents standing with walkers, or in chairs. Railroad sat as still as a statue a few feet away from Jaylin, awaiting a command. The slight flick of Jaylin's finger and a tiny nod, and Railroad jumped a foot in the air and raced toward a group watching intently. She stopped two feet away from the crowd and sat up on her hind legs, waving her front paws furiously at them. The wheelchair bound clapped and cheered, and the people with walkers laughed and cooed. Kristen observed the spectacle from behind her father's chair. *How in the world did Jaylin teach her to do that?*

Railroad stopped her *waving* and regarded Jaylin for another command. Jaylin and Railroad repeated the process until the whole circle of giggling, laughing, and cheering seniors had been properly greeted. Kristen leaned toward her dad and gently rested her hand on his shoulder.

"Hi, Dad. I see you have entertainment tonight."

"Kristen? Is that you? See that nice young veterinarian?" He pointed toward Jaylin. "She brought her fast dog to meet us, just like you said she would."

"Yes, I see. I'm glad, Dad." Kristen looked up and caught Jaylin's gaze.

Her breath caught and her knees weakened. Jaylin was gorgeous in a pair of threadbare jeans, the ones she probably didn't want to wear to the gun club, and a MSU T-shirt. She had on a pair of running shoes and looked more relaxed than she'd ever seen her. She began planning how to get her alone. *I've got to try.*

❖

Jaylin concentrated on Railroad. She hadn't missed a single command and the residents loved her. Jaylin had expected to see Kristen when she'd made plans to bring Railroad to the home, but her reaction to the strokes of her gaze amazed her. Kristen hadn't looked away since their eyes met, and Jaylin liked it. She felt seen.

She let everyone pet Railroad before she headed to the nurses' station. She looked for Kristen, but she and her father were gone. It left her feeling somewhat bereft.

"Thank you, again, Dr. Meyers. Everyone loved meeting Railroad. We look forward to having you visit every month. We'll put you on the schedule for the third Sunday."

Jaylin leaned on the wall next to the nurses' station and sipped from a bottle of water. She tipped the bottle and filled her hand so Railroad could take a drink before clipping on her leash and leading her out to her car. She rested her head on the driver's seat and closed her eyes. She wanted to go back inside and look for Kristen. She wanted to grab her by that sexy denim shirt and pull her into a searing kiss. She acknowledged that her feelings had definitely developed beyond friendship, and anxiety and anticipation twisted a knot in her stomach.

"You okay in there?"

Kristen's voice floated through the open window and beckoned to her soul. She pulled herself out of her semi-sleeping state, sat up straight, and cleared her throat.

"Yes. I'm fine. It's been a long week, and I guess I was more tired than I thought. I must have dozed off." She looked at the clock on her dash and discovered she'd been napping for ten minutes. She glanced at Railroad, who was sound asleep on the backseat. "I guess entertaining took a lot out of us." Jaylin smiled and fought the urge to lean into the invitation of Kristen's lips.

"Think you'll be able to make it to the barrel race Saturday?" Kristen reached through the open window and swept her fingers over Jaylin's cheek.

"I'm not sure." *No. I should say no.* She should end this now, before either of them got hurt. "I'm not sure." She repeated again, unable to find more words, afraid to say the ones on the tip of her tongue. *Yes. And then I want you to go to bed with me.*

"I hope you do." Kristen cupped Jaylin's chin, leaned through the window, and brushed her lips across hers.

"Mm, no kissing." Jaylin slid her hand behind Kristen's head and entwined her fingers in her thick hair. She clenched a bundle and drew her closer, crushed their lips together, and slipped her tongue into the heat of Kristen's mouth. Kristen skimmed her fingers over Jaylin's thigh and leaned further into the car. She moaned and sucked Jaylin's tongue while she slipped a warm hand under her T-shirt to skate her palm over her stomach.

Jaylin hovered on the brink of abandon. She wanted to feel Kristen in every cell of her body. She covered Kristen's hand with her free one and moved it higher, to the underside of her breast. Kristen repositioned her hand so her thumb brushed over Jaylin's nipple through the silky material of her bra. Jaylin whimpered and tugged harder on Kristen's head until she broke the kiss and turned her head.

"I don't think I can fit through this window, baby. May I get inside and sit next to you?" Her breathing was heavy, her voice thick with want, and Jaylin snapped back to reality.

"Oh my God. I'm sorry." She shifted in her seat and pulled down her T-shirt. "I'm so sorry. We can't do this. I can't do this."

She started her car and sped out of the parking lot, fighting the impulse to see Kristen in her rearview mirror. She knew she'd only turn around, and she couldn't do that.

CHAPTER TWENTY-SIX

Jaylin let Railroad out and plopped onto her couch, refusing to shed her self-pitying tears. She was no longer a victim. She'd taken control of her life and made something of herself despite the many deprecating voices and challenges of her childhood. If she'd found enough courage for that, why was she so scared of giving herself to Kristen? When Kristen touched her, she felt her everywhere. Her touch was a salve on her wounds, her kiss a promise of healing.

If you don't try, you'll never know. Maggie's words came back to Jaylin as she went outside to eat her breakfast. She hadn't stopped thinking about Kristen since her cowardly escape from the care facility. She touched her lips, reliving their last kiss. Kristen's hand on her stomach had been warm and gentle, and it left her craving more. Jaylin allowed the memories of Kristen's touch to wash over her, and the sense of rightness stole her breath. It was so different from what she'd had with Sally. Kristen's touch, her kiss, and her words, all spoke of caring. How was she supposed to convince herself to try? "Maybe Maggie's right, Road. Ha. Maggie's always right." Jaylin sighed and took her bowl into the kitchen. Kristen's riding event started at one o'clock. She'd have just enough time to get there.

"I can sit here and be miserable without her, or I can take a chance. See you later Road."

❖

"Hey, Kelly. I didn't think you were riding today." Kristen led Zigzag to the staging area. She hadn't seen or spoken with Kelly since their evening together, but that wasn't unusual. Over the years, they'd often enjoyed one another on an entirely casual basis, and seeing one another again at their events had never been awkward because of it.

"Yeah. I figured Pogo and I could use a little more practice before Texas. Have you changed your mind about going with me?"

Kristen considered the way Jaylin had abruptly left her standing alone, weak with wanting. Maybe it would be good to get away for a few days. A change of scenery might be just what she needed to take her mind off Jaylin. "What day are you leaving?" she asked.

"Next Thursday. We can fly out together. I'm having Pogo trailered."

"I'll have to get someone to take care of Zigzag and my pony. I'll let you know." Kristen checked her cell phone for the third time, then mounted Zigzag and prepared for her ride, her heart heavy.

❖

The bleachers were starting to fill when Jaylin made her way to the arena. She could see Zigzag outside of the fenced area waiting his turn, but Kristen wasn't with him. She sat on the end of the front row and waited. She pulled her cell phone out of her pocket, hesitated, and put it away. She doubted Kristen was expecting her. After all, she'd never responded to her texts about the event, and after the way she'd left things at Kristen's father's home, she figured she was probably the last person Kristen thought she'd see. She pulled it out again and realized that Kristen was probably about ready to ride around the barrels, and wouldn't get her text until later anyway. She returned it to her pocket. The event was the same as the first one she'd watched Kristen ride in, so she knew what to expect. The palomino quarter horse and Zigzag stood waiting for the starting signal.

Jaylin wasn't surprised to see Pogo and Kelly up next, racing against a sturdy looking bay quarter horse. She thought Pogo might get a run for his money with this one. She watched as Kelly leaned over Pogo's neck and whispered in his ear just before they tore around the barrels, a full length ahead of the bay. Jaylin reluctantly admitted that they were impressive. If Kelly rode that well in the final round, she might beat Kristen again.

She pulled out her cell phone, sent Kristen a text letting her know she was there, and looked forward to the *friendly* lemonade. Kristen might not even reply, but she'd pushed herself to get here and see her, and she wouldn't chicken out now. The outcome of the final matchup seemed inevitable, but Jaylin stayed in her seat and watched as Kelly and Kristen faced off. Zigzag and Kristen were outstanding, but Kelly and Pogo took the winning prize. She stood and hurried to the concession area to wait for Kristen.

"Glad you made it." Jaylin shivered at the feel of the warm breath on her ear. Kristen had a lovely habit of coming up behind her.

"You looked good out there. I'll admit Kelly did, too." Jaylin's voice quaked. The intensity of her response to Kristen's proximity startled her for a moment.

"Thanks. It was a fun event." Kristen sat across from her. No kiss. In fact, Kristen didn't even touch her. "I didn't think you'd come today. You seemed pretty upset the last time I saw you."

"Yeah. About that. I'm sorry I panicked. I feel so much when I'm with you, and it scares me to death." Jaylin reached for Kristen's hand. She needed to touch her.

"Hey. I feel a lot when I'm with you, too. I didn't mean to push you that night. I guess we both got a little carried away." Kristen held her hand and softly rubbed her thumb over her knuckles.

"Hello again, Jaylin." Kelly stepped behind Kristen and rested her hands on her shoulders. She glanced at their joined hands before continuing. "I'm taking Pogo home now. I'll pick you up at eight o'clock Thursday morning. Good to see you, Jaylin. Take care." Kelly sauntered away, and Jaylin extracted her hand to rest it in her lap, jealousy making bile rise in her throat.

It was none of her business what Kelly and Kristen had planned for Thursday, but she wished it could be. Kristen had said she felt things for her. Could she take a chance? Kristen sat across from her, silent. She didn't know how to ask.

"Shall I get us a couple of lemonades?"

"I'll get them. You want something to eat?" Kristen stood.

"Yes, please. Whatever you're having." Jaylin blew out a breath while she waited. *If you don't try, you'll never know.* Damn that Maggie.

Kristen set their drinks and food on the table. "I got us a couple of hotdogs."

"Thanks." Jaylin took her drink and hotdog out of the cardboard holder and set it in front of her. "May I ask you something?"

"Of course." Kristen took a bite of her hotdog and chewed while she waited.

"Never mind."

"Are you sure?"

"Yeah." Jaylin ate her hotdog, drank her lemonade, and people watched. "No. I need to say something." She sat up straight and faced Kristen.

"I'm listening."

"I've been thinking about you all week. I panicked that night at your dad's and it made me realize how silly I was being. I'm scared that I'll make the same mistake I made with my ex, Sally, but that discounts all the work I've done to heal and grow. I guess what I'm trying to say, is that I'll never know if I can trust myself again unless I try."

"I've been thinking of you all week, too. I'll admit that I didn't understand why you left so abruptly, and then seemed to ignore me, but I get that you need time to heal from that abusive relationship. I don't want to push you into anything, Jaylin." Kristen took Jaylin's hand again and gently squeezed it.

"You're not pushing me. I'm resisting paying attention to my heart. I keep repressing my feelings because of my past. I'm done doing that. I'd like us to move on and see where we end up." She covered their joined hands with her free one. She realized another feeling she recognized but had little experience with—hope.

❖

Kristen inhaled deeply, enjoying the scent of the fresh air after a rain. She stood at the end of her covered porch and watched a young robin hop across the damp grass. The week's rains had kept her from being able to cut the lawn, and she needed to get it done before she left for Texas. She'd ridden Zigzag out on her property three times. He'd stood with his head down, probably wondering what they were doing out in the rain, while she'd sat under the canopy of leaves and pine needles. She'd looked at her situation with Jaylin from every angle she could think of and hadn't come up with a resolution. She wanted her, she knew that much, but she wanted her in a way that was deeper than any want she'd ever known.

Kristen wasn't surprised to see Debby sitting on her front porch when she trudged up the steps after putting the mower away. "Hi, Deb. I didn't see you pull in."

"I just got here. I'll get us some water." Debby retrieved two bottles of water from the kitchen and settled in one of the chairs on the porch.

"Thanks, and thanks for coming over. Are you sure you don't mind taking care of Zigzag and the pony for a few days? I'll be home on Monday." Kristen opened her water bottle and took a long drink.

"I told you it's no problem. I'll come over every day and let them run around outside while I clean their stalls. I'd love to go to that event in Texas someday. You just relax, have a good time, and tell me all about it when you get back. I have to say, though, you don't look excited about it. Are you worried about your dad?"

"No. I told him I was going, but he won't remember it. Every day is Sunday for him. He won't even miss me. I'm all mixed up about Jaylin."

"Does she not want you to go?" Debby took a drink of her water and set her bottle on the table.

"She doesn't know I'm going. I feel a little foolish about it, actually."

"Foolish?"

"Jaylin made arrangements with my dad's care facility to bring her dog there for an obedience demonstration. She never even told me about it. I felt her withdrawing after the skeet shoot. I'm not sure if she was bored or what, but she never said anything about it. Afterward, she seemed distant. It was weird, because before she left, after the demonstration, she sat in her car and she kissed me like I've never been kissed before. Then she left. She just drove away."

"Well. It sounds as if she rocked your world and scared herself."

"She never said a word about it all, except that she was sorry and that she panicked and that she felt things for me. I told her I had strong feelings for her, and then we talked. She told me she was afraid she'd repeat her previous mistakes. She ended up telling me that she wanted to try to open up with me and see where it went. Now I'm going to Texas for five days without telling her. I'm acting like a two-year-old." Kristen paced the length of the porch, her hands stuffed in her pockets.

"Yep. You are. Why aren't you telling her you're going?"

"God, I don't know. Maybe because I'm going with Kelly," Kristen said.

"Ah. You think Jaylin will be jealous? It's not like you to play games."

"I care about her. I care about her a lot. I just can't seem to let her know how much. Every time I see her I want to kiss her. It's all so damn complicated."

"I'm certainly not one to be counted on for good advice, but it seems to me both of you are too scared to take a chance on each other. I'm a little surprised that Jaylin is like that, though. She's a brave woman. I never told you that I saw her at the bar one night with a woman who turned out to be her ex-lover. I was minding my own business at the bar when I recognized her. Her ex threw her to the floor and slapped a handcuff on her wrist. And it sure as hell didn't look like a mutual thing."

"Debby! You never told me about that!" *Jaylin didn't either* "Did she hurt her? What happened? Didn't you try to help her?" Kristen shot out of her chair and barely refrained from throwing her water bottle.

"It turned out all right. Sit down. Jaylin let her have it. She had a slick move and stomped on her foot. It was great, and yes, I did step in to help her, but she didn't need my help. And that other woman limped out of the bar with her tail between her legs." Debby pulled her down into her seat. "So, why aren't you telling her about your trip?"

"I don't know, Deb. I suppose I should let her know I'm going, but it almost feels like she needs some space to figure out her feelings. I think I might, too. If I tell her, it's like I'm checking in, or expecting her to want to know, or something. If I don't, then there's no pressure." Kristen hung her head and sighed. Jaylin had grown up with nobody who truly cared about her, nobody who stayed around to love her, and here she was going to Texas without even telling her she was leaving. She was an ass. "Jaylin's a brave woman. Braver than me."

❖

Jaylin was glad for a full day of patients. She finished making notes regarding follow up treatment for a heartworm-infected retriever while forcing aside thoughts of where Kristen and Kelly were, and what they were doing. They'd probably gone riding somewhere. It could be something they do every Thursday now that Kristen wasn't working anymore. Obsessing about it would only drive her crazy. She concentrated on her next patient, an Airedale puppy. She always loved meeting puppies. She checked her watch and looked at her cell phone. Eleven o'clock. No text. She headed to the exam room.

"Good morning, Becky. I'm Dr. Meyers. I understand you have a new puppy." She smiled at the young woman holding the pup.

"Hi, Dr. Meyers. The breeder I got Hector from referred me to you—Julie Winters."

"Oh, yes. I'm glad she sent you to me. Tell her I said hello when you talk to her. Let's take a look at Hector."

Jaylin gave the puppy a thorough physical and made note of his previous vaccinations. She walked Becky out to Sarah's desk and said good-bye before heading to lunch. She wondered if Kristen and Kelly were having lunch somewhere.

CHAPTER TWENTY-SEVEN

Jaylin pulled into the expansive parking lot of the fairgrounds and proceeded to the same arena she'd seen Kristen before. She didn't see Zigzag or any other familiar horse. The racing had begun so she watched until the last contestants readied to ride. She was about to go look for Kristen when a conversation behind her caught her attention.

"It's too bad Pogo and Kelly ain't here. That big bay is gonna take this race."

"Yeah, and where's the App? He always gives everyone a run."

"I think they both went down to that rodeo in Texas. Leo told me he seen 'em talkin' in the barn last week."

"Huh. It sure is more interesting when them two are riding."

Jaylin willed her gut to settle before she stood, her legs shaky, and began the hike across the grounds and past the arenas. She felt her composure slip when she turned toward the woman calling to her.

"Jaylin, hi. Wait up a second."

She recognized the friend of Kristen's who'd offered her help with Sally. "Hi, Debby." She walked to the fence and pasted on a smile.

"How are you doing?" Debby asked.

"I'm good." Jaylin forced the smile to stay in place. "Nice looking horse."

"Thanks. This is Shadow."

Jaylin rubbed his soft muzzle. "I was just heading home. Did you compete today?"

"Yeah. I just finished. We took third place. Were you here to watch us?"

"No, actually I came to see Kristen, but apparently, she didn't ride today." Jaylin shoved away the anger and hurt threatening to suffocate her.

"Um, no. She's not here today." Debby shifted from foot to foot.

"I guess that rodeo in Texas was too appealing to resist." Jaylin clenched her jaw and took a settling breath.

Debby stopped shifting and smiled. "I'm so glad she told you. She was all torn up about it...but she probably let you know that."

Jaylin snorted. "No, Debby. She didn't tell me anything. Not one word about it. I just overheard the news from some strangers in the stands. I'm going home. Take care." Jaylin turned away and headed to her car.

That explained why Kristen hadn't responded to her text messages. She was too busy with that hot little blonde, doing who knows what, in Texas. Jaylin's gut roiled and she finally allowed the tears to flow. Kristen had no reason to feel obligated to tell her where she was going, but after their conversation last weekend, she thought they were close enough she would have. It had felt like they were going to give it a chance. Apparently, Kristen didn't trust that she was serious about trying for more between them, though. *She left. Just like all the rest. She just left.*

Jaylin swiped away the offending waterworks, squared her shoulders, and drove home. This was nothing new. She'd live through it. *Another good lesson. I knew better.*

Jaylin contemplated her options as she drove. Go home. Drink wine. Forget. That wouldn't happen. She considered her response to Kristen's leaving without a word and pondered why it hurt so much. A person walking out of her life was nothing new. She'd obviously invested more in their relationship than Kristen had. But wasn't she the one who started withdrawing after that gun club shoot? Maybe she'd pushed Kristen away. Even though they'd talked and she'd exposed her feelings to her once, it didn't mean Kristen would fall down at her feet. *Maybe I pushed her away for good. Maybe it's too late.*

Jaylin threw herself onto her bed after taking Railroad out for a short walk. She thought long and hard about her feelings, and the mixed signals she'd been sending Kristen pretty much since the day they'd met. Was it too late? Had she been so cautious she'd lost the chance to have anything with Kristen after all? Whatever the outcome, she needed to be honest with both herself and Kristen.

❖

The CoDA meeting had already begun by the time Jaylin slipped into one of the seats at the back of the room. She saw Maggie in her usual spot toward the front. Jaylin knew in her heart that Maggie couldn't solve her predicament. Somewhere around two a.m., she'd decided Kristen might be worth risking her heart. The problem was she didn't know what to do next.

"Hi, Maggie." Jaylin sat at one of the tables with a glass of water after the meeting ended.

"Hey. How's everything going?" Maggie sat in a chair opposite her.

"Not so good. I came here tonight royally pissed off at you, at the whole world." Jaylin finished her water in several gulps, set the glass down, and held it between her hands, anchoring herself.

"Let me guess. This has something to do with Kristen." Maggie smiled and Jaylin relaxed slightly.

"I took your advice and decided to let Kristen know how I felt. I—"

"Jaylin, wait." Maggie frowned. "I try hard not to give advice. I strive to help newcomers work out their concerns by offering my opinion, based on what I hear them say. I hope that I only reflect their fears and offer support by identification. What I love about CoDA, and what has helped me for years, is the connection I feel with members. We can identify with one another's struggles. I hope your decision was based on your recognition of your feelings and your courage to follow where they led, not on something you thought I was saying you should do."

Jaylin sighed and collected her thoughts. Maggie looked uncharacteristically uncertain.

"You're right, Maggie. I guess I just needed someone to blame for a minute. I'm hurting and it's a lot easier to give you the responsibility than to take it on myself."

Maggie took Jaylin's hands in hers and squeezed. "Tell me what happened."

"I recognized the truth of your words the last time I was here. You said 'if you don't try, you'll never know.' I realized that I was miserable enough without Kristen that I was willing to try."

"Did you two talk?" Maggie asked.

"I decided I'd try to tell her how I felt. I went to watch her ride at the fairgrounds in a rodeo event. We talked about our latest intense kissing incident last week that went a little beyond kissing, and I wanted to talk to her honestly about where our relationship might be headed." Jaylin stood to refill her water glass. "You want a glass?"

"No, thanks. I'm good. So did you two talk about how you felt, or about your mutual lust?" Maggie grinned from across the table.

Jaylin chuckled. "Yeah, I'd like to rip her clothes off and ravish her, but even more than that, I want to touch her. I want to touch her deep inside where she's never been touched, where only I can reach. Does that make any sense?"

"Oh, yes. I'd say it's damn sexy. It seems to me you have feelings for Kristen that go beyond casual. True?"

Jaylin sank into her chair. "I'm falling in love with her."

"Ah. I see why you're scared. Did she indicate that she feels the same way?" Maggie placed a hand on Jaylin's.

"She said she had strong feelings for me, I told her I didn't want to repeat my past mistakes, and I wanted to try for more with her."

"That sounds promising."

"Yeah, I thought so, too, but then there's Kelly." Jaylin let out a frustrated sigh.

"Who's Kelly?"

"She's a friend of Kristen's who rides in the rodeo events. She's good and she has an exceptionally fast horse."

"So, what's the issue?"

"She's hot, blond, and sexy, and Kristen went to Texas with her." Jaylin grimaced.

"I see. Well, and this isn't advice, but if it were the woman I loved, I'd go after her. Hot little blonde be damned."

❖

Monday morning, Jaylin placed the file from her latest patient on Sarah's desk. "I'll be outside having lunch if you need anything, Sarah."

"Enjoy your lunch." Sarah's smile did little to lift Jaylin's mood, but she smiled anyway.

She watched the birds flitting about the feeder and made a mental note to take Railroad to visit Roy on Saturday. The thought of Saturday reminded her of Kristen and her riding events. She missed her. She missed watching her as she spurred Zigzag around the barrels. She wondered when Kristen would return from Texas. Maybe she wouldn't. She tried to remember if Texas was a state that legalized same-sex marriage. Kelly was probably a better choice for a spouse than she was. For a moment, she'd considered doing what Maggie said, and going after Kristen in Texas. But she had no idea where they were, and she couldn't stomach the thought of finding that they were actually together.

Jaylin sighed and flung the thoughts away. This Sunday was her scheduled obedience show at the Sundowning Care Facility. Of course Kristen would come back. She wouldn't leave her father. Somehow that thought helped lift the pall she'd allowed to fall over her.

"Hi. I thought I might find you out here."

Jaylin blinked, wondering if her thoughts of Kristen had somehow created an apparition. She stood by the table looking sexy, contrite, and magnificent.

"You're back." Jaylin cringed at the inane statement.

"Do you have time to go to Panera's for lunch?" Kristen's beautiful apparition asked.

"I just need to let Sarah know. We can stop by her desk on the way out. It's good to see you." Jaylin hadn't planned to say the last statement aloud, but she couldn't help it. She walked past Kristen and lightly touched her arm, just to make sure she was real.

❖

The short drive had been silent, tense with words they needed to say, but weren't sure how to. Kristen held the door open for Jaylin and followed her into Panera. Her chest constricted at the memory of exploring her lips, and of the feel of Jaylin's firm nipple as she'd brushed it with her thumb. She shook off the visceral memories and concentrated on Jaylin.

"I missed you, too. I'm sorry I didn't respond to your texts. I was in Texas, at the rodeo event."

"I know where you were and who you were with. I don't understand why you didn't tell me you were going, though. You were gone for five days. A text would have been nice, at least. Did I push you away, Kristen?"

Kristen took a drink of her iced tea while looking outside. She turned back to Jaylin looking serious.

"Was that your intention? Because, yeah, you did seem to withdraw after the gun club shoot. I thought that maybe we were spending too much time together, and it made you uncomfortable. I want to kiss you every time we're together, and we agreed to keep our relationship on a friend only basis, so I tried hard to accept you pulling away. I didn't mean to scare you that night at my dad's, and I was an ass not to tell you I was going. I don't know what's going on between us, and I had hoped some time away would help me get some clarity." She shrugged, the deeper, more intense words blocked by uncertainty. "But I knew the moment I got back I had to see you."

Jaylin sighed and pushed her empty coffee cup from one hand to the other. Then she appeared absorbed in her water glass. She looked at Kristen for a long moment, clearly searching for something. A slow, sweet smile lit her face and she said, "I want to consider this our first date. Would that be acceptable to you?"

Kristen hadn't known what to expect when she'd shown up at Jaylin's clinic, but this took her completely by surprise. She felt her own smile stretch across her face. "I'd love to consider this our first date, but I have a question."

"Yes."

Jaylin's smile liberated some of the blocked words. "Do you kiss on the first date?"

"Absolutely."

❖

Sarah wasn't at her desk when Jaylin and Kristen arrived at the clinic, so Jaylin left her a note. Her next patient wasn't due for an hour, so she grabbed Kristen's hand, led her to her office, locked the door, and fell into her arms.

"Hmm. I think I like this dating thing," Kristen said.

Jaylin cradled Kristen's face with her hands and lightly pressed her lips against hers. Jaylin moaned as the kiss deepened, and she backed Kristen up against her desk. Kristen shifted and slid her thigh between Jaylin's legs, and Jaylin briefly thought that she would have to work the rest of the day wet and horny. She straddled Kristen's leg, and hovered on the brink of losing control. She pulled away enough to recapture her senses, and Kristen held her close as they caught their breath.

"Whoa. I didn't expect that." Jaylin murmured into Kristen's neck. She lightly nibbled the smooth skin and tickled it with her tongue.

"Keep that up and you won't get back to work today." Kristen held her at arm's length. She was still breathing hard, her blue eyes as dark as thunderclouds.

"Work. Yes. I have to get back to work." Jaylin wrestled down her arousal. "I've enjoyed our first date, but there's one thing I need to say. If we're dating, there'll be no kissing hot, sexy, blondes. I want to be the only one you're kissing."

Kristen leaned back and grinned. "Kelly? You think she's hot?"

"I'm serious, Kristen. I need to know what's possible between us." Jaylin waited, holding her breath.

"Why would I kiss anyone else, if I had you? You're the only woman I'll be kissing, baby. I promise."

Jaylin resumed breathing.

CHAPTER TWENTY-EIGHT

Good morning, Tim. How's everything around here?" Kristen had only been gone for five days, but she felt out of touch.

"Everythin's good around here. How was Texas?"

"Hot and dry. Kelly did well with her riding, and it was an interesting event. I wouldn't mind trying it one day. Speaking of events, how're your plans for the regional shoot coming?"

"Couldn't be better. We got it. It'll be the last weekend in June. You can register anytime now."

"Great. I'll sign up today. I guess I better get practicing." Kristen pulled out her mother's twelve-gauge and headed out to the first station. Maybe Jaylin would come on another date. She smiled at the realization that they were dating and disregarded the tiny niggle of fear the thought produced.

"Getting ready to lose again, hotshot?"

"Hello, Rupert. I hope I'll do better at the regional." Kristen forced herself to be civil.

"I see you're using the same gun today that your mom used to shoot. I'll still beat you. The gun doesn't make the shooter."

"We'll see. Are you going to shoot or stand there blabbing?" Her patience snapped, and she decided civility was no longer necessary.

Kristen finished her round, hitting twenty-three out of twenty-five targets. She considered that a good score since she hadn't shot her mother's gun in over a year. She'd get better with practice in the lead up to regionals.

"I told you. You can't beat me." Rupert sneered as he sauntered to the clubhouse.

But Kristen was already trying to figure out where to take Jaylin on their second date, and Rupert's slimy competiveness was no match for the thoughts she was having about Jaylin. *Somewhere private. Maybe a dark movie theater or romantic restaurant.* Her cell phone chime interrupted her musing. Her pulse jumped when she saw a text from Jaylin.

Would you go on a picnic with me? Date number two. J

A picnic? She hadn't thought of that. Her thoughts took her to a secluded, shady area of a pine forest. The soft needles beneath their blanket cushioning their naked bodies as the sun's rays peeked through the branches and stroked their skin. The sounds of the water in a shallow stream serenaded them, keeping time with the flow of their passions. She sent an affirmative reply and waited for more information.

❖

Jaylin's stomach gurgled with apprehension. She'd only told Kristen they were going to a quiet, park-like setting for their picnic. The truth was that she wanted to introduce her to Roy. He had been such a huge part of her life as a child, as siblings were supposed to be. She'd stepped in front of him to take the brunt of the slaps, and had held him in the dark of night to soothe his fears caused by the shouting and yelling from the next room. She'd made up stories to distract him from the thumps against their bedroom wall. Now, all she had left of him were her memories and the image in her mind of the fine young man she'd hoped he'd grown up to be. Either Kristen would understand or she wouldn't. It would be a telling adventure and their second, or last, date.

"Hey there." Kristen strolled to the outside table and sat next to Jaylin. She leaned and kissed her lightly.

"Thanks for meeting me here. I had to check on a dog I spayed yesterday. She seems to be doing fine, so you ready to go?"

"Sure. Are you going to tell me where we're going?"

"I can, or it can be a surprise. Which would you prefer?" Jaylin stood and Railroad crawled out from under the table to sit by her side.

"Let's go. I like surprises, so I'll find out when we get there."

Jaylin reached for Kristen's hand and led her to her car. *Please, please let this work.*

❖

"A cemetery?" Kristen turned to Jaylin and smiled.

"Yep. My brother's buried here. I come to visit him every so often." Jaylin turned in the driver's seat to face Kristen. She wouldn't bother getting out of the car if Kristen didn't want to be there.

"You told me about your brother and growing up in foster care, but I don't remember you telling me that he died. I'm sorry, babe." Kristen took her hand and kissed her palm.

"I'm not even sure how he died. The last time I saw him I was five years old. Come on. I have a couple of chairs, and I brought us Panera sandwiches. The cooler has a few beers, a bottle of wine, and some water."

"Let's have a picnic."

Kristen carried the chairs and cooler while Jaylin carried the picnic basket and led the way.

"Here he is." Jaylin stopped and set the basket down at the foot of Roy's grave.

Kristen opened the chairs and set them off to the side, next to a large spruce tree. After positioning the cooler between the chairs, she sat in one and reached for Jaylin. "Come sit. Tell me about him."

Jaylin sat in the chair next to Kristen, and Railroad lay at her feet. They sat in companionable silence as they ate their sandwiches and Jaylin debated where to begin the story.

"Shall I open the wine?" Kristen asked.

"Thanks. That sounds nice. I'm glad it's a nice day. They predicted rain for this afternoon." She tipped her head back and followed the few clouds drifting across the sky. She turned to take the glass of wine Kristen offered.

"I love cemeteries. They're peaceful," Kristen said.

"Well, I'm certainly glad of that. I worried that a picnic in a cemetery wasn't appropriate for a date." Jaylin turned to watch Kristen. She'd mimicked her pose and had her eyes closed. She was beautiful. Jaylin squelched a twinge of fear at their intensifying relationship. She'd decided Kristen was worth pushing past her fears, but apprehension still stirred her insecurities.

"I think it's perfect. Any place is wonderful as long as we're together." Kristen lifted the wine glass to offer a toast. "To Roy. May he rest in peace."

Jaylin lifted her glass and gently touched it to Kristen's, and they both took a sip together.

"There's not much more to tell about him. He was smart. The last time I saw him was when I was in kindergarten, and he was only three years old. I used to read to him as best I could and tell him stories. He'd remember all the names in the books and stories and repeat them to me. One day I came home from school, excited to share a new coloring book I'd gotten from my teacher. There were two strangers in the living room, and my foster mom was stuffing my brother's meager belongings into garbage bags. I think the only reason they told me what was going on was because I cried so loudly they wanted me to shut up. I asked about him for years, but either no one knew where they'd taken him, or they didn't want to tell me."

Kristen stood and moved the cooler aside and slid her chair next to Jaylin's. She put her arm around her, and Jaylin leaned into her. Kristen kissed her softly on her forehead.

"How did you find his grave?"

"By sheer luck. I had a friend in college who was studying mortuary science. He was constantly researching cemeteries, and he let me know when he found a Roy Meyers listed in this one. I drove out here and found his grave marker. The birth date matches, so I'm pretty sure this is his grave. I just wish I knew how he died, and why so young."

"It sounds as if you were a good big sister. I'm sure he never forgot you."

Jaylin sighed and sat up in her chair. "I like to think he didn't. Sorry, this isn't very sexy date conversation. Maybe we should have gone somewhere else after all."

"I think it's perfect. I think this date is perfect. I'm with you, and that's perfect. Seriously, thank you for trusting me enough to bring me here." Kristen took her hand and kissed it softly.

❖

It was nearly dark by the time they returned to the clinic. Jaylin went inside to check on her surgery patient and Kristen followed her. The date choice had surprised her, but she hadn't lied about it being perfect. The more time she spent with Jaylin the closer she felt to her.

She opened herself to Kristen more each time they were together, and Kristen cherished the trust that must take. She admonished herself again for heading to Texas without telling her. The time spent at the rodeo had turned out to be interesting, and Kelly had sensed the shift in their relationship and had arranged for separate rooms without complaint. They'd enjoyed their time there as friends, and it had given Kristen plenty of time to think.

"How's she doing?" Kristen stood behind Jaylin, wrapped her arms around her waist, and nuzzled her neck.

"She's fine. Mm…that feels nice. Her surgery site looks good. Oh, yes, right there. I'll have to change her blanket. She peed on this one… Oh my." Jaylin pushed back against Kristen and reached back to pull Kristen's head tighter to her neck.

Kristen couldn't resist. Jaylin's breasts were too tempting. She moved her hands to cup them and groaned as Jaylin lowered her hands and covered Kristen's. "God, I want you. We'd better slow down here. I'll help you clean her cage." Kristen forced herself to release her hold on Jaylin. This wasn't how she wanted to make love to her, especially not the first time.

"You're right." Jaylin's voice wavered, and she stepped away.

Kristen's resolve faltered when she saw her own desire reflected in Jaylin's eyes. She feathered a fleeting kiss on her lips and went to collect clean bedding for the dog. She returned to find Jaylin gently cuddling it. She pulled out the urine soaked padding and wiped down the cage with disinfectant before she put the fresh bedding down. Jaylin nestled her patient in the cage and secured the latch.

"Thank you for the fantastic date. I enjoyed it very much," Kristen said. She held Jaylin's hand as they walked to their cars, and the feel of their hands entwined made her feel like a teenager again.

"I enjoyed it, too. I get a little sad every time I visit Roy. It helped having you there with me," Jaylin said.

Kristen leaned against the car and pulled Jaylin against her. She held Jaylin loosely around her waist. "I'm glad you asked me. There's another skeet shoot coming up at the end of the month. Would you join me as my guest again, for our next date?"

"I'd love to be your guest. Could I come toward the end, closer to dinner?"

"Sure. I got the impression you weren't thrilled about sitting around waiting for us to finish shooting the last time. I'll let you know what time when I get the schedule." Kristen pulled Jaylin against her body intending to kiss her, but Jaylin raised her hands with her palms against her chest.

"You're right, I'm sorry. It was fun for a while, watching you shoot, but once I understood how it worked, I got bored with it. I'm sure it's more fun to be shooting than to sit and watch." Jaylin rested her hand on Kristen's cheek.

"I get that. How about if you join me for dinner after the shoot? Hopefully, we can celebrate my win."

"There's one more thing," Jaylin said. "The end of the month is a long way away. Do we have to wait that long for another date?"

"I agree. I'm riding again this weekend. Would that be soon enough?" Kristen watched Jaylin wrestle with the decision and wondered if Kelly was an issue. "Do I need to tell you that there's nothing between me and Kelly? There used to be, but it's over. I didn't lie when I told you that you're the only one I want to kiss."

Jaylin smiled and pressed her whole body against Kristen, pinning her against her car. "That's what I wanted to hear. Come pick me up for that date. That way you can't waltz off to Texas again without an explanation."

CHAPTER TWENTY-NINE

Jaylin swept her arm across her body and watched Railroad race toward the jumps she had set up in the home's dining area. She'd brought three different height levels and a small weave pole unit. The residents cheered and clapped as Railroad perfectly executed the jumps and poles.

"Railroad is still new at agility skills, but she loves to show off for all of you. She'll do the weave poles first, then go over the jumps in the opposite direction this time," Jaylin said.

The room was large enough for a small demonstration but not large enough for Railroad to run at full speed. She missed a couple of poles, but none of the residents seemed to notice. They cheered louder than the first time and even Dr. Eckert clapped and laughed, but the highlight of the event turned out to involve Trixie. She'd been sitting peacefully until Railroad went over the first jump, then she flew off Doris's lap and chased Railroad through the course, scooting under the jumps and running in circles around the weave pole unit. Railroad seemed taken with the little dog and chased her from one end of the room to the other. Trixie's short legs were no match for Railroad's longer ones, but her valiant effort had the residents and the nursing staff laughing and cheering them on.

"Look, Dr. Meyers. Isn't Trixie robust? Look at her run!" Doris was beaming as she pointed at Trixie and clapped.

Jaylin laughed along with the rest of the group and let the dogs run for another few minutes before calling Railroad to her. Trixie seemed to appreciate the break, and she stood on her back feet so Doris could lift her up.

"Thank you for letting us come and show off. I hope you all enjoyed it as much as Railroad and I did." Jaylin flicked her hand and Railroad stood and bowed to the group. Through the sound of more clapping and cheering, she heard Kristen's mellow voice.

"Thank you for coming to entertain us again, Dr. Meyers. We love watching you and Railroad."

Jaylin shuddered at the visceral memories of that voice as it whispered in her ear. She commanded Railroad to stay while she gathered the jumps and poles and carried them to her car. When she returned, Railroad was in the spot she'd left her, and Kristen sat on the floor beside her, scratching her ears.

"You've got a friend for life now," Jaylin said. She sat on the floor on the opposite side of Railroad, afraid that if she got too close to Kristen, she'd tackle her to the floor right there in the dining room.

"Do you have to go home right away?"

Jaylin glanced at her watch. "It's only three o'clock, and I have my CoDA meeting at six, so no. What do you have in mind?" She watched Kristen's eyes darken and her pulse quickened.

"I thought I'd buy you an early dinner. Wherever you'd like to go." Kristen ran her fingers lightly over Jaylin's hand.

"What if I stop and pick up Chinese takeout and we eat at my house? You need to know where I live so you can pick me up next weekend anyway."

"Sounds good to me." Kristen stood and gave Jaylin a hand up. They shared a shy smile as their bodies came into contact and both of them made a noise of appreciation.

❖

"This is nice." Kristen followed Jaylin into the three-bedroom ranch house. The front door opened into a moderate sized living room. A faded blue sofa sat against the wall next to a bay window. The rainbow colored throw pillows matched the rainbow colors in the oriental style rug covering up most of the hard wood floor. A small flat-screen television rested on a refinished 1960s style TV stand. Two mismatched rockers with matching throw pillows positioned on either side of the couch made for an inviting seating area. A refinished coffee table was the perfect distance away from the couch for resting your feet. One end table with a floor lamp was located at the right of the couch.

"Thanks. I like it. It's bigger than I need, but I love the location. Wait until you see the cozy backyard." Jaylin pulled out plates, silverware, and napkins while Kristen placed the cartons of food on the kitchen counter. "Shall we eat first while it's hot, and tour later?"

"Sure." Kristen stepped behind Jaylin and wrapped her arms around her. She'd refrained from touching her at the care facility, and now she burned with the need to feel her against her body.

"Hmm. I wonder if we could eat without moving." Jaylin pushed against Kristen and held Kristen's hands against her. "I love the way I feel when you hold me."

"That's good, because I love holding you." Kristen kissed behind Jaylin's ear and ran her tongue along the edge of her ear. "We'd better eat, before I get carried away."

They filled plates with their food and sat at Jaylin's two-seat dining table. "I don't have an outside table, but the kitchen window is open," Jaylin said.

"This is great. So what is this CoDA meeting you go to?" Kristen picked up her fork and spoke between bites.

"CoDA is Codependents Anonymous. It's a twelve-step group based on the principles of Alcoholics Anonymous, except our purpose is to develop healthy relationships. My therapist recommended it. I started attending meetings before I met Sally. I have a wonderful sponsor who's helped me for years to deal with my insecurities."

"I'm glad you have that. It sounds as if it's a group most everyone could benefit from, including me." Kristen set her fork down and regarded Jaylin. It took real bravery to admit a need like that one.

"It's been a lifeline for me. I struggled with my self-worth for years. When I got involved with Sally, I thought I'd found happiness. The group helped me find value in myself after she turned out to be abusive." Jaylin finished her chicken chow mein and turned sideways in her chair to stretch out her legs.

"So, what made you change your mind about our friends-only arrangement? I mean, given what you've been through," Kristen asked.

Jaylin's lengthy pause started Kristen wondering if she'd overstepped herself.

"Sally shattered my trust in myself. I don't have all the answers, but I've decided I can't live my life based on fear and mistrust. What we've shared so far feels as though we could have something special, and I don't want to spend the rest of my life fearful, wondering if I'll ever be able to trust myself, and lose whatever we might have in the process." Jaylin stroked her hand. "Why did you?"

Kristen hadn't anticipated the question. Why *had* it been so easy to ignore her reservations? Could she find the courage to face her feelings and see where their relationship would go? "Because you offered to let me in. I hadn't realized how much I wanted that. Needed it." She stood behind Jaylin's chair to nuzzle her neck. "This is so much more than mere sexual attraction. I want to get to know you, to be with you. It's more than I've felt in a long time."

"Yeah. It is," Jaylin said. "It's a lot more than just sexual. I don't know where it's going, but I look forward to finding out." She turned her head to capture Kristen's lips in a smoldering kiss of promise.

❖

The room was nearly empty when Jaylin took a seat behind Maggie. "Where is everyone?" she whispered.

"It's June. I suppose quite a few people are on vacation. Shall we talk later? I'm glad you made it today," Maggie said.

"Yeah. I want to talk."

Jaylin poured two cups of coffee, sat at one of the tables, and waited for Maggie. She wondered if there would come a time when she wouldn't feel the need to ground herself with this group. Maggie had been the one enduring relationship in her life, available to Jaylin from the time she'd walked into her first meeting. Jaylin had come to depend on the security and support she offered.

"You look a million miles away," Maggie said.

"Just pondering. Things are going well." Jaylin leaned forward in her chair and cradled her cup in her hands. "Kristen and I are dating. So far, it's working well."

"Judging by the sparkle in your eyes and the grin, it's going very well." Maggie tipped her head and waited.

Jaylin sighed. She knew Maggie wouldn't push for more information. She struggled to sort out her conflicting emotions before continuing. It had taken all her resolve not to blow off her meeting and drag Kristen to her bed. It was what her body wanted, and she was sure Kristen wanted it, too, but was it too soon? Would it fall short of their expectations and ruin their growing connection? Was she brave enough to find out?

"I took her to visit Roy's grave with me. It was comfortable, and Kristen enjoyed it." Jaylin considered the feelings her statement evoked. Surprise, relief. Love?

"That sounds good. I was hoping she'd turn out to be worthy of you. It sounds as if she is. So, no more hot blondes?" Maggie grinned.

Jaylin laughed and turned her hand to interlock their fingers. "We're going to Kristen's riding event Saturday, and Kelly will probably be there. But Kristen says there's nothing between them anymore, and I believe her. I'll let you know if I feel the need to break any of her limbs."

Maggie nodded. "Seriously, Jaylin. Does Kristen feel the same way about you as you do about her?"

"You know, this might sound odd, but I recognize what I'm feeling for her, and if she doesn't feel the same, it seems safer if I don't know. Then it can't hurt me."

Maggie sat quietly for a full minute before responding. "That makes perfect sense. As I said before, this isn't advice, but for me, there would come a time when I'd need to know how she felt. It would hurt more to be with her and be unsure of her feelings, and find out they weren't reciprocated later, when I was really invested, than it would to walk away. You may not be wired that way, but I do like that you took the chance to date her. It sounds as if you're both allowing yourselves to see who you are together. I'm happy for you."

"Thanks, Maggie. I don't know where it's going, but it feels right. I just hope my courage holds up to see it through."

❖

"Your first patient today is a cat, Jaylin. The woman who called said she rescued him from the Humane Society, and now she thinks there's something wrong with him. She'd like you to evaluate him. Her name is Joyce and the cat is Thumbs." Sarah turned from her computer and shrugged.

"Thumbs. Interesting. What time is she coming in?" Jaylin set a bag of warm bagels on Sarah's desk.

"Nine thirty. Thanks for the bagels again. I'm totally spoiled now, and Dr. Berglund even sneaks in to get a bagel once in a while, when he isn't running all over working with patients in the field."

"You're welcome. I'll have to find out his favorite and pick up a couple extra. Let me know when Joyce and Thumbs get here." She'd rarely seen Bill since she started at the clinic. She sometimes heard him talking to patients, or saw his car coming and going. He'd popped in and asked how things were going and to say he was hearing great things about her. Other than that, it was like working with an absentee boss, and it suited them both well. Jaylin took a bagel to the clinic and poured a cup of coffee before going to the outside table. She watched the birds on the feeder while she had her breakfast. The only thing missing was Kristen. She stood to go to her appointment when her phone chimed.

I wanted to let you know I was thinking about you. I hope your day goes well. See you Saturday. K

Jaylin smiled at the text message. Kristen was here after all.

"Good morning, Joyce. I'm Dr. Meyers. Sarah says you have a new rescue cat."

"It's nice to meet you, Dr. Meyers. I rescued Thumbs from the Humane Society yesterday. They told me that he was up-to-date on all his shots, was neutered, and was healthy. After I got him home I noticed that something seemed wrong with his front paws." Joyce opened the cat carrier and pulled out a large, green-eyed, bicolored cat. He began to purr loudly.

"Well, you're a handsome fellow." Jaylin checked that it was a neutered male and began a thorough examination. First, she looked at his front paws.

"See what I mean? I worried that these were tumors or something. Do you think I should take him back?" Joyce looked distressed. She hadn't moved her hand from his back and he arched and purred louder. The two had obviously bonded already.

"What you have is a polydactyl cat. He's perfectly healthy; he just has a couple of extra toes. It's a congenital physical anomaly and not dangerous, just not extremely common. The Humane Society probably sees so many cats that it's common to them, so they didn't mention it. Cats normally have five toes on each front paw and four on each rear.

Ernest Hemingway was fond of these types of cats. He had a bunch of them. It just gives you an extra couple of nails to trim." Jaylin looked into his calm eyes and checked his ears for mites. "He looks great. You have a nice cat here, Joyce."

"Polydactyl huh? That must be why they named him Thumbs. He's a wonderful cat. He settled right in when I brought him home. He checked out every room and closet in my apartment and then sat in the middle of the kitchen waiting for food. Thank you for seeing him today."

"You're welcome. Bring him here anytime. I can keep him up on his vaccinations for you."

"Polydactyl. It sounds as if he's some prehistoric creature." Joyce giggled and hugged Thumbs before loading him in his crate.

"Take care, Joyce. It was great to meet you both."

Jaylin considered the bond between pets and their owners. She understood it better now that she had Railroad, and she wondered how it extended to humans. Joyce loved her rescued cat despite his abnormalities. She didn't expect perfection, only unconditional love. Could falling in love with Kristen work the same way? *Could she love me in spite of my imperfections?* Jaylin gave Sarah Thumb's chart and went to her office to return a text message.

CHAPTER THIRTY

Kristen pulled into Jaylin's driveway and sat for a minute. She'd thought of little else all week except seeing Jaylin. She suppressed her anxiety at seeing Kelly, while being with Jaylin. Kelly knew that their physical relationship had ended, but she worried that Kelly might not be ready to see her with someone else. She hoped it wouldn't come down to a confrontation. She cradled the fresh flowers and strode to the door.

"Hey." Jaylin stood at the door regarding her.

"Hey, yourself. These are for you." Jaylin captivated her. She wore her sexy threadbare jeans, scuffed leather boots, and a butterscotch colored knitted shirt that reflected the gold specks in her eyes.

"Thank you. Come on in. I'll just put these in a vase and I'm ready." Jaylin stepped out of the doorway for Kristen to enter.

Kristen followed Jaylin into the kitchen and waited until she had the flowers in a vase before pinning her against the counter, clasping her head in her hands, and covering her mouth with her own. Jaylin grabbed her around the waist and pulled her even closer. She shifted and her thigh slid between Jaylin's legs.

"OhmyGod." Jaylin writhed against her, pumped her hips, and shuddered in her arms.

Kristen felt Jaylin go limp and realized she'd gone too far, pushed too hard. "I'm sorry, baby. I didn't mean to attack you. But God, you're so sexy." She kissed her gently and enfolded her in her arms. Jaylin's tears were her undoing. Her stomach constricted. "Oh, baby. Don't cry. Please don't cry." She rocked her gently, not knowing what to do or say.

"I'm all right, sweetheart. I'm just completely embarrassed. I can't believe that just happened. You do scary things to me." Jaylin wiped the tears from her face and smiled.

"I didn't mean to—"

"Kristen, hey. You didn't do anything wrong. Did you hear me telling you to stop? No. Because I didn't. I wanted you. I still want you. I want you inside me, everywhere." Jaylin clasped her face in her hands and immobilized her with a kiss.

"You sure you're okay? I didn't mean to—"

"Enough already. We're going to be late for your event."

"Jaylin, I don't care about being late. I want to be sure you're all right."

Jaylin stepped out of Kristen's hold and spun her around so she was against the counter. "I'm fine. I think you might not be, however." She pushed her thigh between Kristen's legs and Kristen's knees buckled. "I want to finish what we started. But later. Properly."

"God, baby. I have to ride my horse in an hour."

"We'd better get going then." Jaylin kissed her and turned toward the door.

❖

Jaylin sat in the same seat on the bleachers that she'd been in the week she overheard that Kristen was in Texas. The same group of people sat behind her, and she looked forward to hearing their conversation this week.

"Hey. Pogo and Kelly are back. They're gonna take this race."

"Oh, no. There's my App. He'll be giving them a run for their money."

"I'm sure glad they're back from that rodeo in Texas."

"Huh. It sure is more interesting when them two are riding."

Jaylin thought so, too. She settled down to watch and grinned at the thought of Kristen wet in her saddle. She wasn't surprised when Kristen and Kelly faced off for the final race. If Kristen's aroused condition interfered with her riding, it didn't show. She and Zigzag raced out of the course a full neck ahead of Kelly and Pogo. Jaylin heard the back slapping and cheering behind her.

"See. I knew my Appaloosa was going to win."

"This week. Wait til next week."

Jaylin hopped off the bench and made her way to the concession area to wait for Kristen.

"Hi, baby. Zig did well, didn't he?" Kristen gave her a swift kiss.

Kristen was glowing and Jaylin took a second to enjoy her enthusiasm. "Definitely. You both did well. You looked great out there, and Kelly and Pogo looked good, too." She could at least be civil.

"I'll grab us a couple of drinks and burgers."

Jaylin watched Kristen stroll away. She was such a sexy mix of strength and softness. Her firm ass swayed just enough to be inviting but her stride was solid and confident. Her breasts filled out her shirt exquisitely, and Jaylin couldn't wait to feel their weight in her hands and their firm nipples tickling her palms. She felt a rush of heat between her legs and shifted in her seat. As easily as she'd come with Kristen only pressed against her, she worried she might spontaneously combust if she moved too much now.

"She's going to burst into flames if you keep looking at her that way," Kelly whispered.

Jaylin jumped, startled and embarrassed at being caught cruising Kristen. "Oh. Hi, Kelly. Great riding today."

"Thanks, Jaylin. I'm glad you could make it to cheer for us. Pogo did well in Texas, but we both prefer our little small town rodeo."

"Hi, Kelly." Kristen returned with the drinks and food and set them on the table. "Good ride today."

Kelly laughed. "Yeah, thanks, but we'll take you next week."

Kelly laughed again, and Kristen and Jaylin joined her. Any tension there may have been, dissolved.

"I'm going to lunch with Debby before I take Pogo home. You two enjoy yourselves. I hope I'll see you next week, Jaylin. When Pogo and I win." Kelly strolled away toward the barn.

Jaylin noted the distance she'd kept from Kristen and her genuinely friendly attitude and conceded that Kelly's limbs were safe. She also acknowledged that her heart wasn't. She knew she was in love with Kristen, and she desperately wanted to make love with her. If she offered the gift of her heart, would Kristen refuse to accept it? Would she offer hers in return?

"You doing all right?" Kristen asked.

She looked nervous and Jaylin grinned. "I'm fine. She's nice, isn't she?"

Kristen visibly relaxed and nodded. "Yes, she is nice, and I'm glad you two are getting along. Let's eat before these burgers get cold."

❖

"Thank you for a nice day," Jaylin said.

She let Railroad out the sliding door to the backyard and turned to lean on the door and face Kristen.

"I'm glad you enjoyed it. I love knowing you're there watching me." Kristen held Jaylin loosely by the waist.

Jaylin moved into her arms, cupped her face in her hands, thoroughly kissed her, and then leaned far enough away to explore her gaze. "I want to make love with you tonight."

"I'd like that very much," Kristen whispered. Kristen pulled her into a searing kiss and pushed her gently against the door.

"Wait." Jaylin pushed her away, panting. "I'll let Railroad in, and then I want you in my bed." She slid the door open far enough for Railroad to enter and closed it swiftly as she grabbed Kristen's hand. She led her down the hall to her bedroom and didn't stop until they were standing next to her bed.

She gently pushed Kristen onto the edge of the bed. She held her shoulders and straddled her lap before bending to kiss her. Kristen gripped her ass and moaned into the kiss. She lay back and pulled Jaylin down on top of her without breaking their connection. She slipped her hands under Jaylin's shirt, and her hands were warm and gentle. Her touch reignited Jaylin's desire from their earlier encounter. She rolled off Kristen to catch her breath and Kristen turned onto her side and nuzzled her neck.

"I want to be naked with you." Kristen tickled the hollow of her throat with her tongue.

"God, yes." Jaylin kicked off her shoes and inched further onto the bed. She unbuttoned Kristen's shirt and pulled it out of her jeans. Jaylin reveled in the feel of her warm, smooth skin and her muscles twitching beneath her fingertips. She inched her fingers lower, past the waistband of her jeans. Kristen moaned and lifted her hips into her touch, and Jaylin unbuttoned Kristen's jeans and lowered the zipper. She longed to feel her slippery heat, but first, ignoring Kristen's protest, she got off the bed and pulled off Kristen's boots. Kristen crawled further onto the bed and held Jaylin down with gentle pressure on her chest. She unbuttoned the top button of her blouse and kissed the exposed skin under each button, kissing her way down Jaylin's chest to her belly. She flicked her tongue on the spot just above the button of her jeans and Jaylin groaned.

"I've wanted you for so long." Kristen kissed her lightly and nibbled on her lower lip, then she slipped off the bed and stood next to it to slowly remove her shirt and unclasp her bra.

Jaylin could only whimper as Kristen exposed herself to her. Her breasts were as gorgeous as Jaylin had imagined they would be. Her nipples puckered and Jaylin ached to run her tongue around them. Kristen continued to bare herself as she lowered her jeans and briefs from her hips and stepped out of them. The curly patch of reddish-brown at the apex of her thighs glistened with her arousal, and Jaylin's whimpers turned into noisy moans. She sat up and with one swift motion removed her own shirt and bra, then shimmied out of her jeans and lay back down. She wanted Kristen to be the one to reveal her. She reached out to Kristen in a silent plea.

Kristen crept onto the bed to nestle next to her. She ran her fingers along the waistband of her panties, slowly pushed them off her hips, and pulled them down her legs, tossing them to the floor. Jaylin thrust her hips into the air spreading her legs wide. She grabbed the sheets and twisted them in her fists, her passion unleashed. Kristen rotated to settle on top of Jaylin and slid down to capture her essence with her tongue. She sucked the prominence of her clit into her mouth and flicked her tongue across the engorged tissue. Jaylin writhed in her arms, crying out her ecstasy.

"Oh my God, baby. You're amazing." Kristen kissed the inside of Jaylin's silky thigh before pulling her into her arms.

They dozed off together, Jaylin falling asleep to the steady, sure beat of Kristen's heart.

Jaylin blinked as awareness seeped into her consciousness. Kristen's naked body cleaved to her back and her arm wrapped her in a possessive embrace. Her faint snoring was the only sound in the dark room. She snuggled closer to Kristen, to the woman to whom she knew she would offer her heart. Panic threatened her serenity for a heartbeat at the fear of rejection, and Maggie's words played through her mind again. *If you don't try...* Was she opening herself up to be hurt? Was loving Kristen worth the chance? She closed her eyes and let sleep quiet her doubts.

❖

"Mm, that's nice." Kristen opened her eyes in a state of semi-sleep and fell into the depth of Jaylin's gaze. She felt the first beats of her orgasm begin at the top of her swollen clitoris. How long had Jaylin been awake and touching her? She rarely slept so soundly. Kristen half sat up and whimpered as she trembled with orgasmic aftershocks.

Jaylin grinned and pulled Kristen into a scorching kiss. "I can't seem to get enough of you." She nibbled on Kristen's lower lip.

"I can't believe I have to go."

Jaylin froze. She looked stricken.

"Oh, baby, no." Kristen wrapped her tightly in her arms and kissed her bare shoulder. "I have to go pick up Zigzag. I texted Debby last night to ask her to have him bedded down at the fairgrounds, but I need to pick him up by noon."

Jaylin's grin spread across her lovely face. "Noon? We have plenty of time then." She pushed Kristen onto her back and straddled her hips.

CHAPTER THIRTY-ONE

Kristen leaned forward, set herself for the recoil of the shotgun, and yelled *pull*. She felt loose and comfortable as she followed the target with her eyes and pressed her cheek against the stock of her mother's twelve-gauge. Using her mother's gun always made her feel as though her mom was watching. She was on track for a perfect round.

"Pretty good shooting. You mind if I join you for the last two stations?"

Kristen hadn't noticed Rupert slink up behind her. She'd rather have nothing to do with the sleazy man, but he was a member of the gun club, and she knew she'd run into him again. She emptied the spent shells from her gun and shrugged before replying. "Suit yourself." Then she stepped away from the station to let him shoot.

"Thanks." Rupert loaded his Fabbri and stepped to the station. After he cleanly broke all targets, he turned to Kristen with a feral grin. "I can shoot pretty good, too."

Kristen nodded and proceeded to set herself on the next station.

"I got a message for you," Rupert said.

Kristen turned to look into his dark eyes. "Yeah?"

"You aren't going to win the regional shoot." Rupert narrowed his beady eyes as he spoke.

Kristen clutched her loaded shotgun and pushed aside fleeting images of Rupert running away with lead shotgun pellets blanketing his rear end. She deliberately unloaded her gun and stepped away from the station. "Maybe I won't, Rupert, but I want to practice today if it's all the same to you." She reloaded the gun and set herself on the station.

"You go ahead and practice all you want. You still aren't going to win. Who knows? You might not even make it to the shoot." His evil sneer transformed his beard stubbled, pockmarked face to repulsive. Kristen concentrated on the next target.

She wondered about his remark about not making it to the shoot as she walked to the clubhouse and turned around.

"What's that supposed to mean, Rupert?" She glared at him.

"Nothin'. I just mean sometimes things happen, that's all."

"You can count on me being there." Kristen turned her back on him and continued to the clubhouse. The threat felt empty, like an impotent boast, but it left her feeling vaguely uneasy. She briefly debated mentioning it to Tim, but figured he had enough on his plate, with the upcoming competition and everything else he did to run the place. She tried to put it out of her mind and focus on something else.

She waved to Tim and ordered a cup of coffee and a bagel. Her thoughts went to Jaylin and sitting with her at her outside table at the clinic, sharing coffee and bagels. Their night together had been spectacular. She'd lost count of how many times they'd made love after awaking throughout the night and in the early morning light. She regretted not planning better for Zigzag because she would have liked to spend the whole day with Jaylin instead of returning to the fairgrounds to pick him up. If she were honest with herself though, she had to admit she welcomed the chance to take a step back from the intense feelings being with Jaylin brought up.

Images of Jaylin bombarded her. Jaylin treating a patient, intense and gentle. Jaylin holding back tears as she spoke about her baby brother. Jaylin's eyes flaring with desire. The feel and taste of her lips, her body softly molding to her own. Their tongues dueling for dominance. When did it happen? When had she fallen in love with her and what should she do about it? She pulled out her cell phone.

Thinking of you. Looking forward to seeing you next weekend. K

Kristen put her phone away. She'd wanted to sign it *Love, K*, but a text seemed too impersonal. She wanted to say it aloud, or better yet, whisper it into Jaylin's ear.

❖

I miss you. J

Kristen read the text for the sixth time. She wanted to rush to Jaylin's clinic and gather her in her arms, but Jaylin was working, and if she didn't practice with her mother's shotgun again, she wouldn't do well at the regional shoot. She wasn't sure what it was about Rupert and his arrogance that bothered her so much. She couldn't care less about the guy personally, but something about the fact that he'd known her mother drew her in and compelled her to push beyond her usual efforts. His veiled threat nagged at her consciousness, and she wondered if it was only his loss of a spot on the Olympic team that triggered his wrath. *Could there be more to the story?*

She shook off her musings and typed a reply to Jaylin.

I miss you, too, baby. I'll see you Saturday. Bring Railroad and an overnight bag? K

Kristen hoped for a positive response as she put her phone away.

"How's your dad?" Tim asked.

Kristen jumped. She was so lost in her reverie she hadn't seen Tim approach her table.

"Hi, Tim. He's good. I saw him yesterday, and he was alert and seemed happy. I guess that's about all I can ask for."

"Good. You tell him I said hi. You don't know what he might understand. I gotta go. You gonna be here at ten Saturday?"

"I'm planning on it. Don't forget my dinner guest, Jaylin. She's coming in the afternoon."

"Got her on the list. She's kinda special, isn't she?"

"Yeah, Tim. She is."

"I'm happy for ya." Tim patted her hand before walking away.

Kristen picked up her mother's gun from the rack and mused that she still thought of it as her mother's gun. She knew her mother would have wanted her to have it after she died. She had no official paperwork stating that it was bequeathed to her, but her father had insisted that it not be sold and that it now belonged to Kristen. She remembered his quivering voice as he told her, "She would've wanted you to have it."

She walked to the first station and set her stance, determined to make her mother proud.

❖

Jaylin watched the baby birds squawking for their meal at the feeder and smiled. She read Kristen's text again and finally settled on a reply.

Railroad and I will see you Saturday about three o'clock. I'm looking forward to seeing you. J

She finished with her last patient and considered the Wednesday CoDA meeting. It would be nice to see Maggie, but she was tired. It surprised her how much she missed Kristen not only in her life, but in her bed. She'd never known the simple pleasure of waking up enveloped by the woman she loved. With Sally, she'd rolled over in the morning to an empty bed because she'd always be off doing whatever it was she did from the moment she woke up. Jaylin hadn't missed her because she wasn't present even when she *was* physically there, and a small part of her had been glad it worked that way. Kristen was different. She'd let Jaylin know how much she cared and how much she wanted to be there with her, but it wouldn't hurt to go to a meeting. She headed home to let Railroad out and change her clothes.

Maggie sat at a table with a newcomer when Jaylin walked in. She chatted with a few people before sitting at a table to wait for Maggie.

"Dr. Meyers, it's good to see you." Maggie reached out for a hug and Jaylin stepped into her embrace.

"It's good to see you, too, Maggie." Jaylin hugged Maggie and moved to sit at the table.

"So, how's the love life?" Maggie grinned.

Jaylin considered her answer. The easy answer would be to say it was fine, but Jaylin knew there was nothing easy about it. "It is effortless but not easy. Does that make any sense?"

"Whoa. Yes, it does. Let me see. I'd say you've never felt so moved or so touched. She seems to know who you are and what you need. You've probably slept with her and it was wonderful, but you're scared that it won't last and that she'll leave. She probably hasn't told you she loves you. Am I close?"

"Geez, Maggie. How do you do that?"

"So, I'm close huh? I've been there, Jaylin. It's a scary place to be, but if she's the right one, she'll let you know, and it will be magical." Maggie grasped her hands and squeezed.

"I'm seeing her on Saturday, and I plan to let her know exactly how I feel. I guess I'm scared that I've misinterpreted her feelings."

"You are an intuitive woman. I'd be willing to bet she'll turn out to be as genuine as you feel she is. You deserve someone who cares about you and is honest with her feelings. Do not forget that!" Maggie shook her hands and pulled her into a hug. "I'm here if you need me."

❖

"Here we are again, Railroad. I need to decide what to wear to a gun club." Jaylin chose a pair of black trousers and a cream-colored silk blouse from her closet and sat on the bed. "I guess this will do." She dressed and quickly packed an overnight bag. She checked that Railroad's water and food bowls were in her car and drove to the gun club. She hoped Tim would be more cordial this time. She wiped her sweating palms on her pants, and worked to decipher if she was nervous or excited to see Kristen, considering what she planned to say to her.

"Hey, Tim. My name's Jaylin. I'm a friend of Kristen's."

"I remember you. Did Kristen come with you?" Tim looked stressed, and Jaylin wondered what was going on.

"Isn't she here? I was supposed to meet her here this afternoon."

"No. She ain't here and the event started at noon. She was plannin' to be here at ten. Rupert is pressin' the rules. He's claimin' he's ahead and Kristen's disqualified 'cause she ain't here. I tried callin' her three times and didn't get an answer."

"I don't know, Tim. I heard from her this morning. She was looking forward to this, and we planned to meet here for dinner." Jaylin paced along the length of the small entryway. "Is there any reason you know of that she might've changed her mind about shooting today?" Jaylin cringed at the thought that Kristen didn't want to see her, and then dismissed the thought. This wasn't about her. Something was wrong.

"No. I know she wanted to shoot today. She had her momma's gun, and she was gonna kick butt." Tim followed her pacing and ran his hand through his hair.

Jaylin punched Kristen's number into her phone and counted the rings before getting her voicemail and leaving a message. "She didn't answer. I'll go to her house and follow the route she probably took. Maybe—"

Tim interrupted. "You go. I'll stall Rupert. Oh, and take this." He handed her a card with the gun club's phone number on it. "Call me when you know anythin'."

Jaylin rushed to her car and sped toward Kristen's house, surprised that she remembered the way. She had almost reached the entrance to Kristen's driveway when she saw the red and blue flashing lights. Every muscle in her body tensed, and she clenched the steering wheel until her knuckles turned white. She inched her vehicle to the shoulder of the road and turned off the engine. It could be someone else. It might not be Kristen. She took a deep settling breath, bolted out of her car, and ran toward the EMS unit. She scanned the area for any indication as to what car was involved. She saw the tow truck backing up to the scene. The winch cranked, and Jaylin held her breath.

CHAPTER THIRTY-TWO

Time stood still as Jaylin watched the mangled Boxter begin to be pulled out of the woods. From the look of the dented top and smashed front end, it had rolled over. She gasped, her knees weak, but noted gratefully that Kristen had the hard top attached.

"You have to stay away from this area, ma'am." The burly police officer held his hand in the air as if pushing her away.

"Where's the driver? Where is she?" Jaylin wrestled down her panic. *Maybe it isn't Kristen's car.* She knew it was.

"Do you know the driver of this car?" the officer asked.

"Kristen Eckert. Where is she?" Jaylin suppressed a scream and resisted grabbing and shaking him.

"The driver was taken to Community General Hospital this morning. We returned to retrieve her car."

Jaylin didn't wait for any more information. She couldn't ask the obvious question, because she couldn't bear to hear the answer. She turned and ran to her car. "Hang on, Railroad." She made a U-turn and headed into town, ignoring the speed limit. *Please be okay. Please be okay.*

Jaylin let Railroad onto the patch of grass next to the hospital parking lot, silently urging her to hurry before she put her into the car and left a window open a crack. Images of the crushed Boxter kept flashing through her mind, and she felt like she might be sick any minute. She sprinted across the lot and pushed through the emergency room doors. She scanned the waiting area and released a relieved breath when she saw a familiar face.

"Debby. Have you seen her? Is she all right?"

"Jaylin, hey. Sit down." Debby grabbed her shoulders and pushed her into a seat. "She's in the ICU. I saw her for a minute when I got here."

"Intensive Care." Jaylin's stomach roiled. She took a deep breath to keep from vomiting. "Where is that? How can I get in to see her?" Jaylin stood and paced. "What happened?"

"Jaylin. Sit down. You're as white as a sheet. She has a concussion for sure. They said it was a car accident. She was unconscious when they brought her in and she hasn't regained consciousness yet, at least not as of an hour ago. They found my number in her cell phone listed as an emergency contact and called me." Debby rested her hand on Jaylin's shoulder. "I'm sorry I didn't call you, but I don't have your number."

"God. She has to be all right. She just has to be." Jaylin covered her face with her hands and leaned on Debby.

"They're taking care of her. She's where she needs to be. How did you know about it?"

Jaylin pulled herself up in her seat, remembering Tim and his request to call him. "Kristen was supposed to shoot today. We had a date for dinner afterward, so I went to the gun club, but she wasn't there." Jaylin took a settling breath before continuing. "Tim told me she never showed up to shoot. I have to call him." She got out the card he gave her and dialed with shaking fingers.

"Hello, Tim? This is Jaylin. Kristen's been in a car accident... No, I don't know anything yet. She's in the ICU at the hospital...Yes, I will." Jaylin ended the call. "I saw her car. It's a mess."

"Debra Johnson?" A dark-haired man in a white lab coat called from across the room.

"I'm Debra Johnson." Debby stood and Jaylin glued herself to her side.

"I'm Dr. Wilson. I understand you have medical power of attorney for Kristen Eckert. Is that correct?"

"Yes, I do," Debby said.

Jaylin feared her legs would give out. Why was this doctor asking about that? *What kind of decision needs to be made and why can't Kristen make it?* She straightened her shoulders. She would be there for

Kristen no matter what happened. She held out her hand. "I'm Jaylin Meyers. Kristen's...lover. What's her condition, please?"

"Well, I'm sorry to meet you under these circumstances." He looked at Debby as he continued. "I just wanted to verify the DNR order in her chart. It's only a precaution. She hasn't regained consciousness yet, and we're monitoring her closely."

Debby nodded. She looked as scared as Jaylin felt. "Yes. She insisted on a do not resuscitate order. She didn't want to be kept alive with machines." Debby slid into a chair.

"Can you tell us anything else, Doctor?" Jaylin asked.

"She's banged up, but she's stable and—"

His beeper interrupted their conversation. "I have to go. I'll let you know if there's any change in her condition." Then he was gone, and Jaylin settled in the seat next to Debby and grabbed her hand. *She's stable. That's something, right?*

"Kristen's pretty tough. I've seen her thrown off a horse, stand up, dust herself off, and get right back on several times," Debby said.

"How long have you been friends?"

"Since high school. I used to spend a lot of time with her and her dad's Appaloosa's. She's the reason I learned to ride."

Jaylin couldn't imagine what it was like to have a friendship of so many years, but she was glad Kristen had Debby.

❖

Kristen opened her eyes and immediately regretted it. It felt like shards of glass were poking her eyeballs. She closed her eyes and unsuccessfully willed her head to quit throbbing. She struggled to take a full breath and grimaced at the pain lacing across her ribs.

Fuzzy memories nudged the edge of her consciousness. No brakes. Her little sports car that she kept in pristine condition had no brakes. Then there was nothing. No movement. No sound. Only a still, numbing darkness. She listened to the beep of the monitors and realized she was in a hospital. More memories tumbled behind her closed eyelids. The skeet shoot. It seemed Rupert got his wish. She certainly wasn't any competition for him lying here in a hospital bed. Her dad. Jaylin. *They must be frantic.* She had to get out of there, but she couldn't move.

Why couldn't she move? She lay still, assessing her bruised body. She wiggled her toes. Good. Next, she moved the fingers of her right hand. Then her left. All good. She tried to lift her left hand and felt the resistance. She tried bending her left leg and something tugged at her ankle. She was restrained. She wondered why, but realized it must mean she shouldn't move them. She drifted back to sleep, unable to fight the wave of darkness sliding over her. Maybe she'd dream about Jaylin.

❖

"She's conscious," Dr. Wilson said.

Jaylin and Debby sprung from their seats. Jaylin spoke first.

"Can we see her?"

"I said that she's conscious. That's a good sign, but she's asleep now. We're going to keep her in the ICU overnight to keep a close eye on her. You two can go home and get some rest. I expect she'll be moved to a regular room in the morning. Visiting hours start at seven a.m."

Jaylin watched Dr. Wilson walk away and tamped down her frustration.

"Let's go, Jaylin. I'll come back tomorrow and check on her," Debby said.

"I'll be here at seven. Is there anything that Zigzag or the pony need tonight? I'm staying at Kristen's. That was our plan, so I can take care of things there if I need to."

"Oh. She told me you two were dating, but it sounds a little more serious than that." Debby smiled as they walked through the emergency room doors.

"Yeah. I'm totally in love with her. It's serious for me, anyway. I can't believe I have to wait until tomorrow to see her." Jaylin looked back at the hospital in frustration.

"The doctor said she's sleeping. Maybe by tomorrow she'll be awake enough to know that you're there. Come on. I'll follow you to Kristen's and make sure the animals are fed."

❖

"Thanks for coming, Debby. I appreciate it, and thanks for being there for Kristen. I'm glad she has you for a friend."

"She'd do the same for me. I'm glad she has you now, too. She won't admit it, but she's been lonely. You're a lucky woman. When Kristen loves, she puts everything she has into it. I'll probably see you tomorrow at the hospital. Get some rest."

"Good night, Debby. Thanks again." Jaylin locked the door behind Debby, put Railroad's water and food bowls on the kitchen floor, and walked through the house to familiarize herself with the light switches. She checked the locks on all the doors and went in search of a bedroom.

She flicked on the light switch to the right of the door in what she thought would be Kristen's room. A lamp next to the bed cast a soft glow. It illuminated the area enough to read or get dressed without being harsh. A beautiful patchwork quilt covered the queen-sized poster bed. It appeared to be handmade. Folded neatly and resting on one of the pillows was a pair of flannel boxers and a cotton T-shirt. She'd take those to Kristen in the morning. She quietly closed the door and found a guest room. She wouldn't sleep in Kristen's bed until they were in it together. Right now, it would only be a reminder of the fact that Kristen was alone, in a hospital.

Jaylin awoke to the sounds of bird songs outside the open window when her alarm went off at six. There was no way she was going to be late for visiting hours. She stretched and rolled to her side. An odd sense of correctness overtook her, as if she were meant to be there. "Not without Kristen." She spoke aloud and Railroad whined. "Okay, girl. Let's go outside." Jaylin popped a K-cup in Kristen's coffeemaker and pushed the brew button before letting Railroad out into the front yard. The morning sun cast its rays across the property, and the water in the pond sparkled. Jaylin took a deep breath in an attempt to capture the serenity in an effort to calm the simmering panic that had stayed with her all night. Her gut twisted at the thought of Kristen waking up alone in a hospital room. "Come on in, Road. I've got to go."

❖

Jaylin arrived at the hospital ten minutes before seven and went directly to the service desk to inquire about Kristen's room. She was allowed into the room exactly at seven o'clock. Kristen was warm. Alive. Her breathing was slow and steady. She seemed to be sleeping peacefully, and a tiny bit of Jaylin's anguish melted away. She scooted a chair as close to the bed as she could, slid her hand under Kristen's shoulder, and rested her head on the bed next to Kristen's side. It was as close as she could get, but she'd take it.

Jaylin awoke to the caress of Kristen's gaze. Her hand was asleep, but she didn't care. Kristen was awake and smiling at her.

"What are you doing here?"

"Where else would I be? You're here." Jaylin reluctantly pulled her hand out, flexed her fingers a few times, and then stroked Kristen's cheek.

"This wasn't exactly how I wanted to wake up with you this morning," Kristen said. Her voice cracked, and Jaylin reached for her water cup.

"Here, sweetheart. Have a sip of water."

Kristen drank some water, laid her head on the pillow, and groaned. "Thanks. My head feels like it's going to explode."

"The doctor said you have a concussion. You were in the ICU all night. Did they tell you anything?"

"Dr. Wilson talked to me this morning, or maybe it was last night. I don't know. He said that I was in a car accident, and that I hit my head on something when the car rolled over. I didn't have any brakes. I take such good care of that car, and it didn't have brakes when I needed them." Kristen groaned again. "My ribs hurt like hell, but I guess my airbag and seat belt probably saved me from being hurt worse. I've got a few bruises that will heal, but I think I'm driving my truck from now on."

"Good idea. I don't think your car will be in any shape to drive anyway. It looked pretty bad."

"You saw it?" Kristen tried to sit up but only made it partway before plunking back.

"I went looking for you when Tim told me you hadn't shown up for the shoot. The police were pulling your car out of the ditch when I got there. You were lucky you weren't hurt worse. You must've managed to swerve away from the trees." Jaylin's throat tightened at the thought of how quickly Kristen could have been taken from her.

"Did they say anything? I don't remember exactly what happened, but I know my brakes gave out. Nobody has been here to question me." Kristen shook her head.

"No. Nobody asked me anything. When I saw your car, I nearly panicked. I was so worried you were hurt, and I didn't think to ask any questions. I turned around and drove directly to the hospital." Jaylin took Kristen's hand in hers. She wouldn't let go unless forced.

"I couldn't move when I woke up. I thought I was paralyzed until I realized I must have a concussion, and they'd restrained me so I wouldn't get up and hurt myself, which I nearly did. I wanted to find you to tell you I was all right." Kristen squeezed Jaylin's hand.

"I'm here now. You rest. I'll be here when you wake," Jaylin said.

CHAPTER THIRTY-THREE

Y ou didn't have to take more time off to do this, baby. Debby offered to pick me up." Kristen kissed Jaylin lightly.

"Sarah rearranged my schedule, and I'll go in on Saturday to make up some appointments. It's not a problem, and this is where I need to be. With you." Jaylin stroked her cheek. "Bill said he'd be by next week, and you're supposed to 'get well soon.' He said he'd continue Zigzag's worming schedule, take care of his teeth, and get in touch with the farrier. You're to do nothing but take care of yourself."

Take care of myself. Kristen had spent the last few years of her life taking care of her sick mother, and then her declining father. Her mom was dead, and her dad faded further away from her every week. She loved shooting skeet and riding Zigzag, but those were fun, a diversion from life. Working with Jaylin had revived a need to be productive and had reminded her how much she enjoyed working with animals.

"What do you think about me coming back to work with you once in a while?" Kristen took Jaylin's hand as she spoke.

"I think it'd be great, but not until you're healed. What brought that on?" Jaylin gently squeezed her hand.

"I could've sustained worse injuries or been paralyzed from this accident. That, and working with you, has stirred my need to do something with my life besides play. I miss nursing a colicky horse back to health, or helping Dr. B deliver a foal, and I even miss assisting you with surgery patients. Dad's where he needs to be with good care, and he seems to be happy. Bill's told me numerous times that I'd have a job if I ever wanted one. I want to go back to work."

"Whenever you're ready, honey." She gave her a lingering kiss. "Let's get you out of here."

Kristen sat in the requisite wheelchair and relaxed as the nurse maneuvered it to Jaylin's waiting vehicle. Her headache had subsided to an occasional dull throb, and her ribs only hurt if she pushed on them. They hadn't been broken, only bruised from the airbag deploying. She'd spent three days in the hospital, and she was ready to get home to sleep in her own bed. With Jaylin.

"Will you stay tonight?" She didn't care that she sounded pleading. She desperately wanted Jaylin by her side.

"Of course, sweetheart. If you want me to." Jaylin smiled and squeezed her hand.

Kristen closed her eyes and rested on the trip home. She contemplated what home would be like with Jaylin. In her semi-dozing state, it was perfect. She felt a gentle touch on her forehead and cheek, and then a warm breath and soft kiss on her neck.

"We're here."

The sexy voice drifted into her consciousness and tugged her awake.

"I think the pain pills they gave me at the hospital have kicked in." She pushed the door open and stepped out of the car.

"Hang on. I'll help you." Jaylin put her arm around Kristen's waist and guided her into the house.

"Railroad's here." Kristen laughed at her frantic tail wagging.

"She loves your yard. I had to keep her away from Zigzag and the pony, though. She tries to herd them. Zigzag doesn't seem to care, but your pony gets scared. I don't think she's ever seen a dog before." Jaylin steered Kristen to a chair.

"Nope. She never has. I'm glad you're making yourself at home, baby. I like having you here. No, that's not right. Damn pain meds. I *love* having you here." She held Jaylin's face and carefully kissed her.

"Come on. Let's get you comfortable in bed. You can sleep off the pain medication." Jaylin took her hand and led her down the hall to her bedroom.

"Why is the door closed?"

"I closed it. Sorry, I didn't think to open it before I left this morning." Jaylin opened the door that had been shut for three days.

Kristen walked to the bed and turned to Jaylin. The room was exactly as she'd left it, minus her sleep clothes, which Jaylin had been kind enough to bring to the hospital for her. She didn't see any of Jaylin's things. "Didn't you sleep in here, baby?"

"No."

Kristen pulled Jaylin into her arms. She nuzzled her neck and stroked her back. "Why not?"

"I hadn't been invited."

"Oh, baby. Consider yourself invited now. I want you in my bedroom, in my bed, in my life. I love you."

Jaylin sagged into her arms. "I was so scared I'd lost you. When I saw your smashed car pulled out of the woods, my world collapsed. I'd finally found real love, and I was so scared. I love you, too, forever and always."

Kristen's and Jaylin's tears mingled as they kissed, lay down on the bed, and held each other.

❖

Jaylin gently pulled the quilt up over them. Kristen had fallen into a sound sleep shortly after they'd snuggled under the covers and her soft snores soothed Jaylin's unrest. She cuddled closer to her and rested her soul.

The sunshine streamed into the bedroom along with the birds chirping their morning calls and Jaylin savored the bliss of waking up this way. *She loves me.* She gently snaked her arm around her waist, mindful of Kristen's sore ribs, and pressed the front of her body against her back. *And I love her.* She would've been content to stay in this spot, in this position, for the rest of the day, but the ringing of Kristen's cell phone interrupted her luxuriating. She wrestled with the appropriateness of answering it. It could be important, and Kristen still snored beside her.

"Hello. This is Jaylin answering Kristen's phone."

"Jaylin? This is Debby. I wanted to see how Kristen was feeling."

"She's asleep right now. The pain medication they gave her hit her hard. Can I give her a message?"

"No. I'm glad you're with her. Is she better than yesterday?"

"I'd say yes. She's been asleep since we got home last night. I'll have her give you a call when she wakes up."

"Sounds good. Did I say I'm glad you're there with her?"

"Thanks, Debby. I'm glad, too."

Jaylin disconnected the call and kissed Kristen's neck before quietly sliding out of bed.

She sat on the front porch and watched Railroad sniff every corner of the yard and then roll onto her back and wiggle. Jaylin sighed and sipped her coffee. She'd have to go to work tomorrow and make up for the two days of cancelled appointments, but all she wanted to do was stay with Kristen. She'd begun to form ideas of making love to her that didn't involve intense activity when Kristen wrapped her arms around her from behind and kissed her neck.

"I woke up and missed you."

"You were sleeping so soundly I didn't want to disturb you. How do you feel, love?"

"Much better. Even though those pain pills made me loopy, I think they helped. My head isn't pounding anymore, and I want a cup of coffee. Then can I convince you to come back to bed for a while?"

"Oh, yes. Not much convincing needed for that. Sit. I'll get your coffee." Jaylin stood, kissed Kristen lightly, and turned toward the door.

Kristen clasped her wrist and tugged her into her arms. "I love you, Dr. Meyers. I think I can forgo the coffee for now. I need you." Kristen kissed her and Jaylin relaxed into the safety of her arms for a moment before following her to her bedroom.

❖

"Oh my God, yeesss!" Jaylin rolled her hips as she soared into another orgasm. Kristen's mouth was hot on her sex, and her tongue was relentless. Kristen had promised to stop if she felt any discomfort, so she'd given up worrying over Kristen's injuries. They'd tossed the pillows off the bed, and Kristen reclined on her back while Jaylin kneeled over her. Kristen clutched her ass and pulled her against her tongue. Jaylin felt the ripples building to another climax.

"Come with me this time, baby." Jaylin spoke between breaths. "Touch yourself."

Kristen moved one hand off Jaylin's ass to reach herself. Jaylin fondled her own breasts and squeezed her nipples. Their eyes locked and they spilled over together.

"I think I'm all healed now, baby. Your love is all I need." Kristen nibbled Jaylin's earlobe.

"Well, I have to be able to walk tomorrow, and we both could probably use some hydration, but yeah. I need your love, too. Ready for a shower?" Jaylin traced the curve of Kristen's breast with her finger and brushed her nipple.

"Can you finish what you're doing first?" Kristen arched into her hand, and Jaylin had no desire to resist.

❖

Jaylin watched intently as Kristen scrambled eggs and chopped vegetables. She placed two pieces of toast in the toaster and returned to the heated pan to toss the vegetables into it. "You're good at that." She spoke with reverence.

"It's only scrambled eggs." Kristen tilted her head and smiled shyly.

Jaylin sensed the question in her look. "You're the first person ever to cook breakfast for me."

"What about your foster moms? Didn't they cook breakfast?"

Jaylin chuckled, pointed to the refrigerator, and said, "'Milk's in there.'" Then she pointed to the cupboard and said, "'Cereal's in there. Don't get into any trouble today.' Then they were out the door. I got good at filling bowls with Cheerios for me and Roy."

"Well, those days are over, baby. We are going to dine on vegetable omelets and whole wheat toast. You can be in charge of making the coffee."

Jaylin blinked back tears. "I can do that."

They were sitting on the porch finishing their coffee when Kristen's cell phone rang. "It's Tim," Kristen said. "I'll grab us some more coffee while I talk to him." She stood and took her phone into the house.

Jaylin rested her head back in the chair and let her thoughts drift. She reflected on how much her life had changed since her decision to move to Novi. She was happy, and that was a wonderful feeling.

Kristen returned with two fresh cups of coffee.

"Thanks, sweetheart. What did Tim have to say?" Jaylin set her empty cup aside and took the full one Kristen handed her.

"He wanted to tell me that Rupert won the shoot Saturday. No surprise to me. He also said that Rupert was being an asshole. He strutted through the gun club bragging about beating me, even though I wasn't even there to compete." Kristen shook her head.

"When I talked to Tim Saturday, he said Rupert was pushing him to disqualify you."

"We all had designated starting times to keep the event moving along. Tim had the right to shift shooters to a different time if necessary. Rupert would have known that. I wouldn't have been disqualified until after the last group of shooters was called to begin."

"It sounds as if he was nervous," Jaylin said.

"Huh. I don't know. Could be. Tim told me something else about him. Besides his blustering, he was drinking heavily in the clubhouse after the event. Before Tim could kick him out, he went on a rant. He was insisting he could have beaten my mother, 'the cunt,' and he'd showed her by beating her 'cunt dyke' daughter. I'm thinking there was more to his rage than just wanting to beat me at skeet shooting. He sounds homophobic. I got another call when I was inside. The police report regarding my accident is finished. They concluded my brake lines were cut." Kristen looked pale and her hand holding her cup shook slightly.

"Oh my God, baby. Who would do that?" Jaylin sat up straight in her chair. Fear constricted her throat. Was someone after Kristen? "What about that Rupert guy?"

"I don't know for sure. I don't know who did it, or why, but I told them about Rupert's remark about me might not even making it to the shoot. They're going to pick him up for questioning."

"What's this about a remark about not making it to the shoot?" Jaylin moved her chair closer to Kristen so she could touch her. She needed to feel her, to remind herself that she was, in fact, safe and really there with her.

"He said something to me when we were practicing the other day, about me not making it to the shoot, that he was going to beat me for sure. I didn't think much about it then, but I'm glad I mentioned it to the police. They'll investigate him. It'll be okay, baby." Kristen leaned to kiss Jaylin. "Tim told me that Rupert quit the gun club before Tim could throw him out. It seems his only goal for joining was to beat me."

"How did this idiot know your mother?"

"I guess he tried out for the Olympic skeet team in nineteen ninety-two and my mother beat him out of a spot. Apparently, he's been carrying a grudge ever since. What a waste of life." Kristen reached for Jaylin's hand, kissed her palm, and entwined their fingers. "I don't want to think about sleazy Rupert. The police will take care of him. What I want to think about is that I have you here for the rest of the day, and I don't plan to waste a minute of it. I'll grill us a couple of steaks later and we can go for a walk or a ride—"

"Honey, you just got out of the hospital yesterday. Maybe it would be best if we chilled out today. Give Debby a call to let her know you're all right. She called earlier while you were sleeping. I'm content just to be with you. I love you." She smiled and felt the glow of what she'd said spread through her. "I love you. And I'm never going to let you go."

Kristen relaxed in her chair and squeezed Jaylin's hand. "Yeah. You're right. I'll admit, this whole Rupert thing shook me up. I can't believe he tried to kill me, but I won't be surprised if they prove it was him." She trembled at the memory of the total loss of control as her car careened off the road.

Jaylin kissed her hand and hugged it to her body. "It'll be all right now. Rupert's gone."

Kristen took a deep calming breath and exhaled before she spoke. "You are so precious to me. And every moment I have left on this earth will belong to you. You, me, us. Forever. I love you, too. Thank you for being brave enough to give us a chance." She kissed her softly, tenderly.

Jaylin sighed happily. Life was more than she had dared dream it could be, and now, sitting next to the woman she loved, she felt free and valued for the first time in her life. She knew she could be the woman she'd always wanted to be, and all it had taken was the courage to try.

About the Author

C.A. Popovich has never lived outside of Michigan but enjoys traveling and hopes to, someday, visit every national park in America. She writes full-time, hates spiders, loves to read, spend time with her family, and attend as many Bold Strokes Books events as finances allow. She discovered the romance writer Radclyffe in 2009 and has been hooked on reading and writing happily ever after romances ever since.

capopovichfiction@aol.com
http://capopovichfiction.weebly.com

Books Available from Bold Strokes Books

Break Point by Yolanda Wallace. In a world readying for war, can love find a way? (978-1-62639-5-688)

Countdown by Julie Cannon. Can two strong-willed, powerful women overcome their differences to save the lives of seven others and begin a life they never imagined together? (978-1-62639-4-711)

Heart of the Liliko'i by Dena Hankins. Secrets, sabotage, and grisly human remains stall construction on an ancient Hawaiian burial ground, but the sexual connection between Kerala and Ravi keeps building toward a volcanic explosion. (978-1-62639-5-565)

Keep Hold by Michelle Grubb. Claire knew some things should be left alone and some rules should never be broken, but the most forbidden, well, they are the most tempting. (978-1-62639-5-022)

The Courage to Try by C.A. Popovich. Finding love is worth getting past the fear of trying. (978-1-62639-5-282)

The Time Before Now by Missouri Vaun. Vivian flees a disastrous affair, embarking on an epic, transformative journey to escape her past, until destiny introduces her to Ida, who helps her rediscover trust, love and hope. (978-1-62639-4-469)

Twisted Whispers by Sheri Lewis Wohl. Betrayal, lies, and secrets—whispers of a friend lost to darkness. Can a reluctant psychic set things right or will an evil soul destroy those she loves? (978-1-62639-4-391)

Deadly Medicine by Jaime Maddox. Dr. Ward Thrasher's life is in turmoil. Her partner Jess has left her, and her job puts her in the path of a murderous physician who has Jess in his sights. (978-1-62639-4-247)

New Beginnings by KC Richardson. Can the connection and attraction between Jordan Roberts and Kirsten Murphy be enough for Jordan to trust Kirsten with her heart? (978-1-62639-4-506)

Officer Down by Erin Dutton. Can two women who've made careers out of being there for others in crisis find the strength to need each other? (978-1-62639-4-230)

Reasonable Doubt by Carsen Taite. Just when Sarah and Ellery think they've left dangerous careers behind, a new case sets them—and their hearts—on a collision course. (978-1-62639-4-421)

Tarnished Gold by Ann Aptaker. Cantor Gold must outsmart the Law, outrun New York's dockside gangsters, outplay a shady art dealer, his lover, and a beautiful curator, and stay out of a killer's gun sights. (978-1-62639-4-261)

The Renegade by Amy Dunne. Post-apocalyptic survivors Alex and Evelyn secretly find love while held captive by a deranged cult, but when their relationship is discovered, they must fight for their freedom—or die trying. (978-1-62639-4-278)

Thrall by Barbara Ann Wright. Four women in a warrior society must work together to lift an insidious curse while caught between their own desires, the will of their peoples, and an ancient evil. (978-1-62639-4-377)

White Horse in Winter by Franci McMahon. Love between two women collides with the inner poison of a closeted horse trainer in the green hills of Vermont. (978-1-62639-4-292)

The Chameleon by Andrea Bramhall. Two old friends must work through a web of lies and deceit to find themselves again, but in the search they discover far more than they ever went looking for. (978-1-62639-363-9)

Side Effects by VK Powell. Detective Jordan Bishop and Dr. Neela Sahjani must decide if it's easier to trust someone with your heart or your life as they face threatening protestors, corrupt politicians, and their increasing attraction. (978-1-62639-364-6)

Autumn Spring by Shelley Thrasher. Can Bree and Linda, two women in the autumn of their lives, put their hearts first and find the love they've never dared seize? (978-1-62639-365-3)

Warm November by Kathleen Knowles. What do you do if the one woman you want is the only one you can't have? (978-1-62639-366-0)

In Every Cloud by Tina Michele. When she finally leaves her shattered life behind, is Bree strong enough to salvage the remaining pieces of her heart and find the place where it truly fits? (978-1-62639-413-1)

Rise of the Gorgon by Tanai Walker. When independent Internet journalist Elle Pharell goes to Kuwait to investigate a veteran's mysterious suicide, she hires Cassandra Hunt, an interpreter with a covert agenda. (978-1-62639-367-7)

Crossed by Meredith Doench. Agent Luce Hansen returns home to catch a killer and risks everything to revisit the unsolved murder of her first girlfriend and confront the demons of her youth. (978-1-62639-361-5)

Making a Comeback by Julie Blair. Music and love take center stage when jazz pianist Liz Randall tries to make a comeback with the help of her reclusive, blind neighbor, Jac Winters. (978-1-62639-357-8)

Soul Unique by Gun Brooke. Self-proclaimed cynic Greer Landon falls for Hayden Rowe's paintings and the young woman shortly after, but will Hayden, who lives with Asperger syndrome, trust her and reciprocate her feelings? (978-1-62639-358-5)

The Price of Honor by Radclyffe. Honor and duty are not always black and white—and when self-styled patriots take up arms against the government, the price of honor may be a life. (978-1-62639-359-2)

Mounting Evidence by Karis Walsh. Lieutenant Abigail Hargrove and her mounted police unit need to solve a murder and protect wetland biologist Kira Lovell during the Washington State Fair. (978-1-62639-343-1)

Threads of the Heart by Jeannie Levig. Maggie and Addison Rae-McInnis share a love and a life, but are the threads that bind them together strong enough to withstand Addison's restlessness and the seductive Victoria Fontaine? (978-1-62639-410-0)

Sheltered Love by MJ Williamz. Boone Fairway and Grey Dawson—two women touched by abuse—overcome their pasts to find happiness in each other. (978-1-62639-362-2)

Asher's Out by Elizabeth Wheeler. Asher Price's candid photographs capture the truth, but when his success requires exposing an enemy, Asher discovers his only shot at happiness involves revealing secrets of his own. (978-1-62639-411-7)

The Ground Beneath by Missouri Vaun. An improbable barter deal involving a hope chest and dinners for a month places lovely Jessica Walker distractingly in the way of Sam Casey's bachelor lifestyle. (978-1-62639-606-7)

Hardwired by C.P. Rowlands. Award-winning teacher Clary Stone, and Leefe Ellis, manager of the homeless shelter for small children, stand together in a part of Clary's hometown that she never knew existed. (978-1-62639-351-6)

No Good Reason by Cari Hunter. A violent kidnapping in a Peak District village pushes Detective Sanne Jensen and lifelong friend Dr. Meg Fielding closer, just as it threatens to tear everything apart. (978-1-62639-352-3)

Romance by the Book by Jo Victor. If Cam didn't keep disrupting her life, maybe Alex could uncover the secret of a century-old love story, and solve the greatest mystery of all—her own heart. (978-1-62639-353-0)

Death's Doorway by Crin Claxton. Helping the dead can be deadly: Tony may be listening to the dead, but she needs to learn to listen to the living. (978-1-62639-354-7)

Searching for Celia by Elizabeth Ridley. As American spy novelist Dayle Salvesen investigates the mysterious disappearance of her ex-lover, Celia, in London, she begins questioning how well she knew Celia—and how well she knows herself. (978-1-62639-356-1)

The 45th Parallel by Lisa Girolami. Burying her mother isn't the worst thing that can happen to Val Montague when she returns to the woodsy but peculiar town of Hemlock, Oregon. (978-1-62639-342-4)

A Royal Romance by Jenny Frame. In a country where class still divides, can love topple the last social taboo and allow Queen Georgina and Beatrice Elliot, a working class girl, their happy ever after? (978-1-62639-360-8)

Bouncing by Jaime Maddox. Basketball Coach Alex Dalton has been bouncing from woman to woman, because no one ever held her interest, until she meets her new assistant, Britain Dodge. (978-1-62639-344-8)

Same Time Next Week by Emily Smith. A chance encounter between Alex Harris and the beautiful Michelle Masters leads to a whirlwind friendship, and causes Alex to question everything she's ever known—including her own marriage. (978-1-62639-345-5)

All Things Rise by Missouri Vaun. Cole rescues a striking pilot who crash-lands near her family's farm, setting in motion a chain of events that will forever alter the course of her life. (978-1-62639-346-2)

Riding Passion by D. Jackson Leigh. Mount up for the ride through a sizzling anthology of chance encounters, buried desires, romantic surprises, and blazing passion. (978-1-62639-349-3)

Love's Bounty by Yolanda Wallace. Lobster boat captain Jake Myers stopped living the day she cheated death, but meeting greenhorn Shy Silva stirs her back to life. (978-1-62639-334-9)

Just Three Words by Melissa Brayden. Sometimes the one you want is the one you least suspect. Accountant Samantha Ennis has her ordered life disrupted when heartbreaker Hunter Blair moves into her trendy Soho loft. (978-1-62639-335-6)

Lay Down the Law by Carsen Taite. Attorney Peyton Davis returns to her Texas roots to take on big oil and the Mexican Mafia, but will her investigation thwart her chance at true love? (978-1-62639-336-3)

Playing in Shadow by Lesley Davis. Survivor's guilt threatens to keep Bryce trapped in her nightmare world unless Scarlet's love can pull her out of the darkness and back into the light. (978-1-62639-337-0)

Soul Selecta by Gill McKnight. Soul mates are hell to work with. (978-1-62639-338-7)

The Revelation of Beatrice Darby by Jean Copeland. Adolescence is complicated, but Beatrice Darby is about to discover how impossible it can seem to a lesbian coming of age in conservative 1950s New England. (978-1-62639-339-4)

Twice Lucky by Mardi Alexander. For firefighter Mackenzie James and Dr. Sarah Macarthur, there's suddenly a whole lot more in life to understand, to consider, to risk...someone will need to fight for her life. (978-1-62639-325-7)

Shadow Hunt by L.L. Raand. With young to raise and her Pack under attack, Sylvan, Alpha of the wolf Weres, takes on her greatest challenge when she determines to uncover the faceless enemies known as the ꞇdow Lords. A Midnight Hunters novel. (978-1-62639-326-4)